PENGUIN BOOKS
SNAPSHOTS

Shobhaa Dé describes herself as an 'obsessive-compulsive writer'. Columnist, commentator, and author of fourteen books, she lives with her family in Mumbai, a city that she considers a 'character', not just a locale, in her work.

She is currently planning her next book, a novel.

Snapshots

SHOBHAA DÉ

PENGUIN BOOKS

PENGUIN BOOKS
Published by the Penguin Group
Penguin Books India Pvt. Ltd, 11 Community Centre, Panchsheel Park,
New Delhi 110 017, India
Penguin Group (USA) Inc., 375 Hudson Street, New York,
New York 10014, USA
Penguin Group (Canada), 90 Eglinton Avenue East, Suite 700, Toronto,
Ontario M4P 2Y3, Canada (a division of Pearson Penguin Canada
Inc.)
Penguin Books Ltd, 80 Strand, London WC2R 0RL, England Penguin
Ireland, 25 St Stephen's Green, Dublin 2, Ireland (a division of Penguin
Books Ltd)
Penguin Group (Australia), 250 Camberwell Road, Camberwell, Victoria
3124, Australia (a division of Pearson Australia Group Pty Ltd)
Penguin Group (NZ), cnr Airbone and Rosedale Roads, Albany, Auckland
1310, New Zeland (a division of Pearson New Zeland Ltd)
Penguin Group (South Africa) (Pty) Ltd, 24 Sturdee Avenue, Rosebank,
Johannesburg 2196, South Africa

Penguin Books Ltd, Registered Offices: 80 Strand, London WC2R 0RL,
England

First published by Penguin Books India 1995

Copyright © Shobhaa Dé 1995

Typeset by Vans Information Limited, Mumbai
Printed at Baba Barkhanath Printers, New Delhi

To
*women friends past & present
and to Dilip
for interpreting them for me*

One

Prem liked to make love in public places. The first time he'd suggested it to Aparna, they were weekending in Goa. It was the tail-end of the monsoon. The sky was smoke-grey like the colour of Prem's unusual eyes. It was drizzling lightly as they walked along the beach hand in hand.

'Amazing how many people from Bombay one meets in Goa during the rains,' Prem commented, pushing back a strand of hair from Aparna's wet face.

'Cut-rate tourists,' she said laconically, 'like us.'

Prem kicked idly at an empty Bisleri bottle and laughed. 'Did I hear you right? Cut-rate? And you? What does that make me, boss lady?'

Aparna looked straight at him. 'A hanger-on? Side-kick? Sycophant? *Chamcha?* Kept-man? Adulterer? Take your pick, Prem.' For a minute his smoke-grey eyes looked darker and smokier. His smile, which had temporarily frozen, picked up at the corners. He ran his fingers through his wet hair, threw back his head and laughed. 'I like your style, Aparna. I really do. You know something? You are the first woman I've met who has balls. Balls of steel. You clang as you walk. Bet you didn't know that. Maybe that's what keeps me interested . . . and working for you.'

'Fuck off, Prem,' Aparna said affectionately as they resumed strolling along the stone parapet of the Taj Village. 'You work for me because I pay you top dollar. More than your market value. Let's face it—you've priced yourself out of the job bazaar.'

Prem pulled at her bikini clasp playfully. 'I render services your other execs don't or can't. I think we have a fair deal.'

It was incredible how many familiar faces they encountered on this one strip of beach. 'Has the entire ad community moved to Goa for the weekend?' Prem asked.

Aparna surveyed the scantily-clad bathers before saying, 'It is a long weekend. Besides, we don't exactly own this place.'

Prem smiled, 'At the rate at which you're going, Aparna, you soon might. Your ambition, man, that's something else. I like it. I like it. But it's kind of scary.'

Aparna dug her toes into the loosely packed wet sand and wiggled them. 'Prem, I get the feeling you just paid me a compliment. Correct me if I'm wrong.'

Prem caught her by the shoulders and whirled her around, to face him. 'Let's fuck,' he said, his eyes like the rain-laden monsoon clouds above.

'Right now? And here?' Aparna asked with a laugh in her voice.

'I'm serious, Aparna. Come on. Stop being such a tight ass.'

She took a quick look around. 'Well . . . why not? There are only about two dozen people we know here. Perhaps we could issue tickets.' He held her wrist tightly and led her into the sea. 'Prem,' she cautioned, 'it's dangerous . . . have you seen the waves? Monstrous ones.'

Prem placed the flat of his palm on her bottom. 'Dammit . . . I know it's dangerous. That's the way I like it.'

'But the currents . . . the undertow . . . so many people drown on this beach during the rains,' Aparna stammered.

'Amateurs,' Prem said crisply. 'Besides—sorry to sound crass—I've done this before. Trust me.'

A gigantic wave crashed against them as they waded into the churning waters. It was a time of year when even local fishermen stayed on shore and mended their nets quietly. Aparna was amazed at herself. What was she doing with the unpredictable Prem—a brilliant but lunatic adman who was married to someone else?

Why was she so meekly following him into this notoriously perilous sea that dragged the unsuspecting to their watery deaths each year? And she wasn't even a good swimmer. But Prem had that effect on her. She hated him for it. She often hated herself too.

No, Aparna was definitely not in love with the man. She knew that for sure. But she needed him—both at work and at play. Prem was a convenience. A cold-blooded one. But what the hell. It worked the same way for him too. What's more, he got paid for it. She rather liked that. Prem—her creative director. Prem—her imaginative lover. Good equation, that.

They were waist-deep in violently swirling water by now. Prem had a manic gleam in his eyes as he held on to her hand and pulled her in deeper. The water had reached their shoulders. Aparna's feet were sinking into the rapidly moving sand. The rain had stopped. There was an eerie yellow glow in the overcast sky. A strong breeze blew salt spray into her face as she shut her eyes to prevent them from stinging.

Prem held her by the waist and instructed, 'Remove your bikini bottom. Keep one arm on my shoulders. I'll steady you. Don't worry. It's easy . . . even if you do lose your footing.'

Aparna threw back her head. She was tempted to laugh—in sheer fright. Prem looked at her unblinkingly. They could hear shrieks of laughter as a group of noisy teenagers frolicked in the shallows. Two pale-skinned

4

foreigners were valiantly attempting to windsurf and falling into the rolling waves. Aparna undid the bright pink strings that held the bottom of her lycra bikini up. Within seconds she was naked waist down. Her hand clutched the bikini-half under water. Prem reached for it and took it from her. 'Can't afford to let it float away in a moment of abandon, can we? Imagine walking into the lobby starkers.' Aparna watched as he unzipped a small pocket on his swimming trunks and stuffed her swimwear into it, 'Now for the top . . . Go on . . . off with it. Let's play mermaid.'

Aparna was bobbing up and down in a vain effort to combat the sharp slap of the waves. Her torso was well above the water most of the time. 'Don't be silly, Prem. I don't want half of Bombay to see my boobs.'

Prem looked over his tanned gym-worked shoulder. 'No one's looking. I swear. Do it. Take it off. Or else, I will.' Before Aparna could respond, he'd unclasped the top and fastened it around his own waist. 'Ready?' he asked, reaching down and caressing between her legs. He forced her knees open and she found herself experiencing the most incredible sensation as the cool water splashed right into her creating strange rhythms of its own. She shut her eyes while Prem drew her to him. She found her legs, lighter than ever in salt water, float up as if defying gravity—and wrap themselves around her lover's trim, taut waist. He reached out and supported Aparna's neck as her body arched gracefully backwards and her hair floated on the surface of the sea.

A shaft of sunlight tore through the clouds and shimmered over the waves that barely covered her naked body. Prem had deftly arranged his briefs so that she could feel him growing against her inner thigh. With one hand, he massaged her breasts in gentle circular strokes. Aparna allowed her mind to float. She blanked everything out—her work, her troubled past, even her uncertain future. The moment was here and now. She wanted Prem with the sort of ferocious urgency she'd never experienced. Not even with her ex-husband Rohit at the time she was in love with him the most. And she didn't even *like* Prem. Well . . . that wasn't true. She must have liked him to be here in the first place. But Prem made her feel almost uncomfortably wanton. Something Rohit rarely did for fear of 'spoiling' her with his sexual attention. 'Don't want to have a broad with an "I'm-so-sexy" complex hanging around demanding more,' he'd once told her, a nasty edge to his voice. Prem desired her so openly, it made her feel naked in the office. It was a new sensation. One that she rather liked.

At that moment in the sea, Aparna experienced lust. No-strings-attached lust. She hated to think of it as a 'need'. Did women 'need' sex? Aparna had always scoffed at the notion. No, she'd say, women need love. And caring. And tenderness. Prem had stood all these ideas on their head the day he made love to her for the first time, in an empty office, on the dusty floor, with carpenters working just a thin partition away.

*

'Concentrate on your body,' he was saying, as he touched her with his thumb and pushed her legs wider. 'Hold my hands and stretch yourself out. You won't drown. Have faith.' Aparna followed his orders, floating on her back, flocks of foam crowning her pubes, her breasts like orbs, gleaming in the water, playing peek-a-boo with the ripples. She felt Prem's supple feet on her thighs and over her bottom. He turned her over and held on to her ankles. In one smooth move, he was over her body, his hands cupping her breasts, his mouth tearing at the back of her neck hungrily. 'Stretch out your arms and float,' he whispered, 'keep your legs straight.' She could feel him now as he reached between the cheeks of her bottom with his fingers. 'Relax . . . relax,' he repeated, while she clenched and unclenched her muscles. 'Not yet . . . I have to enter you . . . and then.' He flipped her around easily. 'Let's lock legs,' he crooned as he lifted her thigh and encircled her waist with his knee. The water was slightly warmer now and lapping gently into her. It was so gently insistent, Aparna felt herself coming in waves. 'Wait,' Prem rasped, as he entered her rapidly

7

and set up his own rhythm to synchronize with the movement of the turbulent sea.

Aparna saw the sky spinning over her head. She thought she was about to lose consciousness. She heard herself moaning aloud, as she clung on to Prem's powerful neck and thrust her pelvis aggressively into his. Prem's eyes had changed colour. They looked like pieces of coal—glowing embers. His large hands covered her bottom and held it in place as he dictated the pace—slowing Aparna down or accelerating her tempo in a manner she found maddening.

'Stop that, Prem,' she finally called out, 'it's driving me nuts.' Prem persisted, with a deliberation Aparna found unbearable. At that moment, she didn't care if her wildly thrashing body bobbing in and out of the waves was visible to the entire population of Goa. She was only concerned with what was happening to her . . . inside her. It was like nothing—nothing—she'd ever experienced. A liquid ferris-wheel ride or a roller-coaster trip in the depths of an ocean. Prem increased his own rhythm and used his hands to clasp her waist and synchronize their bodies till they were like a human canoe—up one minute, down the next. Soon—a bit too soon—or it could have been an eternity—Aparna felt him sliding out of her body. The water was still cold outside. But he had left a warm gush inside. She could feel it trickling out and joining the sea. She moved her limbs languorously and swam a short distance away from Prem. Aparna was still naked. And she liked it.

*

Aparna had grown up with shame. Shame about her body. Shame about her adolescent looks. Shame about her background. Shame about practically every aspect of her life. It was the environment she was raised in. Guilt was its defining feature. She couldn't recall a time when she wasn't made to feel acutely conscious of every small pleasure—emotional or physical. And here she was with an employee, a married one at that, enjoying what was popularly known as a 'dirty weekend'. Goa in the rains was irresistible. She'd made it an annual ritual with her husband, Rohit. And now she was there on the well-loved, broad strand of beach with a man she admired but didn't particularly like. What had made her suggest it in the first place? It was so unlike her to take the initiative and come on this strong with a near-stranger. She considered herself reserved, aloof, a bit of a dragon lady. That was the popular image at any rate. Prem wasn't even her type. He was basic. She liked men with high ideals and lofty ambitions. Men like Rohit. Or like her father. But, as she looked back bitterly, it was Rohit who had let her down. Left her high and dry. She was through with his sort. With Prem there was no bullshit. They both knew the score.

9

As colleagues they worked well together. And as lovers . . . well, Aparna was only just beginning to discover her sexual potential.

*

It had started on a floor covered with sawdust and wood shavings while Prem and she tore off each other's clothes greedily and made sex—not love—to the sound of nails being hammered less than ten feet away. That was the first time. Since then, they'd established a pattern. And Aparna had been astonished to discover just how abandoned she could be. And just how uninhibited. It had to do with Prem of course. Prem was brash, arrogant and nauseatingly sure of himself. Instead of feeling intimidated by his prowess, Aparna had found herself responding. . . almost craving for the chemistry their bodies created whenever they were together. She'd stopped trying to analyse her out-of-character conduct. 'If I'm being undignified, so be it,' she'd found herself giggling in a swanky restaurant once, when Prem, sitting across her had skilfully manipulated his bare foot all the way up her legs under her sari, hooked his big toe into the top of her panties and removed them. And through the entire operation both of them had continued to make smooth conversation with a potential client from Delhi and his starched dull-eyed wife.

On another, similar occasion—a formal sit-down reception, he'd instructed her to leave her panties at home. This time, he'd switched table-placings and sat beside her.

Aparna, certain that everybody at their table knew about her nakedness, had stared fixedly, self-consciously at a woman's bouffant across the room, while Prem had used his pat of butter to lubricate his fingers. As the first course was served, he had reached under the long damask tablecloth, lifted the layers of her crêpe de Chine sari, and found the spot he had been looking for. Gently, cleverly, he had brought her to a climax over and over again, while the boring party continued around them and the colour kept rising in Aparna's cheeks.

'Bet these are the biggest O's you've ever had,' Prem had whispered charmingly as he'd leaned over to smile into her eyes. Aparna had flushed and automatically handed him her starched napkin. 'What's this for?' Prem had asked, puzzled.

She had hissed, 'To wipe your fingers, stupid.'

He had thrown back his head and laughed. 'Are you kidding? This is going to be my dessert.' Aparna had watched aghast as Prem had licked each sticky finger with obvious relish and added, 'Mmmm . . . better than Miss Daruwala's chocolate mousse.'

*

Then came the lunch invitation which Aparna had nearly turned down. At first glance, the hastily scribbled note which was almost illegible didn't make the slightest sense. The only thing she could make out was the signature, Reema. Just that. Reema. Impatiently, Aparna cast it aside. Which Reema? How presumptuous of whoever the sender was to expect the receiver to identify the note-writer by just a first note. Aparna knew at least three Reemas. One, a colleague. That ruled her out. Why would she send a note when she could call? The second her manicurist. No, that little chit of a thing wouldn't have the gall to write to her. And then there was her sister-in-law. The hateful one. This wasn't her writing. In any case, they hadn't spoken in years.

Aparna picked up the discarded note again. Handmade paper. She couldn't stand the sight of these ethnic notelets any more. Especially the ones with little glittering thingies stuck on them. Like this one. She looked at her watch. Ten minutes to go. She was late. Aparna ticked herself off mentally. Two mornings in a row now she'd been arriving at her office past 10 a.m. She glanced at herself in the mirror over the telephone. A quick check to see whether she needed a fresh hair-rinse. Oh-oh. She spotted a few tendrils of grey. She was going to fight this going grey thing, she vowed, as she glanced irritably at the note once again. She began to decipher the untidy scrawl.

Dear Aparna,

Remember me? Reema Chandiramani (now Reema Nath). We were at school together. It has been a long, long time. I was the one with the plaits that reached the hem of my uniform. Now do you remember? Anyway, this letter is to invite you to my home. Lunch on Tuesday. I've tried to reach a few other girls. It's to meet Swati Bridges. You know who she is, of course. She phoned from London to say she'd be passing through Bombay. She asked whether I'd be able to round up a few friends—you know, from the old gang. I'm sure you are dying to meet her like we all are. You must come. Swati will be most disappointed otherwise. See you then.

Love,

Reema

Aparna re-read the note, a slight frown creasing her forehead. She removed her glasses and stared blankly at the painting in front of her. A glass painting from Macau, given by Rohit on their first anniversary. But Aparna's eyes weren't really looking at its fine lines and pale colouring. She felt momentarily absent from her immediate surroundings. The phone rang sharply startling her enough to make her jump with fright. It was someone checking on her defective P.C. Without meaning to, she snapped at the caller and looked at her watch in alarm.

Briskly, she gathered her filofax, files and roomy handbag. She called out to her cat, took a quick look around her neat apartment, picked up her car keys and left. Reema, Reema, Reema. Of course she remembered her. Such a bore. And so untidy. Ink blotches on her uniform. Paint on her socks. Unpolished keds. Filthy fingernails. Books without covers. Tattered schoolbag. And a silly giggle. A really, really, silly giggle. Funny that Reema had mentioned her plaits. Obviously, she was proud of them. But when they were at school, the plaits had been Reema's tools of torment. *Chotiwali* they used to call her. And tug her braids till she squealed with pain.

Aparna walked out of her apartment block and towards her Maruti 1000. She ignored the salaams of the building's security staff. Aparna was thinking of Swati. Swati Bridges. Hah! Married to some Brit writer. Or was he a publisher? Aparna tried to push the image away. What was Swati doing in India? And Bombay? A documentary? A movie? A book? Or was she just showing off her latest, newest, whitest husband?

Aparna reversed out of the spacious compound and headed for Gameplan, the ad agency she'd floated only a year ago, with two partners. It was a small outfit. But a smart one. Aparna looked at the flow of traffic and reckoned it would take her twenty minutes to make it to her office on the seventeenth floor of a high-rise. That is, if the serpentine queues waiting for the eight

high-speed elevators were shorter this morning. She
caught her reflection in the small car mirror and looked
away quickly. Help! She wasn't feeling great and it
showed. Neglected eyebrows, carelessly kohl-lined eyes,
no lipstick, and a bindi that was clearly mismatched.
What would Swati think if she saw her now? But then
again, Aparna mused, what was she going to make of
Swati when they met? Rather, *if* they met. She wasn't
sure she wanted to go to this lunch thing. Why had
Swati phoned Reema of all people, and not any of the
others? Why not *her?* Reema and she hadn't been at
all close. Or was there another angle to it? Catch Swati
doing something spontaneous. But if there was a twist,
what *could* it be? Aparna had been out of touch with
'the girls' for over fifteen years now. Ever since college
in fact, where most of them had chosen to be together
after eleven long years at school. Swati, of course, had
pushed off midway to join drama school in England.
That hadn't surprised anybody. She had been the
undisputed star of every school and college annual
production since class five. But Aparna had drifted away
from the crowd much before it actually disintegrated
through marriages, transfers and unshared interests.
Reema, as far as she could remember, had never really
been a part of the inner circle. She was a fringe person,
vague and woolly, who just went along with the rest
without anyone registering her presence. Nobody
noticed or cared whether Reema was around.

15

And yet, Swati had picked her for the 'honour'. Why? Aparna decided to check that one out. A couple of possibilities occurred to her as she parked her car absently and strode towards her office building, her maroon dhakai sari catching the sea-breeze. Reema was the most harmless of the lot. A sweet, soft-spoken person without any real opinions. Maybe Swati felt comfortable with her. Everybody did. Reema had a way of behaving like the *chamchi* of the person she was with. That was flattering, if a trifle tiresome. But Swati was probably used to just that—unreserved, undiluted, unconditional adulation.

As Aparna waited in the queue, she tried to remember what Swati looked like these days. Of course, she sort of knew—everyone did. Her publicity was perfectly organized. She probably paid a big, fat fee to her agent. But Aparna couldn't come up with a clear picture. She was gorgeous, of course. Even Aparna had to admit as much. But not conventionally so. With a wry smile, Aparna recalled that in school, the competition for the best-looking girl invariably narrowed down to the two of them and often Aparna emerged the winner. But that was then. Twenty years had gone by. Swati still looked smashing. At least in her photographs. And Aparna? Well, she was striking all right. People told her so constantly. But in a formidable sort of way. Perhaps 'handsome' was the right word. Tall, long-limbed, strongly built—almost muscular with a no-nonsense attitude that kept even the most ardent admirers at bay.

Swati was shorter and plumper. At least, that's the way Aparna remembered her. But she had those eyes, and that hair, and above all, the dimples—two of them. Plus, the mouth that was constantly in motion—large, generous, half-open, hungry. Not much of a body, Aparna concluded, staring down at her toes in the crowded elevator. A small waist for the rest of her and slightly stubby legs. But put together, Swati stole the show—any show. Vibrant, energetic, given to flamboyance, there was something about the way she used her hands, the angle at which she cocked her head and the intimate manner in which she locked eyes with strangers that drew people to her and kept them there. As Aparna walked into her neat, modern office and greeted the receptionist, she knew she'd made up her mind about Reema's lunch. She'd go.

Two

Reema was in a flap. She was always in a flap. Swati was making this difficult. The lunch was all organized. Four had accepted. She'd got the menu worked out. Plus the linen and everything. Now Swati had called with another brainwave. Not that she minded. But it meant phoning up all the girls. She hated that. As it is she'd spent three days chasing addresses and phone numbers. Damn Bombay telephones. And that irritating recorded voice that announced yet another number change. And now this. She'd have to repeat the whole drill. But Reema had to admit the idea was good. Why not? All of them would be meeting after years. How much could they possibly catch up with over just one lunch?

'Snapshots,' Swati had suggested. 'Tell the girls to bring snapshots. Albums. Old photographs. New photographs. Mementoes of their innocent pasts.'

Why hadn't she thought of it herself? Reema looked around her fussily-appointed home proudly. She wouldn't need to pull out untidy albums—her living-room was already crowded with frames. Silver frames. Such great pictures too. But that's not what Swati had in mind, she reminded herself. Old pictures, school pictures. Isn't that what she'd said?

'Tell the girls to bring souvenir shots, Reema darling. Tell them I asked. They'll do it. Won't it be fun looking through funny old photographs? Let's all have a really big giggle, shall we? I'm dying to meet everyone. I can't tell you how excited I am. But . . . remember the snapshots. See you soon, sweetheart.' And Swati was gone.

Reema wasn't sure she'd kept any school pictures. Or if she had, she'd probably left them in her bedroom at her mother's house. Funny, she thought, she still thought of that old room as *her* room. The one that her younger sister, Kritika, grabbed the day she got married. Maybe Kritika had thrown out all the stuff when she rearranged the room? Just the thought of calling up her father (now that Mummy was dead) put Reema off. Really, he was becoming such a demanding so-and-so. Complaining constantly, cribbing about the servants, moaning and groaning about his health. And the bulging bills. Why couldn't he just watch TV like everybody else? Anyway, since it was obviously so important to Swati, she'd have to make the effort somehow.

Reema sat back heavily on her crushed silk cushions. She was due at the health club in forty-five minutes.

If only Swati had written earlier, she'd have managed to get into some kind of shape. She pinched her midriff and winced. The aerobics instructor had said, 'Three to four months, madam. I'm not promising anything. Plus, you will have to go on a strict diet. No pakoras.' Reema hadn't been entirely convinced. Just ninety days to take off twenty years of compacted fat? Impossible. But her teenage daughter had urged her: 'Please, Mummy, lose weight. All the other mummies are so slim.' Reema's husband, Ravi, had regarded her critically. But at least he had looked. It seemed like ages since he'd noticed her body. 'Why not?' he'd encouraged, taking time off from his unending phone calls to say that. 'Why not start with your own belly first,' she'd been tempted to retort. But Reema knew better. In any case, with or without his hairy belly, the man didn't interest her. Never had.

Self-consciously, Reema had gone off to a small boutique, Eternity's End, to pick up the mandatory leotards for the Club. 'The largest size,' she'd said not daring to look the trim salesgirl in the eye. 'Here, Aunty,' the brat had said, her jaws working overtime on the gum in her mouth. 'Aunty, indeed,' Reema had silently fumed as she struggled to pull the fluorescent leggings over her squishy hips.

A month of sweating it out had helped a little. She felt better. And her kitty party friends told her she looked it too. No more ice cream, she'd reminded herself at the weekly gathering of wives, at the chosen five-star venue. She'd taken to smoking instead. Ravi had come home, sniffed the air suspiciously and asked, 'Have the servants started smoking inside the house?' To which Reema had responded airily: 'No, darling, I have.' A week's argument later, he'd given up. But then Ravi had given up on everything that concerned his wife. Even sex.

Reema wondered just how good Swati looked now in person. Judging by her pictures, she looked great. Unbelievably so. Mrs Mehra, whom she had visited some days ago, had been dismissive. 'Forget it, *yaar*. These days anybody can look like a bloody movie star. You just have to know the right stylist.' Reema had studied the picture of Swati they were discussing more closely. OK. So, the lines had been painted over with make-up. But what about the rest? The expression in her eyes? The teasing way she'd arranged her matt lip-sticked mouth? The sophisticated cut of her perfectly-streaked hair? The great jewellery? The clothes? Everything so smart. So sexy. Reema had instinctively reached for the five carat diamond ring she constantly wore. It always reassured her. She'd walk into a kitty party uncertain of her latest salwar-suit, but feel perfectly confident knowing she had more solitaires than all the other women in the room. They knew it too. And it kept them in their place.

She looked around her spacious home for the hundredth time since Swati's letter. Of course, it was grand enough to impress Swati. All their friends thought so. Her husband was one of the biggest brokers playing the market. He still preferred to operate out of a dump. ('Why spend more than necessary on an office?') But she had convinced him to make the move out of their former cramped suburban flat into a terrace flat on Worli seaface—all five thousand square feet ('Built-up,' he'd explain proudly) of it. She only wished they'd done it earlier. Maybe their marriage would've worked better if they'd left the joint family when she was expecting Shonali, their daughter. Maybe not. Ravi's big turn-on in life was money. More and more of it. She enjoyed it too. But the cold glint of her solitaires often mocked her loneliness as she slopped around watching *Maine Pyar Kiya* for the fifteenth time waiting for Ravi to get home. And start his phone calls. Which was her cue to watch a re-run of *The Bold and the Beautiful*.

Reema loved her new home. She couldn't stop showing it off. Or getting it decorated. She knew it was childish of her, but the minute she met someone new, someone worth impressing, she'd invite the person home. 'I've done it up myself. No interior designer,' she'd lie proudly as she escorted visitors around the place, pointing out her bonsai collection, the ceramic pots she'd painstakingly moulded in craft class, the fibreglass sculpture she'd commissioned, and the collage she'd put together herself from broken bangles, discarded sequins, sari borders and dried leaves. Reema looked at her handiwork and felt nervous for the first time since moving in. Would Swati approve?

*

Aparna's day at the office was a real bitch. The presentation hadn't gone off as well as she'd have wanted it to. 'Hey—what gives?' Krishna, her partner at Gameplan, had teased. 'I can see you didn't eat your full quota of nails for breakfast this morning.'

It was true. Aparna was uncharacteristically distracted. Not sufficiently in control. She ran her fingers through her short hair. 'Too butch,' Krishna had commented when she'd lopped it off impulsively. 'Practical, baby, practical,' she'd smiled, staring sidelong at her image in a shiny chrome award they'd won for the 'Most Creative Campaign of the Year'. Aparna was lying. She'd cut her hair to spite Rohit. Or to show him how completely indifferent she'd become to his reactions. That is, if he still kept up with her busy life. He had fallen for her glorious tresses when they'd first met in art school. Her 'White Lucknowi Kurta' days. Both of them had discovered just how similar their tastes were, quite by accident. Rohit was an architecture student, two years her senior. They'd run into each other at a film society screening of *Jalsagar*. She'd noticed the long-haired man in a white Lucknowi kurta. And he'd noticed the long-haired woman in an identical one. A coffee and two cigarettes later they'd declared themselves in love. And Rohit had said, 'Either you chop off six inches of your hair, or I'll grow mine. Then we can pass off for each other and confuse the world.' 'You grow yours. I refuse to touch mine,' Aparna had replied. And Rohit had done just that.

They were the most attractive couple on campus. Always dressed in white, with glossy brown hair hanging over their shoulders. 'This is disgusting,' Aparna had commented when they'd stumbled upon yet another shared passion—haikus. 'We must've been separated at birth or something.' 'Sure,' Rohit had responded. 'With two years between births.'

It was when they found out that they also shared a common sun sign (Gemini) that the joke had become serious. 'Uncanny. Weird,' Aparna had said seriously.

'Yeah—two split personalities make four. And if we have two kids with the same sign, that will make us a family of eight. No sweat.' It had taken her a minute to realize that Rohit had actually proposed. Another to accept. And a third to formalize it by going off to Chor Bazaar and getting two antique silver rings. 'That's done,' Rohit had said with enormous satisfaction as they sipped faloodas in a nearby juice shop. 'And now let's get on with life.'

*

After the divorce, Aparna had methodically dug out every single white kurta from her wardrobe and thrown it away. She'd got rid of her blue jeans, camel hide jootis, crudely crafted sling bags, Jacques Brel records, haiku volumes and Begum Akhtar's CDs. It hadn't helped. The bastard. Two years later, the rage was undiminished. There wasn't a waking moment when she forgot. Or forgave. The unexpectedness of his decision to leave her was what she couldn't get over. No signs. No warnings. No hints. Nothing. Or if Rohit had been scattering them around, Aparna had completely missed them. Sure, they had had their squabbles, sulks and walk-outs—but that was only to be expected given their respective temperaments. Aparna considered the stray storms perfectly normal. For a person who didn't forgive easily, she forgave everything where Rohit was concerned, leading to the establishment of a pattern that suited them both. He erred—she forgave. It was taken for granted that all differences were to be settled in just one way—his. And each time they fought, it was Aparna who was left feeling rotten and vaguely guilty as though the whole thing was somehow her fault; that it was her intensity that came in the way and spoilt everything;

that it was she who expected too much; demanded too much; that men weren't supposed to be a hundred per cent honest, or sincere; that it was unrealistic of her to hope for that with Rohit. Wives, she often heard, were better off being somewhat indifferent. Husbands preferred that to an obsessive interest in their lives. Curiosity. Questions. Learn to overlook details, Aparna was told. Don't pry. Block out. Ignore. She'd tried. Trained herself to keep quiet even when it killed her. But what could she possibly do to the expression in her eyes? Rohit often said he felt accused and suspected—not by what she said but by the way she looked at him. Aparna practised 'neutral' expressions in the mirror, made a conscious effort to appear calm and cheerful when Rohit rolled in. No nagging. No explanations. No strain. That didn't work either. Rohit found her responses cold and mechanical. Stop being unnatural, he'd say. Unnatural. What a harsh word. Aparna smiled wryly at the memory. It was true. She'd been entirely 'unnatural' vis-à-vis Rohit. And that's why he'd left her.

One morning, Rohit asked for his coffee and while she showered, he casually packed. When she emerged from the bathroom, she found him dressed and ready to leave. She towel dried her hair and asked unsuspectingly, 'Going somewhere?'

'Yes,' Rohit replied, lighting a cigarette.

'You didn't tell me. Baroda again?' Aparna continued.

'Yes,' he said coolly.

26

'How long?' she asked looking for something in her wardrobe.

'For good,' he replied picking up his bag.

Aparna continued rummaging for the right bra in her messy drawer. She turned around after a moment. With a smile on her face: 'Ha! Ha! Like it's that easy,' she grinned, throwing her wet towel at him.

'It is,' he said ducking. 'Watch me while I leave.' And with those words he'd picked up his Samsonite and walked out of her life. No explanations. No apologies.

Aparna still seethed when she recalled that horrifying moment. How foolish he'd made her feel. Oh God! How desperately small and foolish. Years later, she still didn't know why or where she'd failed. Yes, the failure was hers. That's what he'd managed to convey to her without saying a thing. The shock of his absence had lead to a depression she had thought she would never pull herself out of. For four days she hadn't dared to leave their smart, stark, impersonally efficient flat. She'd remained in bed with the Japanese lantern swinging maddeningly over her head. She couldn't eat. Or drink. Or smoke. Or think. Or even mourn. She missed him so deeply, so physically, every bit of her being ached.

Was it their decision not to have children that had driven him away? Aparna surveyed her neat office table and asked herself the question for the umpteenth time—the question that had been gnawing her insides since Rohit's departure. She fiddled with the ashtray and reached absently for a cigarette. Force of habit, she sighed as she tried fruitlessly to go back to the muffed campaign. Like almost everything else in her life. Everything except Rohit. The one thing, one person, she never took for granted. 'Are you looped or pilled?' She remembered this tactless question of his on their wedding night, spent on a cane divan in his P.G. digs. 'Neither,' Aparna had replied, lying back uncomfortably against worn sweaty cushions and a frayed bedspread. 'No babies, sweetheart. We can't afford them,' he'd said stepping out of his kurta-pyjama. And that's how it had stayed. No babies. Well after they could afford them.

Till one day, Aparna had teased, looking at him over the crystal rim of her wine glass. 'How about tonight? Let's try and make a baby.' Rohit had swirled his cognac around in its snifter and looked dreamily out at the sea through the large windows enclosing the plant-filled balcony. 'Why do you want to spoil it all? This is perfect. I'm enjoying life. I'm busy. You're busy. Let's stick to fucking and forget kids.' Aparna had looked disbelievingly at him, the man who was now an established, sought-after architect in the fast track, with enough contracts to see him through the next five years. 'But . . . but, Rohit. I *want* kids. I like kids. I want to be a mother. I thought you wanted them too.'

'Yeah, I do like kids, other people's kids. I did want them. In the past tense. Not now. Who has the time for that shit? I mean, come on, Aps, you've got your career to think of. You're up for a promo soon. Accounts Supervisor. This is no time to fuck up.'

The evening had ended with Aparna listening moodily to Brel's *Ne me quitte pas*, while Rohit worked late into the night on a time-share holiday resort near Goa. Did the marriage end that day, Aparna asked herself, fiddling with loose threads trailing from her dhakai sari. Or did it end the evening she had discovered Rohit and Swati (yes, Swati on one of her visits to India and her house) in a suspiciously cosy mood. She'd fought with her husband and her schoolfriend that day and had never got over the suspicion that perhaps Swati had succeeded in seducing her husband. Well, she had always wanted to win, to take, and why not Rohit as well. Aparna had even confided her anguish to her diary. But then, as always, she prefered (stupidly, as she now thought) to forgive Rohit even if he'd actually been unfaithful to her.

Rohit was a selfish man. She knew that before they were married. Selfish and vain. But Aparna believed all men to be the same. All the men she'd known were both selfish and vain. Including her handsome father. It wasn't Rohit's self-absorption that bothered her as much as his ruthless streak. He had a grand design for his own life—people either fitted into it or didn't. So long as Aparna recognized that she was merely a point on his agenda, the marriage stayed on an even keel—'Don't rock the boat, baby,' he'd tell her if she ever demanded indulgence. She recalled, with some bitterness, the time they'd had his star clients over to dinner. She'd had a rough day at work, rushed home to get organized only to find she'd forgotten to pick up the wine from the Club.

As she got busy with the salads and main course, chopping spring onions till tears streamed from her eyes, Rohit had returned from work in a jaunty mood and opened the fridge for water.

'Where's the wine?' he'd asked.

'I forgot. I'm sorry, but I forgot. I was so rushed at the office today—the secretary had bunked—and I had to get the presentation ready for those blasted new batteries—you know, the new account I was telling you about last week?'

Rohit had stared at her coldly. 'Fuck you. And fuck your new account. When I tell you to make sure there's wine in the fridge, baby, you bloody well make sure there's wine in the fridge. Now, if you know what's good for you, you'll get your ass out of here. Go to the Club and pick the fucking bottles up.'

Aparna had flung down her knife and challenged him: 'What if I don't?'

He had walked out of the kitchen casually saying, 'Find out, if you have the balls. I warn you, the consequences won't be pleasant.'

Aparna had jumped into a pair of old jeans and driven halfway across town for the wine cursing Rohit all the way. Forty-five minutes later, she was back in the hot kitchen with just enough time to finish dinner. Rohit hated 'food smells' in the living-room. Aparna had sealed herself into the tiny functional kitchen, switched on the exhaust fan and slaved while Rohit listened to jazz in the air-conditioned comfort of their bedroom. It was at times like these that she hated the fact that she was a woman.

Often, they'd argue about their respective roles in marriage. She'd taunt him: 'I thought you were the New Man. I expected you to care and share. But you're like any other husband. The same old double standards. The same hypocrisies.' Rohit would smile back sadistically, 'Too bad you miscalculated. Sure I have double standards. I bring home the bread. You cook. Easy.' Aparna would retort furiously, 'Don't forget I bring home the bread too. I am a serious career person. When we married, you respected my priorities. You knew what you were getting into. If you'd wanted a housemaid, you should have married one.'

Stalemate. That's where each argument ended. And yet, on one level, Aparna knew how proud Rohit was of her position in the agency. He'd boast to his friends about it and bring out clippings from back issues of *A & M* profiling her. That's what had led to the eventual confusion. 'Don't send mixed signals,' Aparna would

31

plead. 'Either you are proud of me and what I'm doing or you aren't. Make up your mind.' That would lead to another flare-up, with Rohit stalking out of the flat and heading for the Gym Bar.

*

Aparna figured that Rohit had changed. Marriage had changed him. She had changed too. 'Become more macho,' as colleagues often teased her. It was the pressure of life in Bombay, she reasoned. After a point, it took its toll. Rush-push rush-push. One just never got off the bloody treadmill. Like right now. Another campaign to visualize. Another client to woo. Plus this stupid lunch invitation to deal with.

Aparna stared moodily out of the large glass windows that gave her a sweeping view of the bay with the governor's colonial bungalow balanced on the outer edge. Yes, she thought, Bombay was a beautiful, beautiful city. But such a bitch to survive in. Nobody had time any more. Not even for a light flirtation. Or love-making for that matter. A tired sigh escaped her lips. She thought of her last bed-encounter with Rohit, the night before he abruptly walked out of her life. It had been a disaster, even though it had started out promisingly. Rohit had brought her a chilled glass of smuggled Schwepps with a dash of Baccardi—a perfect drink for a muggy Bombay pre-monsoon evening. Aparna had just finished her twenty-minute workout clad in black underwear. Rohit had appraised her body and commented, 'Not bad for an ageing broad,' to which she'd joked back, 'Seen your paunch lately, Rohit?' And then he'd lunged at her, taking the panties off swiftly, not bothering with the bra and making love on the smooth chatai spread over their bedroom floor. Rohit was an intense, almost violent lover. Aparna liked that aspect of their couplings. That night he'd been more physical than usual, hurting her in the bargain. Roughly, he'd turned her over, seen the chatai pattern imprinted onto her smooth, tanned back, and inspired by it, added a few scratches of his own before binding her hands with his discarded pyjamas. 'Hey, hey, hey,' Aparna had protested mildly. 'Aren't you going a bit too far?'

Rohit's eyes were ablaze and almost manic as he had breathed, 'With you, it isn't far enough. You need a real man . . . a real fuck. You need pain.'

Aparna had suppressed a scream as he'd entered her harshly—almost as if he wished to subjugate and humiliate her into submission. She hadn't experienced the slightest pleasure—just a searing, burning sensation that had left her sore and hurting. Rohit had walked away into the bathroom without bothering to untie her. They'd eaten dinner silently—she was too bruised to speak. And he was unable to meet her swollen eyes. But, as she'd consoled herself later in bed, at least they'd done it—it—whatever it was, and howsoever brutal.

Most of their friends had stopped even making the attempt and formed a 'No Kids, No Sex' club. They spent their time either working or working out. But rarely making love. Which reminded Aparna that she hadn't been with a loving man for a long, long, time. Hadn't missed it either. Women were like that, she told herself. They were partner-specific. Not men. Any woman would do when the good old hormones were on the boil. She wasn't looking for a fuck. She didn't need sex (no shortage in that department). She wanted laughter and touches. Small, intimate moments. What she wanted was a steady, warm, attentive companion. No, if she were to be honest with herself, she'd admit it more readily—it wasn't just a man she missed—it was Rohit, her husband. She hated herself for continuing to think of him in those terms . . . husband, husband, husband. Awful word. Aparna blamed her mother—all those years of conditioning and brainwashing. She recalled her voice and words, 'Remember, a woman in our society is nothing without a husband. Study as much as you wish. Win prizes. Get a good job. But don't let all these things affect you, give you a big head. You may be the prime minister of India tomorrow, but when you come home, you automatically become your husband's wife. If you forget that, you are finished. Your marriage is finished.' How right her mother was. How depressingly accurate. Back to work, baby, Aparna reminded herself, as she stared listlessly at a small pile of cheques that required her signature.

Old pictures. Mementoes. What was Swati up to now? Another one of her games? Aparna sighed as an art director walked in with rough visuals for a TV campaign. She couldn't concentrate on his spiel. Her thoughts were scattered, going back and forth from her last encounter with Swati to the one that was scheduled for the next week. She could've opted out of the lunch so easily. So convincingly too. A business trip, perfectly timed to coincide with the event. An emergency meeting at the office. Oh, just about anything. Career women had countless alibis. Such convenient ones too. Maybe Reema would've grudged her absence. Held it against her, called her a 'ditcher' in her usual childish way. Reema hated people turning down her invitations—at least that's how Aparna remembered her. But would Swati? Yes—of course. Given her ego, Swati would see it as a personal insult, a deliberate slight. Coming from one of the other girls, maybe not. But coming from Aparna, surely. They were back to their old games. Games Aparna had fervently hoped were behind them now that the nasty business was finally over. Or was it? With Swati one never knew. And then again Aparna recalled the last time she'd met Swati. Aparna pushed the image out of her mind and stared unseeingly at the artworks on her table. 'Give me a break,' screamed the headline. Yeah, give me one too, she said to herself sardonically.

Three

Surekha was busy with the dhobi when Reema's note arrived. She looked at the fancy paper and put it aside. It was probably someone inviting her daughter to a birthday party. Or a shoe sale announcement. Surekha wasn't used to receiving mail, personal mail in particular. The only letters that ever came for her were from her sister, the one in New Jersey. And they were written on air mail forms. She went back to squabbling with the sullen man sitting at her feet surrounded by a pile of soiled clothes, mainly her daughter's messy uniforms and her husband's six towels (he repeated a towel on Sundays only). Surekha washed the rest of the clothes including her mother-in-law's severe white saris and lace-edged petticoats in her brand new washing machine. She glanced at the gleaming blue object ('with spin dryer' she always told friends) displayed prominently near the kitchen.

She went back to grumbling, 'How can you charge ninety paise for hand towels? I can understand if you'd said that you'd raised your prices for bedsheets and big towels.' The dhobi continued the clothes-count, hunkering on the polished floor. Reema's invitation lay forgotten on a small stool near the telephone.

The bell rang again. It was the fruit vendor. Surekha looked up from her dhobi book irritatedly. 'No, no go away. I've got oranges from Crawford Market. Wholesale. You charge too much. Don't think you can cheat me. Last week, two of the chikoos were rotten.' The man stood there stubbornly. 'I'll replace the chikoos. But I've brought disco-papayas for baba. He likes them.'

Surekha screamed, 'Can't you see how busy I am? You want to wait, then wait. Otherwise, come back next week.' She looked up as the hiss of the pressure cooker interrupted her dhobi work. The driver was waiting impatiently for her husband's dabba. She still had chapattis to make. And she'd forgotten to set the dahi for dinner.

Surekha got rid of the dhobi, retaining half the unwashed clothes. What was the machine for? Most of her neighbours did the sheets and towels plus the children's soft toys and tennis shoes in their machines. She put down her reluctance to use the machine more fully to her usual nervousness about electrical gadgets. No, that wasn't entirely true. She was scared of something going wrong with the machine. Even that wasn't true.

She was scared of her mother-in-law. What if the machine broke down? Her mother-in-law would be furious, so would her husband, Harsh. And her daughter would laugh at her.

Back in the kitchen, she hastily prepared the chapatti dough. Her mother-in-law would be returning from the mandir any minute. And the sight of the driver waiting would elicit the usual remarks. Surekha wiped her hands on her soft 'home sari' and got down to rolling out four, perfectly round chapattis. Her husband was very particular about their appearance. He hated even the smallest burnt spot on them. And her bath! The morning had gone by in a blur. She'd forgotten to switch off the geyser. She packed the chapattis hurriedly and rushed into the bathroom. She made it in the nick of time. The doorbell rang, announcing her mother-in-law's arrival.

'Surekha. Did the dhobi come?' She heard the sharp, rasping voice as the old lady went to her room to put back her keys and take off her chappals. Surekha braced herself to answer the barrage of questions about why some of the clothes had been left behind. And if they had, why on the floor near the entrance where everybody's dirty feet would trample over them? The driver suppressed a sly laugh. She caught the look on his face as she handed him the dabba. She rushed back into the kitchen to get a fresh napkin for the tiffin box. Last week she'd forgotten it and Harsh had been angry.

Her mother-in-law came shuffling out. It was her telephone hour. Between now and lunch, she phoned her Vile Parle kirtan friends. Surekha told her she was going in for her bath. The old woman glared, staring pointedly at the clock in the living-room. 'So late?' she asked walking to the phone.

Surekha was about to bolt the bathroom door when she heard her name being called: 'You've left your letter here,' the old lady cried out, 'on the stool. Where will I sit?'

Surekha redraped her sari and went back to the narrow passage. Letter? What letter? she wondered. Her mother-in-law held Reema's invitation out, using just the tips of her fingers. Surekha took it from her almost absently. It had obviously been sent to her by mistake but she didn't want to argue. She looked again at the name, just as she heard her mother-in-law say, 'Surekha Shah—*wah*—don't the senders know you are a married woman with a new surname? Shah! Hah!'

Surekha flushed as she took it from her hands. 'Open it, open it. Don't worry. I'm not looking,' her mother-in-law taunted while dialling rapidly with her bony forefinger.

Reema Nath. Formerly Reema Chandiramani. Surekha suppressed a smile. Of course she remembered Reema. And Swati. And Aparna. And Noor. And some of the other girls from their class. Swati most of all, of course. But then, who could forget Swati? Either then, or now. She kept staring at Reema's large, childish writing, memories flooding her mind as her mother-in-law continued to glare while carrying on a long conversation with another, equally ferocious widow in a distant suburb.

Instinctively, Surekha's hand flew to smoothen her untidy hair. She was back in school, laughing with her friends, as Swati swaggered across the courtyard, chewing gum and brazenly imitating the dragon woman—their hated headmistress. Surekha had been dubbed the 'Gujju Goody-Goody' by Swati after she'd refused to go along with a class prank. But somewhere down the line after that incident, Swati and she had become friends—a friendship that didn't endure beyond two school terms. But then, that was Swati—fickle, *matlabi*, manipulative. And yet, Swati had ruled. She had just to say the word and everybody followed. Resentfully perhaps but follow her they did, such was her hold over her classmates. Surekha re-read the invitation several times. On one level she felt immensely flattered—so, they hadn't forgotten her after all. Surprising, given that Surekha had dropped out of view straight after school. She hadn't bothered to maintain any links—except with Dolly who was still her closest friend—and nobody had bothered about her. When the time came to register her own daughter, Surekha had very deliberately picked another school. Why? she asked herself now, still holding Reema's invitation. Lousy memories, she concluded. Yes, Surekha certainly didn't have very pleasant associations with her old school. Particularly the memories of that last bitter year. Bitter because of Swati? She brushed it aside. Why blame poor Swati for everything, she concluded charitably and went in for her delayed bath.

That's when another thought struck her. Even if she did decide to go to Reema's lunch what would she tell her mother-in-law? And her husband? It was something she hadn't done before—ever. They'd be incredulous. Surekha visited her mother's home once a fortnight—but never for lunch. It was a formal visit that lasted no more than two hours. She went alone leaving her daughter to complete her homework. It wasn't a visit she particularly looked forward to or enjoyed. Her mother was a dour-faced woman not unlike her mother-in-law. Even though Surekha's father was alive, she behaved and dressed like a widow. Surekha found that most depressing. And the constant complaining about servants and health. An unending tirade that began before Surekha could put her bag down and which followed her to the narrow, dark staircase down which she escaped.

And now, here was this fancy invitation. Surekha mentally ran through her wardrobe trying to think of something appropriate to wear. She couldn't come up with a thing. Not a single sari that made her feel either confident or presentable. The question of buying one for the occasion did not arise. Her husband would laugh

41

and her mother-in-law would banish the very idea as being far too extravagant. Only her daughter would understand. Surekha looked at her reflection in the mirror above the wash-basin. How puffy and pallid her face looked. Even those almond-shaped dark eyes that had flashed fire seemed lustreless and dead. She trailed her fingers over her plump shoulders and sighed. No. She couldn't face 'the girls' looking like this. She tried to imagine what the rest had grown into and gave up soon enough. She was amazed at herself. She couldn't even remember all the names. Swati, of course, was hard to forget. And though Surekha hadn't exactly tracked her life since school, she had read something occasionally in women's glossies and heard the odd bit of gossip while her neighbours chatted in the lift. Swati, after all, had become an international figure. Surekha couldn't think why Swati had attained fame—or was it notoriety? Was she an actress? Or was she involved in some scandal? As Surekha stepped out of the bathroom, wrapped in a fresh sari that she would drape carefully on the dry floor of her bedroom, she felt a small panic welling up inside her. She wanted very much to go. She'd give anything to be there. And yet, one side of her said, 'Forget it. All this isn't for you. You chose your life when you agreed to marry Harsh. An arranged marriage at nineteen, when all the other girls were busy getting their degrees and enjoying themselves with college boyfriends. You'll have nothing in common with them.

Maybe you never did. It was a mere accident that all of you came together for a few short years of your early school life. That's all. You'll feel a sense of shame. And they'll feel sorry for you. Stay home.'

Surekha heard a sharp knock on the door. It was the part-time servant. 'Bhabhi—phone,' he said, breaking her reverie. Phone? For her? Surekha rushed out after pleating her sari hastily. Was it her father? Daughter? Harsh never called. Or if he did, it was to speak to his mother. Then who?

Surekha pounced on the receiver, her heart pounding. 'Surekha?' the voice asked uncertainly. 'Yes, Surekha speaking,' she answered.

'Hi, this is Reema. Did you get my note?'

Surekha looked over her shoulder to see where her mother-in-law was. She spotted her in the small living-room, pretending to be totally absorbed in the Bhagavad Gita. Surekha lowered her voice when she responded. Reema urged her to come, adding, 'It will be such fun. So many years since all of us met. And don't forget to bring some pictures. I'm sure you can find them. We are all scrambling around looking for forgotten photos. Remember that crazy picnic to Elephanta Caves when all of us wore shorts and shocked the boatman? I think I've got a few of those. And that other trip to Lonavala where we stole some chikkis from the shop on Main Street? I'll never forget the trouble we got into.' Surekha kept listening, her

43

mounting excitement bringing colour to her cheeks. Reema didn't give her much of a chance to speak. But it felt great just listening to a voice from her past. While they talked, Surekha slipped back to those carefree years when she was the class fatty and everybody teased her, including Reema. 'Are you still, you know, plumpity-plump?' she heard Reema asking.

Surekha laughed a full-throated laugh: 'Yes, I'm still a fatty-bambola. What to do? I'm trying to lose weight. But it's so difficult.'

Reema sympathized: 'You're telling me! I go to that Bangalore health farm twice a year. And of course I'm also a member of the health club. My husband would disown me otherwise. I shed ten kilos there. And then I come back and put them all on again. Terrible. Maybe we should go together next time. And get one or two of the girls to join us. It will be just like old times.'

Surekha didn't say anything. How could she possibly tell Reema that she had just suggested the unthinkable? Instead, she asked casually, 'By the way—how is Swati? Any news?'

Reema laughed, 'God knows what she's up to—that woman; it's impossible to keep track of her. All I know is she called out of the blue and asked me to organize this. How could I refuse? Anyway, I thought it would be great to meet everyone again. Good chance, no? So, don't say no. Just come. Swati will be very disappointed if you don't.' Reema rang off with a jaunty,

'See you, fatty,' and left Surekha feeling strangely elated. Why not? she reasoned. She'd go. It was only the girls. Old girls. Not strangers. Surely her mother-in-law wouldn't object? She'd organize everything before leaving. Get up even earlier than usual. Fix the dabbas, part-time bai, everything. Even make the evening snacks before hand. That way nobody could say anything. Not even Harsh. Surekha had a song on her lips and a spring in her step as she went into the kitchen to prepare muramba for the season. The sight of the precisely cut raw mangoes awaiting the annual ritual of pickling a year's supply of sweet, spicy chutney, reminded Surekha of something. Oh yes! Swati used to love the muramba from Surekha's mother's home. She would raid her tiffin-box and lick it directly from its special container, annoying Surekha greatly. 'Don't make everything *jhoota*,' she'd scream at Swati, who'd be nonchalantly picking choice tidbits from everybody's lunch boxes. Surekha decided she'd take a jar full of this season's fresh muramba for Swati. For old time's sake.

Four

Rashmi had just received a call from Pips' school. The headmaster wanted to see her urgently. Rashmi stared at the large face of the kitchen clock. Damn! She'd have to skip rehearsals. Again. Dev would be furious. He'd probably replace her with someone else. The role was small. But it was her big come-back to the stage. How long had it been? Eleven years or thereabouts, she figured. It was around the time she'd decided to get pregnant. Involuntarily she touched her stomach. Flat and hard. Rashmi gulped down her lassi and reached for a cigarette. A few quick puffs would calm her nerves. The flat was a mess. The tiny kitchenette where she was sitting was smelling of stale food. One of these days . . . she reprimanded herself. Yes, one of these days she'd somehow find the time to clean up the place. Make it more liveable for Pips, if not for herself. He'd been complaining lately. He couldn't ask his friends over with a house this untidy. Rashmi hardly noticed.

Without Pips, she'd have been perfectly happy to live out of suitcases and eat out of cans. She did that anyway. Almost. It was Pips with his frequent taunts of 'pigety, pigety' who reminded her of her 'responsibilities'—it was a word Rashmi detested. 'Responsibilities,' her mother would remind her, each time she flung her school books down and started playing her favourite game of make believe. And here was this finicky eleven-year-old making her agonizingly conscious of her motherly duties. 'Why can't you be like other mummies?' he'd demand and Rashmi would be tempted to reply: 'Because I am *not* like other mummies. And you are not like other kids. You, my dear chap, are a bastard. Yes, a real-life bastard. Of course, you do have a father. All bastards do. But he is not my husband. He is someone else's husband. And father. Now do you understand why your mummy can't be like other mummies?' But she couldn't say that to her little boy. She loved him far too dearly. She suspected he knew the truth about his status. Not in those ugly terms. But he knew. What worried her was that he never asked her anything directly. No accusations. No tantrums. Just a huge, big question mark in those depthless eyes of his, which she would have liked to have erased. But it was his silence that stopped her. Counsellors advised against it as well. 'He'll ask when he's ready,' they told her. Perhaps they were right.

Rashmi stubbed out her ciggie and re-wrapped her lungi—the one she'd bought on a beach in Goa five years ago. Pips had enjoyed that vacation, she remembered. He'd even enjoyed Max, the only 'uncle' who'd bothered to befriend the boy. Pity Max disappeared, she thought wryly. He wouldn't have been a bad bet. Maybe he'd have rescued the two of them from the life they were stuck in and taken them to Stuttgart with him. She'd have adjusted. And worked hard. Learned German. Got herself a driving license. Kept house. Oh hell! Maybe that was it. Max was fanatical about a neat and tidy home. He'd stopped visiting theirs after the first couple of times when he'd stayed the night and not been able to find a clean towel. But she'd have changed for him. For an escape. For a better life. Too late for regrets now, she told herself briskly as she dumped her coffee cup into a full basin and rushed for a quick shower.

The doorbell rang just then. Rashmi was sopping wet with suds in her eyes. Damn the fucking bell, she cursed, wrapping her thin lungi around her damp body. She looked through the tiny peephole and kept the security chain on. This wasn't the time for the fisherwoman—she came later. Rashmi saw a uniformed man. A chauffeur? Cautiously she opened the door making sure to keep the chain in place.

'Who is it?' she asked.

'Invitation for Miss Rashmi Singh,' he announced, holding out a small card. She extended her fingers and took it from him, shutting the door quickly. Probably some out-of-town theatre group inviting her for a preview, she figured, flinging the card carelessly next to a pile of magazines stacked by the door. She went back to shampooing her hair briskly. The thought of trekking off to Pips' school didn't cheer her up. Shit! What had the boy done this time, she wondered as she blow-dried her hair hastily and climbed into a pair of worn jeans. She glanced at the card again and something about the rounded, childish handwriting made her pick it up. That, combined with the manner in which it was addressed—'Rashmi Singh'. Nobody called her that any more. She'd sort of forgotten it herself. Curiously, she flicked the envelope open and read Reema's short note. Well, well, well, after so many years, here was an invitation from the snooty bitch. Rashmi's mouth twisted into an ironic smile as she thought of all the times she'd phoned Reema in the past, asking for help, perhaps a half-page ad in her brochures, or a donation for one of the several causes she was involved in—street children, old peoples' homes, Dying with Dignity. Not once had Reema bothered to return her calls or respond to her appeals. Rashmi read the note through again. 'Swati—huh! Big bloody deal. So who the fuck does she think she is summoning her old court, expecting everybody to drop whatever it is they are doing and rush to pay homage? She can go fuck herself, the bitch.'

Rashmi remembered her attempts to contact Swati in London when Pips was really tiny—like an underfed mouse. Rashmi had needed a bit of help—not money—just a couple of numbers. Consultants. She'd written to Swati from India. Then called her on arrival. Swati had been deceptively sweet over the telephone and then become completely inaccessible. Her secretary answered Rashmi's calls with the same monotonous response, 'I'm sorry, Mrs Chowdhary is not available right now. Please leave your name and number and I'll get right back to you.' She never did.

Swati was all over the press that summer. Front-page tabloid news. What a stink she'd created. And how utterly sensational she'd looked. Rashmi thought of her micro-mini skirted pin-up as she left the court on the arm of her jock lover—the captain of the English football team named by Swati's husband as a co-respondent in the messy divorce case that sounded like a made-for-television melodrama. Rashmi remembered the captain's wife—a mousy little woman in a grey coat, standing in the rain clutching three little children. The British tabloids had dubbed Swati 'Dusky Hussy'. And the public couldn't get enough of her. Rashmi tried to think—was Mr Chowdhary husband number one or three? It didn't matter. Not to Swati at any rate. She'd promptly discarded the football player and latched on to a nineteen-year-old rock star with long, blond braids and a stage presence so sexually potent, he had women in the audience pleasuring themselves openly. No, Swati certainly hadn't had the time for her old schoolfriend. As Rashmi prepared to leave her flat, she thought bitterly, 'Well, too bad, baby, I don't have the time for you either.'

*

She found Pips outside the headmaster's office, standing sullenly next to a hard, yellow bench.

'What happened, poppet?' she asked gently, kissing him on the head.

'Nothing,' he answered shortly.

'Then why are you here?'

'I didn't mean to hit him,' Pips replied, turning his face away to hide his tears.

'Not another fight, sweetheart,' Rashmi said wearily. 'Come on, son, grow up. You can't keep bashing the world.'

'Yes, I can, I can. I will,' Pips cried out angrily. 'I hate this bloody school. I hate all the boys. I don't want to study. Why can't I just stay at home and learn music?'

Rashmi sighed, holding the boy close to her. So much like his father, she thought. Stubborn, headstrong, impetuous—and talented. Even she had to admit as much. Strange that he should be a mini-replica of Pips

Sr., the brilliant movie director who'd walked out on her when she was pregnant with Pips. Walked out. Just like that. Not for another woman—Rashmi would've understood that, knowing Pips' insatiable appetite for new women, new experiences—but for a tidier home. A tidier house! It was unbelievable, inconceivable that a man would leave a woman for being an indifferent home-maker. He'd yelled and screamed for months, 'Woman—clean up the mess, or hire someone to do it.' But Rashmi had foolishly ignored him feeling sure he'd never leave her—and the complete bed experience she provided. No man had ever walked away from Rashmi's bed. Not till she gave the orders to march. Why should Pips have been different? All right—he was the star in the relationship. The original Mercurial Man, who took what he pleased, when he pleased, on his terms. But she hadn't invited him into her life. He'd bulldozed his way past a devoted companion of three years, who had meekly rolled over and said, 'Kick me.' Pips revelled in his reputation as the Lover Boy of Filmland. 'I'm bigger and better than any fucker,' was his slogan. The entire industry knew the line. And what was Rashmi? Another ambitious RADA-trained actress looking for a break. 'Go back to where you came from,' he'd bellowed at her when she'd gone for a screen test. 'You are too dark, too stylish and too talented. We don't need girls like you. Come back after becoming fairer, losing your accent and forgetting your talent.'

Rashmi had stormed out of the studio, humiliated and furious.

Pips was a perfectionist. He controlled every aspect of his blockbuster films. He wrote the scripts, operated the cameras, composed the music, designed the sets and often played a key role, besides producing and directing the movie. Though he had all the money in the world, he shunned the usual lifestyle adopted by his contemporaries, preferring to operate out of a hotel suite which doubled as an office. Dressed in black with strands of rudraksha malas around his neck, Pips (short for Parminder) cut quite a figure when he strode into a room, his wild hair held back with a rubber band, his beard brushing his hairy chest. It was this animal-like quality that intimidated and attracted people to him.

Like it had Rashmi.

'Hey, listen woman,' he'd told her during their first encounter in bed, 'I am the original fuck-'em-and-leave-'em guy. Is that clear?' Rashmi had rolled him over, straddled him easily and said, 'Clear. That makes two of us. We should get along just fine.' They had. For nearly six months. It was considered something of a record for both. When Pips moved into her flat, a battered saddle bag in hand, the industry had been stunned. 'He hasn't done that for any woman. This must be serious.'

In a way, it was. Rashmi cared enough for Pips to actually cook breakfast. Pips ate four huge meals a day with a gusto that was awe-inspiring. She hardly ate anything at all. 'You don't eat woman,' Pips commented, 'where do you get the energy to fuck so much?' Rashmi also tried to keep house—disastrously. She was no good at it. It just wasn't important enough to her. 'Shit man, where are the frigging bedsheets in this dump?' Pips had hollered when he noticed the stains on the soiled, unwashed sheets and tried to pat away the creases. Rashmi, between sips of a wake-up Bloody Mary giggled—'I change a set when this one tears. No spares in this house.' Pips had regarded her with something close to contempt. 'Now you know why I prefer hotels—clean sheets. Fresh towels. Room service. Christ! You must've been a bloody scavenger in your last life.'

But the sex was so good, so varied and so intense, nothing else mattered. Pips was hungry all the time—for her and for food. They stayed in bed, ate in bed, fucked in bed and hardly stirred out of the place. Pips was successful enough to keep his career on hold while he enjoyed Rashmi—bathed her, painted her toenails, filed her nails, trimmed her hair, even shaved her armpits. She thought it would last, if not forever, at least for a couple of years. Rashmi didn't push him for a role—she was smart enough to realize that that would drive him away. And she didn't push him for money. Pips had plenty of it. But he didn't give her any. Not even to run the place when he knew

she was short. Rashmi took on the odd assignment—
audio-visuals, commercials, compering jobs, anything
that brought in the much-needed cash. Pips noticed,
but didn't chip in. She found it strange that he could
be so miserly, especially since he was known to be
loaded.

Rashmi was to find out just how loaded he was at a
party in honour of a visiting foreign crew. Pips was
going all out to impress the pompous director hoping
to assist in the making of his next Raj saga scheduled
to be shot in Rajasthan the following summer.
'Pull out all the stops, gang,' he'd told his unit as they
planned the party. 'Let's go the whole hog—hire
elephants, camels, whores, hijras . . . hire the whole
fucking bordello. But let's do it in style. Spectacular
shit is what I want. Gather the low life, parade the
pimps—and don't forget the food. How about wild
bear and roasted peacock?' His stoned out lackeys had
listened through a reefer-haze and nodded away.

Rashmi had dismissed it as his usual over-the-top
nonsense. But later that night, after a bout of frenetic
love-making ('Blow me, baby—and wet your lips') Pips
had pulled out a calculator and got down to work.

'Hey, are you finally going to pay me for services
rendered?' Rashmi had asked.

'Sssh, shut the fuck up woman, I'm concentrating,'
he'd said. A quick call to his financial advisor and Pips

had got back into bed, a smug smile on his face. 'Man, security sucks,' he'd said, 'but find me a better alternative.' Rashmi had snuggled up to him and run her fingers over his hairy chest. 'Hmmm—feels good, feels good, keep doing it,' Pips had mumbled distractedly.

The next morning, she'd overheard his conversation with the moneyman he'd been talking to the previous night. He'd brought piles of files and the two of them were in a huddle throwing figures and statistics around. There was talk of properties all over the place and acres of farmland back in Punjab. Investments and dummy companies, accounts abroad and enough liquidity to float half-a-dozen other film companies. 'Wow!' Rashmi had said half-jokingly as she passed them chipped mugs of lukewarm coffee. Pips had glared at her and gestured rudely. The moneyman had merely placed his arms across the reams of figures spread out on the table and stared expressionlessly ahead.

After he left, Rashmi had teased Pips, 'Hey, you're one hell of a loaded son-of-a-bitch, huh? Piles and piles stashed away. So why do you give me all this shit about being hard-up, strapped for cash and all that?'

Pips had struck her unexpectedly—it was the first time he had. It didn't hurt. Not really. But Rashmi was stunned by the suddenness of it all. 'Stay out of stuff that doesn't concern you, OK?' he'd snapped. Rashmi had retreated to her room and stared in horror at the imprint his bony fingers had left across her smooth cheek.

*

The party for Chris Angelo and his unit was arranged at one of Bombay's best-known brothels off Falkland Road. Pips had 'leased' it for the night. 'Don't cut back on the sleaze-factor,' he'd instructed his boys. 'Keep to the original muck, but just spruce the bloody place up sufficiently so as not to scare these white monkeys. Tell the girls to slap on the goo—really lay it on thick and heavy. Promise them roles, get them boozed up. Jazz up the fucking madam—buy her a new sari—whatever. I want the set-up tacky and authentic. No false frills. Get it?' They'd got it.

The brothel they had picked was off the main strip—away from the notorious cages of Kamathipura. It wasn't even numbered like some of the other dancing houses. Its patrons were well-heeled businessmen who paid well for their pleasures. Most of the girls were hand-picked by Champabai herself. She was known to spot a future beauty from a distance of half-a-mile. She liked her girls young—very young. And clean. She got fresh recruits from Nepal—ten- and twelve-year-old virgins. For the first two years they slept by her side on her gigantic four poster and she guarded them like a possessive mother hen. They were pampered by the older girls, cared for and fed well. A far cry from the abject poverty they'd escaped from in their native country. When the time was right, that is, when the girls attained puberty, Champabai prepared them for the big night with loving attention. Bathed, perfumed and dressed in finery, their faces made-up and hair oiled, they'd be presented to select customers discreetly. And finally go to the highest bidder. Champabai prided herself on the finesse she brought to the brutal act of selling virgins. She claimed she prepared her girls mentally and physically, so that when the moment of truth arrived under the heavy, sweaty body of a patron, the girl did not dilate her eyes in terror, or let a scream escape from her tender lips as was the norm with other novices. Champabai's virgins spread their legs as they'd been tutored to do and groaned seductively—mouths open, bosoms heaving. Word got around so swiftly that Champabai's virgins soon became the most desirable on the market. Interested parties booked them months in advance (via fax now) and were willing to pay any price for the privilege. 'Not for nothing,' Champabai would smile, 'not for nothing.' To be in Champabai's stable was something of an honour. Her girls didn't have to work the filthy streets. Nor solicit custom. Their job was to look after their bodies, stay free of infection and please the customer.

Champabai was the first brothel-owner to go hi-tech. Her premises were air-conditioned, carpeted and linked to the rest of the world via fax. She was also the first woman in her locality to instal a dish so that her girls could enjoy foreign soaps during their leisure hours. The cabins in her establishment were spotlessly maintained and each girl had a personal mini-bar in her small refrigerator. Taking her cue from imported catalogues and hard-core films, Champabai had shrewdly imported assorted sex games and accessories such as nipple clamps, dildos, whips, dog-collars and chains. But as she never tired of saying, 'Our men don't like all this nonsense. They come here for pleasure, not pain. Hitting and beating is reserved for their wives. But anyway, why not keep all this handy—who knows what a man might want and when? Why lose business to someone else? And why send our men straight into the arms of some white woman in London to get whipped and chained when he can get the same thing here for rupees instead of pounds?' It was her very original way of helping the Indian economy by conserving precious foreign exchange.

Pips had decided to stage his event in the main mirrored hall which led to the girls' individual cabins. He had ordered baskets of rose petals which were to be scattered over Champabai's gaudy synthetic carpet and bottles of rose water to be sprayed on his guests. 'Keep the music loud and filmi,' he'd told his boys. 'And hang a couple of extra chandeliers if necessary.'

Champabai had sat back against heavy satin cushions and surveyed the proceedings placidly, the paan in her mouth dissolving gradually and blending deliciously into the smoke bubbling up from her polished silver hookah. Rashmi had found herself so fascinated by Champabai that she had sat and stared not daring to strike up a conversation. It was only on being summoned that she had got up and taken her place by Champabai's side. 'Beti,' the madam had begun, adopting the usual maternal tones affected by brothel-owners the world over, 'what are you doing in this place?'

Rashmi had pointed to Pips and said, 'I'm his woman.'

Champabai had rolled her eyes knowingly and said, 'Woman, not wife?' Rashmi had nodded silently. After pulling on her hookah thoughtfully for a few minutes, Champabai had leaned across conspiratorially and whispered, 'Never give yourself to any man for free. You know why? Men don't value anything they get so easily. That's why we are here: to satisfy their lust, not for sex but power. Power over women. Power over us—you and me. If they buy your sex, pay for you, they feel like kings. Give it to them with love for nothing and they'll kick you in the gut.'

Rashmi had been too flustered to respond. Champabai had turned her attention to someone else. And preparations for Pips' grand evening had swung on.

But the madam's words had stayed with Rashmi. Stayed with her down the years, long after their terrible truth had been experienced and absorbed. And Rashmi had discovered an aspect to herself that sickened her.

She had found out her capacity to tolerate abuse. Champabai's girls put up with the pain inflicted by nasty Madonna-style nipple clamps. But Rashmi didn't mind those for she put up with something even worse— humiliation and insult. Her debasement was complete.

*

Pips' party went off well enough—the whores in tinsel finery danced and sang to a crazy medley that ranged from Hindi film mujra classics to Apache Indian's latest bhangra rap hits. Rashmi noted with some surprise that the girls were very pretty indeed—a far cry from the diseased-looking, undernourished, garishly-painted prostitutes flashed on front pages of dailies after staged police raids. Champabai's girls were obviously handpicked for their beauty. All other skills followed—acquired the hard way through their exacting madam's training. She watched as the girls flung their long glossy tresses across the faces of the men and teased them mercilessly through gestures that were just this side of lewd. Rashmi struck up a conversation with the girl who was sitting out a dance number. She spoke reasonably fluent English and could have easily passed off as a flashy socialite's flashier daughter. Rashmi tried not to sound terribly patronizing as she asked her about her future plans. The girl giggled and said happily,'My future is in

Champabai's hands. Whatever she decides, I'll be happy.'
Rashmi's attention was diverted by another girl clad
in a skimpy harem costume who was sitting in Angelo's
lap and tickling his left ear with her tongue. Pips was
looking immensely pleased with himself as he raised
his glass of rum and toasted Rashmi drunkenly. Rashmi
waved back feigning a cheerfulness she wasn't feeling.
She looked again at Champabai's girls. They seemed
happier by far than she herself. And their futures also
seemed more secure.

Unfortunately for Pips, his investment in Angelo
didn't pay off. The Raj saga did get made the following
summer—but without Pips. Chris Angelo picked an
unknown, low-profile production assistant from a video
magazine and got his job done at one-eighth the price
quoted by Pips. Rashmi wasn't surprised; Pips had
been behaving in a particularly high-handed way with
everybody over the past year. A monumental blow to
his ego was what he needed. But instead of reorganizing
his priorities and getting down to work, he stepped
up his drinking and took to calling Angelo, 'the frigging
Yankee bastard'.

*

Little Pips had grown up in the company of a succession
of 'uncles'—men hungry for sex—who drifted in and
out of his mother's untidy bed. Often, he'd wake up

in the middle of the night and drift sleepily into Rashmi's room to find yet another stranger between her sheets. Most of these 'uncles' were faceless fellows who rarely bothered to acknowledge his presence on the double-bed. And they rarely made any attempt to conceal their irritation. Rashmi was frequently too drunk to do anything more than shift heavily and make a little space for the frightened boy. Often she'd carry him back to his little room and snuggle into bed with him. But Uncle Max wasn't like the others. For one, he was older and kinder to both mother and son. For another, he had actually taken the trouble to speak to the solemn-faced boy staring unblinkingly at his exposed, limp penis.

'What are you looking at?' Max had enquired with amusement.

'That,' Pips had said, pointing.

'Oh that. . . that's my little friend John—John . . . you have one too, don't you?' Max had responded.

Pips had reached down between his legs and felt his own index-finger-sized penis and nodded. Their brief friendship had begun on this note as Max had extended his stay in India and moved in on a semi-permanent basis into their cluttered flat and lives.

It was on their short holiday in Goa that the boy got his first real taste of how fleeting his mother's relationships were even with nice 'uncles' like Max. Before their four-days-five-nights scheme at a seedy but new 'resort' on Baga Beach was over, Max was gone. And a Younes from Algeria had taken his place. The new uncle was too stoned to take notice of or care about the saucer-eyed, slim child clinging on to his mother's gaily-coloured beach sarongs. Younes took Rashmi on the beach, in broad daylight, under the puzzled gaze of her son. Passing fishermen looked and then walked away—another foreign animal fucking one of our bitches in heat. Sights like this weren't uncommon on the more remote beaches of Goa. And Baga in particular attracted down-market budget travellers—riff-raff, in other words—from all over the world.

The night Max moved out and Younes moved in, Pips had clung to Rashmi at night and asked softly, 'Why did that nice uncle leave?'

Rashmi had shushed him gently before saying, 'All men leave, baby. That's the way they are.'

Pips had fallen silent for a while. When he finally spoke his little voice was strong: 'I won't leave you when I become a man. Promise.'

Rashmi had squeezed his small hand and turned her back on Younes lying naked beside her.

She thought back on how Pips Sr. had left. How easy it had been for him . . . .

Six months of struggling to feed him and fuck him on command and Rashmi was ready to give up. She had talked about the crisis over an enormous dinner—pork chops, mashed potatoes, caramel custard, brandy. Pips had looked intensely disinterested as she hinted, finally mentioning the unmentionable. 'Look, baby, the fact is I'm busting my ass supporting you. And now I'm broke. B-R-O-K-E. I can't continue with this arrangement any more ...' she had trailed off, before adding through her tears: 'Besides, I think I'm preggie.'

Pips had continued to eat slowly and thoughtfully. He had asked her to get up and change the music. He had poured himself another snifter of brandy.

Rashmi had exploded, 'Did you hear what I just said—huh?'

He had raised his hand, 'Quiet, woman. I'm not deaf—the prelude hasn't ended. Sssh, listen, it's so beautiful. I love Chopin.'

'Well . . .' she had asked when the Chopin finished, 'what are you going to do about it?'

'Nothing,' he had answered, pushing his plate away and reaching for a cigarette.

Rashmi had broken down and begun sobbing uncontrollably. 'This isn't fair. You're a selfish beast. A brute. You used me.' The accusations had continued for half an hour, while Pips had wandered around her small flat, adjusting picture frames and straightening objects. Rashmi had rushed into her room and locked herself in. Two hours later when she had re-emerged,

65

Pips was gone. He'd scribbled a note on the telephone-pad: 'Hotels don't get pregnant. And they provide clean sheets.' That was it.

*

Rashmi gripped her son's hand firmly in her own. This was it. She'd had enough of this school and those bloody pink cards of theirs. Her little boy was no angel. But he wasn't a delinquent either. He needed a school that understood him—and kids like him. A special school, with flexible rules. Rules that didn't kill the spirit of a sensitive child. Rules that weren't designed to condemn him to a life of guilt for a crime he hadn't committed. She didn't know of such a place. But she sure as hell was going to find it. And fast. Poor Pips, she thought miserably. It couldn't have been easy for him in this rigid, strict school full of snooty 'regular' kids. And those horribly prim, smug mothers who gossiped about her—and worse—refused to invite Pips to kiddie parties. Yes—that was definitely the worst part. The first time he was singled out for exclusion she'd been stupid enough to demand an explanation. After that she had known better than to ask. But not Pips. He would whine like an abused puppy and sulk for days. 'Why can't I go to Ashish's party? Why didn't I get a card? Or sweets? Or a return gift?' His mother had no answers to give as she seethed within at the injustice of it all.

'Come on, let's get the hell out of here,' she said tenderly.

Pips' eyes lit up momentarily. 'We can?'

'Of course we can. We aren't in jail or something,' she told him reassuringly.

'But, what about the headmaster? He'll be angry. He'll punish me tomorrow.'

Rashmi started walking down the stone corridor. 'There will be no tomorrow—not in this crummy school, at least.'

Pips fell in step with her gratefully. 'Mummy, promise me, no more schools.'

Rashmi didn't answer him right away. She was as bewildered as he was. What was she to do with this child? Being a single parent was agonizingly difficult at moments like this, when a second opinion would have helped. Her instincts told her that Pips was justified and that she should support his decision to quit. But on a more practical level, he couldn't stay home as a drop-out either. And no Bombay school would have him with his track record. Rashmi felt drained and defeated as the two of them walked out of the school gates defiantly. She would take him to his favourite fast-food joint for a hamburger, order a coffee herself, smoke and think.

Rashmi preferred her cigarettes and coffee unfiltered. As the smoke curled up towards the false ceiling of Grab A Bite, a sense of hopelessness hit her. She picked

up a soggy finger-chip and dipped it into watery sauce.
It tasted awful. Everything tasted awful. Maybe she
was awful. Maybe she brought out the awful aspect in
people—in lovers. Why else had Pips walked out on
her? It was a convenient enough relationship from his
point of view. He didn't have to spend a dime—free
fucks, free food. How many men were that privileged.
She stared at a little girl in a polka-dotted dress licking
an ice cream and wondered about her parents, her life.
She listened to the laughter around her and asked herself
where she'd messed up. 'Just about everywhere, with
everyone, and everything,' she concluded, as she lit
another cigarette. Pips' short sadistic goodbye note
had been flushed down the toilet years ago. But his
words were branded on her mind. She remembered
the emptiness of the aftermath of his abrupt walking
out. 'It's not true. This isn't happening,' she'd tell herself,
walking round her sloppy flat picking up odds and ends.
For months afterwards, she'd waited for him to ring
the bell and walk in.

Thinking about that desperately lonely period now,
Rashmi didn't feel bitter—merely sorry. It wasn't as
if she'd loved the man truly or anything, she reasoned.
She might have, given more time. But then, given time,
most people are capable of loving anybody. Especially
when there is mutual need, mutual dependency. Maybe
that was it—she didn't make her men feel needed enough.
And consequently they didn't need her. The trick was

to get them hooked. Become an incurable habit in their petty, self-obsessed lives, get them so beholden that they thought they couldn't live without you—or more accurately—without the services only *you* could provide. Mediocre women used sex as a bait. Or food. It was the shrewd ones who used their brains. And schemed throughout their lives to hold their men, keep them enslaved. It was too late for Rashmi to learn. She should've done it to Pips, though he hadn't been worth it. But was any man? She hadn't met one she genuinely felt like sharing her life with. And it wasn't as if she was self-centred. Or mean. She was honest; and, as she had found out, men didn't like honest women. They preferred flirts and flatterers. Even manipulators. They felt more comfortable with them.

Why, she wondered. Was it because those sort of women were like men? Intrinsically, instinctively, intuitively dishonest? She wouldn't really have minded becoming one of them. It was not as if she'd taken a vow or something. Nor was there a moral stand involved. But she just didn't know how. If she put it on, she'd be found out soon enough. And she preferred being a failure to a phoney. A cheap little phoney everybody would see through. As well, she concluded, as she watched her son wipe the last traces of grease and ketchup from around his mouth, that she had never tried. She had her career, such as it was. And she had her so-called independence. The men would come and go. Come and go. Float in and out of her life like wispy cotton balls on a summer day. So bloody what? Was being manless such a shame? As she stuck her chin out defiantly and stubbed out her cigarette, she said to herself, 'Who are you kidding, darling? You know it is. You know it's a fucking shame. A big fat fucking shame. And you'd give anything for a man of your own. Anything at all. So quit the big act and START LOOKING. He's out there somewhere, grab him before some other bitch does. There is a trick to it. A method. Learn it. Perfect it. And this time, make sure you chain him down. Seal the exits. Block all escape routes. Hang on to the man. Last chance coming up, baby. Take it, take it, take it.'

Five

Noor had been about the only person in the class who had actually liked Swati. But then, Noor liked everybody. And everybody liked Noor. She was kind to people, kind to animals, kind even to inanimate objects. She believed fallen leaves and seashells had feelings. And she respected them. Nobody minded. Noor was harmless and sweet, the kind of girl who'd pick up stray kittens on the way to school and pop them into her bag only to have them scratch and mew their way out in the middle of a physics lesson. Noor was artistic and dreamy, spending hours staring at rain puddles or meditating on a rainbow that was visible only to her.

It was Noor's background that was interesting. Her aristocratic mother, known simply as Begum, was an outstanding beauty in the classical mould. The family was royal if slightly impoverished. Noor's father was a wiry, nervous nawab and had declared his independence from the Begum soon after the birth of their two children,

Noor and Nawaz. He lived to play poker, drink and
carouse with like-minded friends. Races during the
season, partridge shooting in winter and relaxing in
the hills in summer. Each time the family was strapped
for cash, out would pop some priceless piece from the
Begum's jewellery locker. Flogged on the market at a
price far below its worth, it would see them through
till the next crunch.

The Begum was a distant, cold woman, entirely
shut off from her family and, perhaps, the world.
She lived in a private sealed off environment, talking
to her pet parrots, getting massaged endlessly with
freshly-ground almond oil and listening to soul-stirring
ghazals. The children saw her only if she was ready to
meet them. At such times they would be escorted to
her wing in the sprawling, broken-down bungalow,
by the faithful Naani, the old maid from Hyderabad
who'd reared them from the time they'd emerged from
their mother's narrow, tight, dry womb. It was Naani
to whom Noor turned for everything—a grazed shin,
a cut finger, and the deeper, invisible wounds inflicted
by uncaring parents.

Nawaz was a different child—he thieved from infancy.
Shifty-eyed, fleet-footed, sly and calculating, he lived
by his wits and his extraordinary good looks. He bore
a strong resemblance to his fragile-boned mother and
made the most of it by playing up to her vanity on the
rare occasions she deigned to grant her son an audience.

'Look, Ammi,' he'd say, holding up an antique silver hand-mirror to her face. He'd boldly pull her chiffon pallav from over her head and cover his own with it. 'Can you tell the difference? Where do I begin and you end? We look like twins.'

His mother would retrieve her pallav and her dignity before shooing him off with a small, frozen smile. But Nawaz knew even at that early age that the way to his mother's heart lay through flattery. Her vanity became his weapon.

Noor would watch him cold-bloodedly reaching for their father's velvet pouch and taking out a few coins, and she'd protest mildly, 'It is not a good thing to steal.'

Nawaz would look at his elder sister disdainfully and say with a deliberation that scared her: 'No? Is it good to have children you don't care about? Answer me.'

'Don't speak like that,' she'd admonish, placing her hands over her ears to shut off his words. Cruel, harsh, accurate words calculated to inflict injury. Yet, Noor loved him. Loved him more than anyone in the world. He knew it. And exploited her vulnerability ruthlessly.

*

Noor was surprised that Swati wanted to see her. Nobody was really all that interested in Noor. Not anymore. Not since that awful accident so many years ago that had left Noor in a coma for two long months. Even the doctors had given up on the palely pretty woman lying in a near-lifeless heap on the huge hospital bed that had seemed larger than it actually was given Noor's tiny form. The Begum had sat wordlessly by her side, delicately chewing pinches of tobacco from her miniature, minakaari paan-daan. The Nawab would weave in late, the smell of a vodka-lunch still on his breath. The Begum would turn her perfectly made-up face away and engage the day-and-night nurse in meaningless conversation. The whole thing had cost the Begum a set of priceless pearls. But at least Noor had lived. Nawaz had missed the entire 'event' (as he always referred to it) by being away in Europe studying 'art history' (a classy description for gambling). When Noor had opened her eyes it was to see the Begum weeping prettily in the arms of a man she'd never seen before. 'Who is he?' were Noor's first startled words, as her mother and her lover had sprung apart guiltily. It was a moment she'd never forget.

She had taken her time to recover. She was not in a hurry. What did she have to make a quick recovery for? Everybody around her noticed a distinct change in her personality as Noor got back to her old, predictable routine. By then she had joined the ranks of perennial researchers. Nobody was very sure what exactly Noor was researching. But diligently, every morning, she'd set off for some mouldy library armed with files, pens and a packed lunch. It was assumed that she was working on Tipu Sultan's biography. But nobody saw the notes.

Naani knew that Noor had changed irrevocably when she came home from the hospital and seemed spaced out. The expression in her eyes had startled the old woman who rushed to convey it to the Begum. 'Don't be stupid,' the Begum had snapped. 'There's nothing the matter with my daughter. She's tired, that's all. Besides, she has always been this way . . . crazy, like her father.' And Naani had got the message. Whatever it was that Noor had suffered, it would remain under wraps—a family secret like so many others she was privy to. She had wisely decided to seal her lips. But that didn't mean she didn't observe the differences. Noor's movements were slower, her speech slightly slurred and her thought process drastically different. Naani noticed it all but was silent. The other servants had gossiped: *'Ladki paagal si hai'* ('the girl seems slightly mad') and Naani had shut them up. But in her heart of hearts she had known Noor would never be the same again.

A few months later, two schoolfriends had dropped in to see her at home. One of them had been Swati. It had taken a while for Noor to recognize her, but when she had, she had been genuinely glad—almost grateful—to see her. 'I thought all of you had forgotten me,' she had whispered as Swati held her hand and comforted her. The other woman had been Aparna—strong, silent and in control, just like Noor remembered her. Swati and Aparna—how great they looked together, Noor remembered thinking. Swati had been wearing a Carnaby Street outfit complete with boots, her hair blunt cut at the Mary Quant salon. Aparna was dressed in her trademark, starched white Lucknowi kurta, with the silver accessories that everybody associated with her. Noor had gazed at them with love and admiration. The evening had gone beautifully, smoothly, with fragrant sherbet and fresh mithai that Swati had gone on and on about. 'This is what I miss the most about leaving India,' she'd declared. 'Why can't the bloody Brits eat more edible food? Do you know, there are days when I actually weep thinking of hot jalebis and creamy shrikhand?'

As usual, nobody had dared to interrupt or contradict Swati as she held forth on food, clothes, fashion, books, sex, movies, music. Noor had hung on to every word, dazzled by the Swati magic. For once, the Begum too had chosen to stay on in her daughter's room, while Nawaz had staged a grand entrance straight from the airport and faked a marvellously stagy reunion with his reluctantly recuperating sister. Aparna had finally cut short the visit by saying, 'I think we are taxing Noor. She needs to rest. All this is too much excitement even for an ordinary person.'

Noor had protested mildly. She could sense that her mother and brother didn't want the party to end. Finally, she had suggested a little weakly, 'Maybe it would be a good idea to shift to the adjoining room while I take a little nap.' Nawaz and the Begum had been all for it. Swati too. She'd clearly been performing for the benefit of the two of them and this was no time to quit. Aparna had very firmly vetoed the suggestion, kissed Noor on the forehead, left her a book of verse and dragged Swati off with her.

*

The scene was perfectly clear in Noor's mind as she thought about the forthcoming lunch. It meant changing her schedule for the week. She hated doing that. Noor lived an orderly life. This sort of adjustment was alien to her. Each Monday morning she spent forty-five minutes organizing her planner. Nawaz invariably laughed when he chanced upon his sister crouched over a fat filofax meticulously making entries for the rest of the week.

'Hey, sister, you seem to be real busy. What is it that takes your time? Here, lemme see.'

Noor would clutch the filofax to her bosom and glare at Nawaz. 'At least I stay out of people's drawers and bureaux,' she would say primly.

Nawaz hadn't changed in all these years. He was busy playing the eligible rake and, what's more, succeeding. He'd built an aura around himself, that of a man of fine taste and rare sensibilities. Women were attracted to him like bees to honey. He preferred the married ones with money. A princess had killed herself because of him. Another had claimed that Nawaz was the father of her son. An ageing movie star had left her devoted husband hoping Nawaz would marry her, and a Pakistani poet had dedicated a fat volume of romantic couplets to him. Nawaz got along splendidly with his father. They were two of a kind, the only difference being their choice of sexual partners. Nawaz had taken to pimping for the old boy whose predatory instincts were dulled by alcohol and age. But they still made a remarkable pair as they swaggered into the club clad in old-fashioned achkans, swinging silver-topped ivory canes and smelling of expensive French perfume.

Noor was simultaneously repelled and fascinated by her brother. She admired his savoir-faire, his devil-may-care poses and the fussy elegance of his appearance. And yet, she backed away from his reptilian eyes and spidery fingers, especially when he got into one of his mischievous moods and began tormenting her about boyfriends she'd never had. Noor would scold him in her high, thin, nasal voice, 'Stop it! You know there's nobody. I hate you when you are like this.' This would be his cue to ask, 'Like what, like what?' and come close to her, his spidery fingers reaching to tickle, to tease and finally to pinch till she winced in pain.

Nawaz had attempted the same thing with Swati. That had been a long time ago, when the girls were twelve. Swati had rewarded him with a stinging slap and flung him easily out of Noor's room, yelling, 'Creep! Keep your tentacles to yourself.' Noor had silently applauded her friend's gesture but felt obliged to declare her affront on Nawaz's behalf. Was that when Swati had stopped talking to her abruptly and stormed out of her house? Possibly. All Noor could recall now was the look in Swati's eyes—disbelief mixed with deep hurt. She'd said nothing but her actions had conveyed her message. She couldn't forgive Noor for siding with Nawaz—her own brother! That was the extent of the sort of unquestioning devotion Swati expected from those she called her *friends*. The next day at school Noor had faced a virtual boycott. Swati had arrived early and provided an entirely distorted version of the events of the preceding day. She'd threatened to ostracize the others if they dared disobey her edict and speak to Noor. It had been yet another demonstration of Swati's powerful hold over the class. The boycott had been lifted eventually, but things had never been the same between Swati and her. Noor regretted it bitterly to this day and held it against Nawaz.

How did he do it? Get away with everything—including brazenly pimping for his father? It was no secret that the old man requisitioned Nawaz's services whenever he needed a woman or an able-bodied young man. 'Just for a massage, that's all,' the Nawab would wheeze, his rheumy eyes lighting up briefly, perhaps at memories of his distant youth when, rejected from the Begum's cold, unfriendly bed, he'd lurch off to seek company elsewhere. It started with bridge partners at the club. Neglected wives of men too busy making money to bother with making love to the beautiful women with cold bodies they'd abandoned back at home. The Nawab could smell them out in an instant—it was a gift he'd passed on to his young son. Over pink gins and Benson and Hedges, he'd pay them courtly attention at a measured pace—never rushing, never pushing. He'd identify their perfumes and present them flacons of their favourite fragrances a few months later; send them exclusive bath oils and ittars from his personal perfumiers in Lucknow; offer garden fresh chameli strings for their slim wrists in summer; and pamper them in small, intimate ways. The Nawab was rarely in a hurry in those days. He knew he had all the time in the world to work on his chosen love, revelling in the slow but inevitable game which would end in his favourite five-star suite—the one with Omar Khayyam motifs and latticework screens.

It was only after the Nawab lost his romantic, rakish good looks and developed something like a hunch due to a chronically bad posture, that Nawaz moved in smoothly.

The first time was at a mehfil organized at Nawabsaab's oldest friend's sprawling old bungalow on Cumballa Hill. The Begum had declined the invitation, declaring that such evenings were far too vulgar for her delicate tastes. The Nawab had accepted instantly—not that he had much of an ear for Urdu poetry—but it was on occasions like these that he managed to meet fresh blood—visiting begums from Hyderabad, simpering dancers from Lucknow, nubile daughters of casual friends. The Nawab had roped in Nawaz and even thrown him a tantalizing bait. 'Tasneem is going to be there—you know that lovely-as-a-magnolia girl from Delhi? Back from some fancy British university—but aah—what beauty! Breathtaking.' Nawaz had smiled slyly to himself. He knew Tasneem. From the squash courts at the club. Knew her intimately, so to speak. A quick grope after switching off the lights in the indoor, enclosed court and then a quick tryst in the deserted ladies' changing rooms. That had been fun, he recalled, especially the marker's knowing smile when the two of them emerged, showered and perfumed twenty minutes later. And now here was the old man trying to entice him with a girl whose tiny breasts had fitted so warmly, so snugly, in his long-fingered hands.

The Nawab had surveyed his son critically on the evening of the party. 'Wear a sherwani,' he'd urged the jeans and T-shirt clad Nawaz, 'it's more suited to the occasion.' Nawaz had hesitated, 'I feel so stupid in that thing and hot too.' But seeing his father's disappointed expression, he had gone off to have his black, beautifully-tailored long jacket ironed. When the two of them entered the large, cool, marble front hall of the bungalow, everybody had turned around to stare. They made a remarkably good-looking pair—noble of brow, aristocratic in bearing. Nawaz had sat through the interminably long poetry recitations, mentally ticking off prospective bedmates. He had noticed his father staring at an elegant woman in her mid-forties. The woman had returned the stare but allowed her gaze to linger on Nawaz. Embarrassed for his father, Nawaz had looked away quickly. He'd been to bed with women of her age, but hadn't enjoyed the experience. Something about their upper arms put him off. And the determined expertise on display. The Nawab was beginning to look dejected. It was obvious that the evening had ceased to have any meaning for him. Nawaz had found himself feeling intensely sorry for his father. How bruised the old man looked. And how desperately unhappy. In a longish break between poets, Nawaz had gone up to the woman as she stood expectantly on the veranda sipping khus serbet.

'You are more beautiful than a moonlit night,' he had said softly. She had turned around and laughed softly. 'Stop pretending, you bastard. You don't mean a word—I saw it in your eyes immediately. So why are you bothering when there are so many young girls around. Tasneem, for instance.'

Nawaz had led her into the fragrant garden silently before saying, 'Since you have been honest with me, I feel obliged to be honest with you. It's my father—he fancies you. Give him a little of your time—that's all I ask. He's a charming man. And an exceedingly generous one too.'

The woman had stared at him mockingly: 'So, that's what you do for a living. Pimp. How charming! And for your father at that. Even more charming. But let me tell you I'm not offended. In fact, I'm rather touched. I think it's awfully sweet of you to put yourself out like this. Really. And just for that I'll go sit next to that randy, old goat—to make you happy. OK? But remember—you owe me one.'

Nawaz had smiled a slow, devilish smile. He had touched her bare arm lightly and traced a long line down the length of it with his forefinger. 'Lady—that's a deal,' he'd said. 'Besides, you have nice upper arms.' He had turned on his heel and walked briskly back into the hall. The woman saw him going up to his father, bending low and whispering something into his ear. The old man had perked up immediately and patted his son's hand. And with his mission easily accomplished Nawaz was gone, leaving a faint whiff of musk in his wake.

*

'I lost her because of you,' Noor had accused Nawaz the day after Swati put her into the deep freeze. 'Who knows when she'll start speaking to me again? It could be months or years.' As it turned out it didn't take too long for Swati to thaw. She had needed to borrow Noor's neatly written English Literature notes. Better still, she wanted Noor to copy them out for her. Swati had put Noor on the job casually, conveying the impression that she was bestowing a rare honour. Overwhelmed, Noor had got down to it promptly and even thanked Swati for 'letting' her. But till the truce took place, Noor had suffered. And suffered deeply.

Nawaz had listened to his sister's accusation with a scornful expression on his face. Picking up a few toasted nuts from a silver tray he had tossed a few into the air, catching them expertly in his open mouth. 'Really?' he'd mocked. 'You mean that horny friend of yours matters all that much? Hey come on, what is this— true love or something? Forget it. She's just another cheap slut turning tricks. Not worth your time—our time. We are different, Noor. Our background is different. Our way of life is different. We don't need to put up with the likes of Swati. I bet she smells—up, there and everywhere. And I'm almost certain the greedy bitch steals. Naani mentioned it. She's noticed a few things missing. If Mummy finds out, that's it. She'll ban your friend from coming over. Next time I see Swati I'm going to ask her about the silver ashtray. And the ivory horse.'

Noor had gazed at her beautiful brother uncertainly— he was right about Swati. She *was* rather low. Nawaz had cracked open a salted pistachio, walked up to his sister and said, 'Good girl—open your mouth. Here's a little present for you. Go wash your face. I'm in such a great mood, I'll take you for a drive. And forget that whore. She isn't worth your tears.'

Gathering her heavy files and books together, Noor remembered Nawaz's words. Swati had certainly lived up to them—she was a whore. A classy one perhaps. But still a whore. Noor took a quick look at herself in the long mirror of the ancient armoire. She looked prematurely old and exceedingly shabby. Her shapeless kurta hung limply below her knees. Her shock of grey hair was cut in some nondescript style ('Just keep it off my face,' were Noor's standing instructions to the Chinese girl who trimmed it). She peered at the world through thick, unflattering glasses even though the Begum had offered to finance a pair of contact lenses years ago. The once laughing mouth now turned down at the corners, and Noor didn't walk so much as shuffle, weighed down with books and, or so it seemed, the burden of life itself. She knew that her mother was extremely ashamed of her appearance and turned her delicate face away to avoid noticing her dowdy daughter. The Nawab barely looked in her direction and when he did, it was generally to cadge small change ('Have to pay the bloody cab, just a couple of coins will do'). That left Nawaz and his constant taunts. 'No wonder you don't have a boyfriend. Which man will want to be seen with a floor-mop?'

Noor stared at her reflection in the low light of the cheerless room. Did she really look all that bad? All that unattractive? She straightened her shoulders, noticed how her breasts swelled out provocatively and promptly assumed her customary slouch. She ran a brush through her stiff hair. It used to be beautiful once—thick and shiny. Before the accident, that is. Noor stopped her critical self-examination abruptly. It was hopeless. Her life was for ever more sliced up like a 'before-and-after' ad: before the accident, after the accident.

*

She should never have accepted Aamir's offer for a ride home. Never. But Aamir was so hard to resist, so hard. Especially when he tilted his head, crinkled his eyes and looked at her in a way that made her wish she were Swati—confident, sexy, flirtatious Swati. But Aamir had asked her—Noor and not any of the other girls. That was a triumph in itself.

Noor remembered each horrifying little detail connected with that ill-fated day. She remembered her smart clothes, her hair streaming in the breeze, and the feel of Aamir's well-muscled shoulder blades rippling under her slim fingers as she clung on to him while the motorbike sped down the highway, picking up speed with each kilometre.

'Faster, Aamir, faster,' Noor had urged, 'let's break a record today.'

Aamir had swerved his way through midday traffic—trucks, taxis, tempos making their way out of Bombay city, heading for distant destinations with overwrought drivers behind the wheel. Nobody at home knew where Noor had disappeared that afternoon. The old driver had waited outside the college gates as usual and finally gone home.

The Begum had looked up from her massage at Naani's distraught face and murmured, 'Don't worry. She's probably at Rashmi's. Or Aparna's. She'll phone.'

Naani had protested, 'It is not like her to do that. She would have told me if she didn't need the car.' She was waved off and told to leave as the masseuse kneaded the Begum's creamy, bony buttocks with warm olive oil.

The call from the public hospital had come hours later. Aamir and Noor had been picked up by a kindly retired advocate on his way home. The two of them had been tossed to the side of the road like discarded dish rags and left to die. Two more victims of Bombay's callous hit-and-run brigade. Noor had become unconscious at the moment of impact, while Aamir had lain a few feet away, doubled up with pain, but fully conscious.

Eventually his broken limbs had knitted faster than hers. Both of them had suffered concussions and internal injuries. But only Noor had received a cranial blow so forceful, that it had brought on the prolonged coma and the subsequent sea change in her personality. The doctors couldn't decide whether to attribute her miserable condition to something physiological or to trauma. Noor was never the same again. Nor was Aamir. He'd gone on to an arranged marriage and prosperity without a backward glance, while Noor had crept back into her dim bedroom and stayed there, often waking up in the night to the sound of crushed bones and the slightly salty taste of blood in her dry mouth.

Six

On Tuesday morning, Reema woke up with one of her famous migraines. Ravi took one swift look at her creased brow and asked for ice-packs. He went out of their gilt-and-marble bedroom to warn their daughter not to disturb her mother. Shonali, the daughter, hastily shoving a packed lunch into her bag, said without bothering to look up, 'She has one of her headaches—right? The servants have had it today.' Reema's headaches were a regular family event that left nobody untouched. The people who dreaded them the most were the servants whom she'd scream at all day for imaginary transgressions.

Ravi peeped into the bedroom to check on her mood. She glared at him and promptly screwed up her eyes to play up the pain. The room smelt strongly of Tiger Balm. Under the quilted silk bedcover ('I spent eight thousand rupees on it') Reema lay motionless. She could've been a corpse, he thought, and wondered for a moment if that's what he'd have really liked Reema to be—dead. In an effort to overcome his guilt at the thought and to show her he was interested and involved in her empty life, he said, keeping his voice friendly, 'Reema . . . it's Tuesday. Your friend's lunch. Remember?'

Reema sat up as if her spine had got an electric shock. 'I know it's Tuesday. I know my friends are coming. Do you think I'm so stupid or what? Why do you think I'm upset? Now everything will be spoilt—my mood, my looks, my clothes, the food. Somebody jealous must have cursed me. I think I even know who it is. That Mithoo woman. Always staring at my rings and eyeing my saris. Jealous bitch.'

Ravi ran out of the room leaving Reema to mutter on. He knew how much the success of the lunch mattered to his wife. This was not the usual kitty lunch which she'd trained herself to handle with such aplomb. Even though he didn't know her schoolfriends, he'd overheard enough scraps of conversation over the years to realize that Reema still had a lot of scores to settle, a lot of points to make. Ravi was indifferent to his wife's disappointments and longings most of the time. It was when they impinged on his life and made him miserable that he felt drawn into her world. Ravi was a practical man. His wife's mercurial moods bothered him only when they had important business entertaining to do. As they did over each busy weekend. Reema on a rampage didn't make the ideal partner for NRI clients with bulging portfolios. He needed her to fulfil the role. And with that at the back of his mind, Ravi wanted his wife's lunch to be a hit. Besides, it wasn't every day that someone like Swati Bridges came over for a meal. His friends were sure to besiege him with questions. It was one story he could eat out on for at least a couple of months. Reema had casually alerted a couple of media contacts. There were chances of their lunch being mentioned in the papers. Somebody from a glossy had already phoned their home to ask about Swati's schedule in Bombay. Reema's self-importance had soared as she'd boasted about the 'very exclusive' lunch for her friend, sounding proprietorial as she jealously guarded her friend's 'privacy' by refusing to divulge details she herself wasn't aware of.

'Shall I organize some flowers for you?' he asked Reema helpfully.

'Don't bother, I've already done it,' she snapped, as she clambered out of bed, her thighs rubbing against each other, her nightie riding high above her dimpled knees. Ravi made his exit quickly. He hated to see her puffy face in the mornings. It ruined his day.

Reema stared balefully at her ungainly reflection in the full-length dressing table mirror. She stepped on the weighing scale and pulled a face. She couldn't bear to look at herself in the mirror after that. Her bedside clock chimed musically. With a start she jumped off the scales and into the shower. Two-and-a-half hours to go, she calculated. She was going to need every precious minute. She popped two Migril tablets into her mouth, threw back her head and swallowed them. No water. Just the sticky, warm saliva that had gathered in her throat was enough to push the pills down her gullet. There. That would settle her. It always did. Till the pain started hammering inside her head again.

Reema went over the menu. She'd decided to hire the hottest caterers in Bombay—a boyfriend-girlfriend team, Tanya and Titu, who specialized in what passed for 'nouvelle cuisine'. She'd been most impressed by their act at Pinky Khemnani's kitty the previous month. Nobody had heard of any of the dishes and almost every woman had gone away hungry, but the impact the two made had compensated for those lapses. Besides, Reema figured, her cook with his repertoire of Punjabi-Moghlai fare wouldn't be able to create the desired effect for this particular occasion. Swati probably wasn't used to eating desi khana any more. She looked so slim in the papers and on TV, Reema marvelled. No woman could stay that way on murg-massalam and chana bhaturas. With that in mind, she'd ordered a selection of salads, using 'foreign' vegetables from Crawford market—broccoli, leeks, baby corn, Chinese cabbage, iceberg lettuce. She'd asked Tanya and Titu to get their cold cuts from the Taj. The rest she'd left to them—cheese and spinach quiche, stuffed mushrooms, ham and asparagus rolls, roast mutton with mint sauce, jacket potatoes and onion tarts. Fresh strawberries (cream separate) would take care of dessert. The coffee had caused a bit of a problem as Reema didn't have the right cups. And she only drank instant coffee. She'd considered borrowing Natasha's bone-china set and Italian percolator but given up the idea (the entire kitty club would find out and snigger). Finally, she'd gone out and bought one from a smuggler in the Heera Panna Shopping Complex. Ravi had raised his eyebrows along with his voice when she'd told him what she'd paid, but Reema had a way of explaining these things: 'Darling, remember what happened when that Dutchman and his wife asked for coffee last year? We had to serve it in teacups. This is an investment—all your foreign friends drink coffee after dinner.' True enough, Ravi had concluded, and shut up.

Reema also gave herself full marks for buying a carton of Perrier. She'd had to go to at least five stores before finding what she was looking for. Everybody said, 'Buy Bisleri, buy Bisleri.' That was like saying, 'Buy local Scotch.' Reema sighed at the memory. Some of these people were so unaware and untutored. As she dried herself, she felt better. Mineral water. Imported mineral water. It was the sort of detail that made the difference. She was sure Swati would ask for mineral water with her meal. And wine, of course. Reema had got the servant boy to clean the crystal yesterday. Ravi had stared as Reema brought down the box from the storage room. 'Hey! We spent a bomb on those in London,' he'd commented, 'where the hell have they been rotting all these years? How come I never get to drink out of them?' Reema had glared at him, 'As if you drink wine. These aren't meant for whisky. Can't you make out from the shape? Look, I've found a book which shows you how to mix cocktails. Here are photographs of the right glasses for the right drink, see?'

Both of them had studied the pictures. Ravi had picked up one of the glasses, looked at it thoughtfully and said, 'This looks like a martini glass, doesn't it? Don't tell me you girls are going to drink martinis tomorrow?' Reema had grabbed it from his hands. 'Don't be silly. This is for wine. White wine. Everybody drinks white wine these days. Everybody. I am sure Swati would like a glass. And red also. I'm serving both.' Ravi had shaken his head and gone to his room. His wife had looked so flushed with excitement, he hadn't wanted to ruin her enthusiasm by pointing out the ridiculousness of the whole thing. Besides, he'd stopped arguing with his wife long ago. What Reema wanted, Reema got. And Swati was a trophy guest after all.

*

Reema asked the maid to fetch her freshly-ironed outfit. Layers and layers of it. Flowered pink chiffon in a flowing design. Like those airy suits Sharmila Tagore wore in

her husband's ads. Feminine, expensive and loose enough
to camouflage figure faults. She was grateful to Mrs
Mehra whose busy tailors had agreed to stitch it at
such short notice. Fortunately Reema had a chiffon
sari lying around. That meant she could save a little on
fabric. Of course, Mrs Mehra had charged her the earth
for the outfit, but it was worth it. Reema had surveyed
her wardrobe and concluded she didn't have anything
suitable for the lunch. She wanted the look to be
sophisticated yet simple. All her stuff was far too dressy,
flashy and overstated. She'd tried to visualize what the
rest would wear, particularly Swati. Something stylish,
something sexy and something red, she'd figured. Aparna?
A dull brown khadi kurta with wooden buttons, or
the trademark Lucknowi kurta. Surekha? An embroidered
organdy with pink posies. Rashmi? Maybe a sari—but
the neckline of her blouse would be plunging. Noor.
Hard to say. In the old days she'd have picked a traditional,
tasteful salwar-kameez. Rather, the Begum would've
picked it for her. But now, she'd show up in a shapeless
something. Maybe even a kaftan. She'd spotted her at
a traffic light months ago clad in one. Thank God Noor
hadn't seen her or she'd have had to pull over and give
her a ride.

Reema had finalized her jewellery last night.
She'd wondered whether her pearls would do the
trick—the pink ones from Hong Kong. Then she decided
to stick to jadav—the simple set her mother had presented

her. Somehow it gave her confidence. Pearls were so commonplace these days. And they all looked fake or Hyderabadi. A woman could never go wrong with jadav. But the earrings were bothering her. The long ones seemed too formal—but they were a part of the set. The small ones got lost against her large face. Diamond clusters seemed excessive. And gold wasn't chic enough. Reema considered calling up her sister-in-law and asking for her South Indian rubies. Ravi would be furious, but what the hell. Finally, her daughter solved the problem. 'What about your solitaires, Mummy. They go with everything.' Of course. Silly she hadn't thought of them herself.

She had a choice of two other looks on the clothes front. A designer outfit from a Delhi boutique in dyed jute with wooden beads or a designer sari from Ravissant with the latest quilted, embroidered, jacket-like blouse. The sari slimmed her considerably but made her appear darker than she was. The salwar-kameez was fun, but she felt a bit like Bajirao Peshwa in it. Reema debated over the sari. After all, it was her lunch, and she was the hostess—she was permitted to be overdressed. No No sari. A salwar-kameez it would be. It made her feel younger, and hopefully, look younger too. The layered look of Mrs Mehra's outfit would make her look both youthful and elegant. Make-up was never a problem for Reema—she was an expert. She'd gone to a grooming class two years ago—the fancy one conducted by an ex-model. She'd picked up all the tricks—how to apply lipstick so her lips looked thinner, how to wear kajal so her eyes seemed larger, how to paint on eyebrows à la filmstar Rekha defining each individual hair so that they appeared longer, how to shade her cheeks with blusher so they acquired contours—oh how she enjoyed cheating with her bag of tricks! Even her daughter knew her secrets now. Ravi, of course, was far from interested or impressed. And since their love-making had fizzled out to a pathetic fortnightly routine, it didn't matter any more that she went to bed with her face lathered with layers of expensive night cream home-delivered by her favourite smuggler.

Reema examined the fine lines under her eyes in Ravi's shaving mirror and with the curtains drawn. Of course they were there. She wondered whether Swati had had hers removed or filled out or injected with silicone or tucked away out of sight or whatever it was that these fancy women did in the West. She certainly looked much younger than all of them in her pictures. And her voice over the telephone! So cultivated, so charming and with such a nice accent—just like a foreigner's. Reema had always envied Swati her musical, well-modulated voice. While practising for the school choir, Swati's contralto would soar over everybody else's off-key contribution, and she'd be singled out to sing the solos. And there was Reema taking singing lessons from a thumri singer. Spending hour after hour with

97

her tanpura and getting nowhere. How effortlessly Swati had managed to leave the others behind.

And it was still the same story. Here they were, the 'girls' from Santa Maria High School, leading predictable, mundane lives of domesticity and imagined bliss. And there was Swati, trail-blazing her way from one exotic locale to another (according to the glossies, that is) from one great lover to another—successful, sexy and having the time of her life. Lucky bitch, Reema cursed silently, as she hastily plucked her eyebrows. She didn't deserve any of this. No way. There were other, far worthier girls in their class. Reema herself, for that matter. She could've been anything she wanted to be—yes, even an actress. It was she who'd won the prize for dramatics in their final year, not Swati. Instead, she'd decided to get married. Why? Because her mother had told her to. 'Just imagine, you'll be the first girl from your batch—everybody will be jealous of you. And think of the boy you're getting! He isn't just any old fellow. Ravi is rich. He is also *kafi* good-looking. Nice family—small. No *jhanjat*. No in-law problem. Good house. Car with driver, servants. Air-conditioned bedroom. Jewellery. What more do you want? Also, you have to think honestly, beti. There are fairer girls in the community. He has chosen you over them. There were families willing to give big dowries. I know Ravi was offered a flat on Peddar Road. And a partnership in the family firm within two years. You're a lucky girl.

Whatever you want to do can be done later—after marriage. These people are broad-minded. They won't stop you.' Reema had fallen for it all. It had seemed so exciting. New clothes, new jewellery, supervised dates with Ravi . . . .

With an impatient snap of her head, she rang for her maid. She had noticed a crease in her outfit. Plus, the bedroom needed straightening out. These servants! She'd tried to train them for years, but the minute they got her routine right, they'd disappear. Walk into the neighbour's flat for a few rupees more. Treacherous lot. And shameless people. Imagine hiring, no, worse, stealing other people's servants. How low! But that was Bombay. Nobody respected ethics.

The door bell rang. It was a man from the Taj florist carrying an enormous arrangement of antirrhinums and gladioli with green ferns at different levels.

Reema snapped, 'I didn't order this.' A quavering servant showed her a card. She glanced at it with growing irritation till she noticed the embossed initials on the envelope—SB. Reema's face changed. The hard lines around the mouth softened as she waved the delivery boy away with a fiver and read the short note:

To my dear and sweet schoolfriend Reema. Just a small way of saying thank you for arranging the luncheon. I hope you like the flowers. I picked them up myself. See you shortly.

Reema was beaming as she waltzed back to her room thinking, 'That's class.' Would any of her kitty wives ever think of such a gesture? Never. They took everything for granted. Forget appreciation and thanks, they tore you apart the moment you left the room. In your own house and at your own party. That's how grateful they were. And look at Swati. She must've spent at least five hundred rupees on those flowers. Not just any flowers. Antirrhinums. Those fleshy, sexy, phallic-looking things which cost the earth. And the arrangement! No cheap cane baskets with plastic containers. This was modern art. High fashion sculpture. As stylish as the sender. Reema would show her that she too knew a bit about such things. Frantically, she dug into her cupboard, behind the clothes and under her sweaters. That's where she hid her foreign perfumes. The unopened ones. She had quite a hoard and she was immensely proud of it. After careful consideration, she picked out Passion. It was expensive and it was still in. Reema loved the ads and she'd always been a big fan of Liz Taylor, ever since she'd seen her in *Lassie*. She rushed to her daughter's room to look for wrapping paper. Reema had also taken classes in gift-wrapping and presentation. She could tie different kinds of bows and do wonderful things with satin ribbons. It took her less than ten minutes to create a compact parcel dressed up in gold and red. Passion looked professionally gift-wrapped.

Reema surveyed her handiwork proudly. Nobody, not even those catty women at the club could deny her skills at presentation. All the kitty wives envied her table. It never looked the same. She devised themes for her parties—themes that were so ingenious and creative, it left the other wives gasping. They all said, 'Only Reema could do this.' It was true. Her sister-in-law never failed to compliment her. 'Where do you learn all these things?' she'd ask staring admiringly at the way the prawns were served in individual straw baskets with pretty paper doilies under them. This afternoon, too, Reema had come up with a picnic theme—everything casual, but stylishly so. Food in hampers, red checked tablecloths, solid red serviettes, assorted breads, a mound of fruit arranged as a centrepiece, with bottles of Chianti propped up on covered boxes. She'd thought of imported paper plates, but given up the idea and brought out her other, less formal china (the one without gold leaf). Even the dining-room looked different, with lots of plants, plastic vines, flowers and palms everywhere. She'd spread straw mats at strategic points over the wall-to-wall carpet in case anybody felt like sitting down for the meal. The music would be appropriate as well—perhaps *The Pastorale* (this had been suggested by her Goan neighbour who played the piano and was familiar with Western Classical music).

Everything was perfectly in place. Reema peeked into the kitchen to check on the caterers. They were busy making tiny onion tarts. 'Smells good,' Reema commented before rushing back to her room for the final touch—a hint of lip gloss over her dry, nervous mouth. There! Now she was ready. Ready to face Swati. And the others.

Seven

The first person to arrive was Rashmi.

'I nearly didn't make it,' she said breathlessly, giving Reema a quick hug. Rashmi seemed flustered and distracted as she pulled out a hair brush and ran it through her matted tresses nervously. Reema noted the occasional grey in Rashmi's hair with some satisfaction. So, she wasn't the only one. She also stared pointedly as the strands fell on the carpet. Rashmi noticed her expression and apologized: 'God! What a mad day!' she muttered, as she bent down to pick up the fallen hair.

'Leave it,' Reema said, sounding sharper than she intended to, 'I'll get a servant to brush the carpet.' She looked at Rashmi closely and felt smug. Sure enough, the neckline was plunging. Rather, there was no neckline at all. Rashmi was wearing a knotted choli like the Bombay fisherwomen. What they used to call a 'ghati blouse'. Her figure was still pretty good, but her neck looked crepey. Maybe she neglected to cream it, Reema thought. The sari must've been pretty when she bought it. Rashmi did have individual taste. What was it? A Chanderi? Or a mulmul? It was hard to tell. Poor girl, obviously didn't possess any jewellery. Her thin wrists had four wooden bangles encircling them. They looked old and worn. Nothing round the neck—no mangalsutra. Not even a chain. And small pearl and gold earrings. The watch was old and cheap. The rings, obvious fakes. Reema looked at Rashmi's sandals—footwear revealed so much about a person. Yes, they were scruffy and cuffed all right. Black. And she was carrying an old brown bag. A huge and ugly one. The sort that could double for an overnight case. Reema adopted a kindly condescending manner, as Rashmi looked around the apartment and exclaimed, 'Well, this is rather grand, isn't it?'

Reema adjusted an antique silver lota and said casually, 'I don't know, my husband and I did it together. We like beautiful things.'

Rashmi walked to the large windows and stared out. 'Great view.'

There was a longish silence before Reema said a bit too cheerily, 'Let's sit down and have a drink while we wait.'

'Good idea,' Rashmi said as she sank into a raw-silk upholstered sofa, her feet sticking out.

Reema asked in her special society voice, 'White, rose or red?'

Rashmi laughed, 'Who cares, *yaar*. Wine is wine. Anything *chalega.*'

Reema fetched two glasses of chilled white and sat down next to Rashmi. 'You're looking good,' she said rather unconvincingly.

'Liar!' Rashmi laughed again. 'I'm looking like a fucked-up hag-bag. You know it. I know it. But you are looking, well, prosperous. Like a smug, snug, bug in a rug. Your boobs seem bigger too. Done something?'

Reema hastened to assure her that the boobs were still the original ones with an extra padding of middle-age fat on them. That's all. Rashmi hadn't changed very much. Still using foul language. Still rough and raw all over. Mercifully both of them were spared further conversation by the sound of the bell. Reema sprang up and went towards the door after arranging her dupatta carefully around her shoulders. Rashmi lit a cigarette and looked out of the window at the sea in the distance.

'Hi!' Reema squealed. 'Hi!' she heard another squeal.

'God! Look at you. Still the same,' Reema was holding a woman Rashmi couldn't see at arm's length. But she recognized her voice. It was Surekha. Rashmi could just about make out an ample outline and the starched sari standing out stiffly around it making Surekha's silhouette appear like a cardboard cutout. Surekha peeped over Reema's shoulder and spotted Rashmi. 'Hi!' she shouted enthusiastically.

Rashmi raised her hand, the one with the cigarette held between the fingers. 'Come, come, come . . . sit . . . it's been ages. You're looking prosperous. Well, both of you are.'

There was an edge of defiance in the comment that made Reema squirm a little. Surekha was looking around, picking up things, marvelling over Reema's acquisitions. All three of them were talking simultaneously. 'I hear your daughter's very pretty.' 'Heavens! My son is a terror.' 'What about your sister—the younger one who had that funny boyfriend?' 'How's your mother's knee? Still bad?'

The bell rang again and the three women stopped talking. They looked expectantly at the door. 'Wonder if it's Swati—she's very particular about time,' Reema said. It wasn't. Noor stood outside uncertainly, fidgeting with her dupatta, a small parcel clutched tightly in her hands.

'May I come in?' she asked timidly, as the others stared wordlessly at her. After a long moment, Rashmi got up from the sofa and went to the door to welcome her with a hug and kiss.

'Is she here?' Noor asked, a nervous edge to the already quavery voice. She seemed totally disinterested in the assembled women or her surroundings and barely glanced around.

Reema pointed to the flowers. 'She sent those,' she said, 'I suppose she got a little held up.'

Noor stared down into her lap. 'I hope she comes soon. I have to give her this and then I must go.'

'Without having lunch? Never!' Reema interrupted her. 'We are meeting after years. Let's enjoy ourselves. As it is nobody stays in touch.'

'That's true,' Surekha said helping herself to toasted cashews. 'I mean, look at me, I meet nobody. We all live in Bombay and we don't see each other. Everybody is so busy. But that is Bombay. After this lunch, we must get together regularly.'

Rashmi pulled a face. 'Where's the fucking time, *yaar*? I don't know whether I'm coming or going. I'm on the run all the time. By the way, what news of Aparna? Is she coming? Reema, have you invited her? I'm dying to hear what she's doing with her life. I read the odd thing in some business magazine or the other. Advertising, right? Good racket to be in.'

Surekha declined the wine and concentrated on the cashew nuts. 'I'm waiting to see Swati. What a life she's been leading! Lucky girl. No problems. Hasn't she married again? I read it in a gossip column. English fellow.' The women exchanged looks that were a mixture of envy, resentment and reluctant admiration.

Reema patted the creases of the kurta stretched across the plump thighs and tried to change the subject by saying brightly, 'Well, let's face it. At least she's having a damn good time.'

Rashmi added dryly: 'When hasn't she? Swati fucking lives for a good time.' Noor had withdrawn further into

herself and was fiddling absently with the parcel. 'What's in it?' Rashmi asked in an effort to draw her out.

'Nothing, nothing. Something small for Swati. Actually, something she'd left behind at our home on one of her rushed visits.'

Rashmi raised her eyebrows but didn't ask further questions. Reema went back into the kitchen to order more snacks. Surekha followed her saying, 'Don't mind, I want to see how you've planned your flat. My kitchen is a big mess. What to do? When there's a mother-in-law in the house, there is no choice. Everything has to be done her way. . . everything.'

Reema was only too glad to show off. 'I've just put in a microwave. It's so convenient. Especially when my daughter comes home. Pop in a pizza and out it comes in seconds. My husband really freaks on it. The deep freeze is also new. We have so many parties, I prefer to stock everything in advance. No last minute problems . . . . Oh that? My brother-in-law sent it. Latest food processor. He also sent that soda-making machine—you know for fizzy drinks. I'll serve some later.'

Surekha opened the fridge and exclaimed, '*Baap re*—so much food, so much food.'

Reema looked at her pointedly and tried not to look embarrassed. 'Poor Noor. She's looking terrible, isn't she? I don't think she has recovered fully. She never will. Rashmi's also looking funny. Did you see her feet?

All cracked and black, as if she works in a coal mine. Or walks barefooted for miles and miles.'

Surekha was staring at the catering duo. 'Who are they?' she asked loud enough for them to hear.

Reema pinched her and led her out of the kitchen. 'Don't ask like that right in front of them. It's so embarrassing.'

Surekha seemed surprised. 'So what? They're only cooks or something, no?'

Reema led her to the children's bedroom. 'See the wallpaper. I got it specially from New York. Such lovely stuff you get there. I wanted to buy the whole floor in the departmental store with the furniture and everything. But Ravi said, "Don't be silly, we can't take all this back. As it is, there is so much excess baggage."'

Surekha sat on the bed and bounced up and down. 'Do you go abroad often? Every year?'

Reema nodded, as she fussed with her daughter's desk and repositioned her pencil box. 'Ravi travels a lot on business. I go once or twice a year. Generally to Singapore or to Hong Kong—we have cousins there. Plus, the shopping is so good. And cheap. I mean compared to London. One trip and I get my year's supply of everything—soap, shampoo, perfumes, bras, panties. So convenient.'

Surekha continued to bounce. 'I have never been abroad,' she said cheerfully. 'Must be lovely, no? I look at Star TV and think foreign countries are so clean.'

Reema stared incredulously at her friend. 'I don't believe this. How is it possible? You mean you have never travelled outside India?'

Surekha laughed, 'Forget India, say Bombay. I can't go anywhere. I have to stay home because of my mother-in-law. She's old, sick and can't be left alone. My husband doesn't like me to go anywhere leaving her at home. And she doesn't want to travel anywhere. Only go for pilgrimages with other widows. Even this lunch was a problem.'

Reema sat down next to her and said, 'Look, this is ridiculous. Come on, what age are we living in? Why can't your mother-in-law stay with her other children? Surely your husband has brothers and sisters?'

Surekha answered slowly, 'I have one sister-in-law. She lives in Ahmedabad. My mother-in-law cannot stay with her daughter's in-laws. In our community, we don't behave like that. It's not nice for married girls to have their people staying with them.'

Reema got up abruptly. 'Well, let's go outside and join the other two. Nice ring you're wearing. Your husband's in the diamond business, isn't he? Must see him one of these days, I need bigger solitaires.'

Noor and Rashmi were talking softly, earnestly, when the other two joined them. Rashmi looked at her watch. 'No trace of Madam Bridges. We can't hang around forever. Maybe she has forgotten. Or maybe she met a man on the way and decided to marry him. Hey, listen, I've got to split. I have a rehearsal, and I'm starving.'

Reema signalled for more wine. 'Let's give her ten more minutes. Besides, Aparna isn't here.'

Rashmi threw up her hands, 'Forget Aparna, *yaar*. She won't come. Not after what happened between Swati and her. In her place, I wouldn't have bothered either. What the hell? Is Swati a queen or something that all of us have to forget the past and rush to pay homage? I'm getting out of here. It was fun seeing you guys but I'll be damned if I'm going to hang around for some fancy lady to show up and show off.'

And suddenly, Swati was there. Standing in the small passage near the living-room. Smiling. Still. Watching. Silent.

'How the hell did you get in?' Rashmi asked incredulously.

Swati winked, 'Magic!'

Reema went up to greet her. 'Hi, Swati. You're looking fantastic. But seriously, how did you enter without our hearing the doorbell?'

Swati whirled around and indicated a bearer, 'He's the culprit. He'd opened the front door to get a crate of beer in, and *voila*, there I was . . . and there you were . . . so, I just walked right in. Sorry about that, girls. I suppose I should have rung the bell. Ting-a-ling-a-ling. H-e-e-e-r-e-'s Swati. Naughty me.'

'Let me take a good look at you,' Reema gushed, turning Swati around. The others gathered as Swati twirled. She was clad in a figure-hugging mini-skirt with a burgundy-coloured silk shirt and a cotton blazer with boots. Her hair hung loose to her hips. The once voluptuous silhouette had been whittled down to a pleasant curvaceousness. Swati was far from fashionably anorexic looking. But it was also obvious to her old friends that Swati worked hard at looking the way she did—athletic, fit and ravishingly attractive in a fresh, natural way. Her face was practically free of make-up and she wore very little jewellery apart from a smart art deco bracelet studded with sapphires and rubies. Even her ring was a simple wedding band.

'Satisfied?' she smiled as she went up to Surekha to kiss her. 'My, just look at you. No change, huh? Same happy face. You must have a great sex life to look so contented.'

Surekha blushed despite herself and murmured something incoherent.

Reema waited for Swati's appraisal of her. But Swati had turned her attention to Noor who had shrunk into a corner. 'Darling girl—how wonderful to see you again. You look so well,' Swati said warmly.

Noor held out the package awkwardly. 'This is for you. I mean, it's not a present or anything, it's something you'd left behind at my place, remember?'

Swati bent down to kiss her. 'Of course I do. How could I forget? Tell me, how is your family? And you?'

Noor shifted uncomfortably, trying to get out of Swati's embrace. 'Fine, fine. Everybody's fine. Nawaz . . . everybody. Mummy, Daddy, yes, we are all well.'

'Good,' Swati said swinging her hair back.

Rashmi piped up. 'Highness, am I allowed to interrupt? I'm in a hurry, see? I'm not a lady of leisure. I bust my ass trying to make a living. Shall we get the big emotional scene over and done with quickly?'

Swati rushed up to her, arms outstretched, 'Rashmi! Stop it. You're still angry with me, aren't you? Don't be, darling. I had my own problems to deal with at that point. And I'm sorry about what happened—rather what didn't. But I'm truly glad to see you. And I'm even gladder to see you haven't changed your choli-style. I always did envy you your great boobs.'

Rashmi's hand flew to adjust her sari pallav. 'Oh quit your bullshit, baby,' she said embarrassedly. But it was obvious she was immensely pleased.

'Someone's missing. Right, hostess?' Swati said to Reema.

'Well, I did invite Aparna, but I'm not sure whether she'll show up or not,' Reema stammered.

Swati shrugged, 'Pity if she doesn't. I was looking forward to seeing her. Anyway, hey, I haven't greeted you properly, Reema. Awfully rude of me.' Swati dug into her Chanel bag and took out a wrapped gift. 'This is for you. Just something small. I really, really appreciate what you're doing for me. Don't open it now.' And Swati pressed the gift into Reema's hand. Then she held her at arm's length and said, 'And now, let me take a long, hard, good look at you. Hmmm, you look great. I love your ensemble. Your skin's looking terrific. You could lose a little weight around the ass—but hey— who couldn't? Can't believe you have such a grown-up daughter—I saw the framed pictures in the corridor. Great-looking. You lucky thing!'

Reema was beaming. 'My daughter will be fifteen this year. I can't believe it myself.'

Swati looked around the living-room, her gaze sweeping over everything. 'I like the painting, and that silver box. Nice. Oh and look at that lamp—that's clever. Your idea? It works so well in that corner. Yes—I love it. Reema, my sweet, you've got a great set-up here.' Reema was flattered that Swati was taking such a keen interest in her bric-à-brac. Till that moment, she'd been most diffident about her own taste. But watching Swati pick up each *objet*, examine it carefully and move on to the next was like receiving a certificate of merit from a professor. Swati seemed to appreciate everything— even the curtains.

Reema stared at Swati's smooth, tanned legs and wondered how it was that she didn't feel shy about exposing half her thighs.

Swati noticed her looking and smiled, 'I'm far too *nanga* for India, right? I realized it straightaway. But this is the length I've been wearing—and I know that's a silly excuse. I could wear saris but, what the hell, I've got great legs. Might as well show them off. But God! You should see the reactions. I thought my old bai would have a fit. She was so shocked! And to think she has seen me starkers. Not just when I was a baby but even later . . . till I left for England. And the watchmen in your complex! The lift boy forgot to ask which floor—he became near catatonic.'

The bearer came and bowed deferentially in front of her. Reema said, 'What will you have? I've got everything. My husband likes a well-stocked bar—wine, Campari, Cinzano, tequila, champagne, white rum—you name it. I've even got imported beer and mineral water.'

Swati thought for a minute. 'How about a Limca? Possible? I remember the old ads. "I like Limca because it's Limca-Limca."' She sang out the jingle and everyone laughed.

Reema said awkwardly, 'I may be out of Limcas, but I thought you'd prefer something stronger.'

Swati replied, 'You bet I would. But I'm on this low-cal diet right now. Strictly no booze. No wine. No champagne. Nothing at all. I'm surprised my agent hasn't struck sex off my list.'

Rashmi butted in, 'Why, darling—does fucking make people fat?'

115

Swati turned to her and said with feigned sweetness: 'Oh baby, you're still as adorable as ever. And still mad at me. I know it. I know it. How can I make it up to you? Tell me. I'll do anything.'

Rashmi lit a cigarette, and blew the smoke ceilingwards. 'Forget it. I don't hang on to the past. And I don't have hangovers. I'm just getting pissed off with your act. All this sweetness and light stuff. Why don't you be yourself for a change? We won't blow your cover, don't worry. Go ahead—be a bitch. It's so much more fun. All of us know you. Have known you only too well. We'd feel most relieved if you dropped this sham and acted natural.'

Swati threw up her hands. 'I *am* being myself. This is me. Natural. Why don't you quit being so hostile?'

Reema interrupted, 'She's right, Rashmi. You are going after her for nothing. Forget it. Let's all relax and talk about old times. There's so much to catch up on—'

Rashmi held up her hand. 'I heard the bell. It must be Aparna.'

It was.

*

For a moment, there was complete silence as the other women stared uncertainly at Aparna. She was standing in the doorway looking defensive and somewhat defiant. Her eyes were fixed on Swati. 'Hi,' she said softly, her voice low, as if it was having difficulty emerging from her constricted throat.

Swati was the first to respond: 'Hello, dearest one,' she breathed huskily as she flew towards Aparna, arms outstretched. Aparna stepped back unconsciously and shrank from her touch. Swati froze in her tracks. 'Oh, oh, oh, what's this? Why am I being treated like an untouchable?'

Aparna stiffened momentarily and then broke into a big grin. 'Shit! Why am I behaving like a turd? Welcome home. You look wonderful, far better than your tarty pictures. Here, let me look at you properly.'

Swati's face was swathed in smiles as she pretended she was a catwalk mannequin parading up and down, humming an MTV hit, 'I'm too sexy.' Everybody laughed. Within seconds the atmosphere altered. Swati announced, 'I'm breaking all the rules today. Summon a slave. It's champagne time. Come on gals, drink up, drink up. This is an occasion. The best. I haven't felt this exhilarated since I lost my virginity—and all of you know how, when, where and with whom that happened. Let's drink to us. Let's drink to school. Let's drink to memories. Let's drink to innocence. Let's drink to fun. Fuck it! Let's just drink. I mean DRINK.'

As the corks popped something popped in Noor's head. And she started to scream. Scream uncontrollably. Like an animal in pain. Her hands flattened over her ears, her mouth wide open. And the screams kept coming

in waves while her frail body shook and shuddered.
And her friends stood around her motionlessly not daring
to move, to react, to help.

*

Reema remembered it was her house and she, the much
acclaimed hostess. Hastily, she took Noor by the arm
and forced her to sit down. As abruptly as she'd started,
Noor fell quiet. Her eyes flew around the room wildly.
'Who are all of you?' she whispered agitatedly.

Aparna took the situation in hand and told Reema,
'I think she needs to calm down without all of us
crowding her.'

Rashmi, the cigarette burned down to a stub, sat
by the phone mumbling, 'What about a doctor? Shouldn't
we get a doc?'

Now the immediate crisis appeared over, Surekha
and Swati, who seemed the least affected by it, turned
to each other and began chatting easily. Swati stared
pointedly at Surekha's midriff and finally pinched it
playfully, 'Too much dhokla and too much sex. Right?'

Surekha blushed. 'Swati, you'll never change. Still
naughty, cracking all your jokes.'

'I'm not joking, Suree,' Swati said, her eyes twinkling.
'But just look at you—tch! tch! A month at a health
farm is what you need.'

Surekha brushed her suggestion aside and said, 'Tell me, are you happy? I mean *really* happy?'

Swati looked straight into her eyes, 'How do I look?'

Surekha shrugged, 'You are an actress. You can look whatever you want to look—happy, sad . . .'

Swati smiled a slow, wistful smile, 'How horrible of you to say that. You make it—me—sound so calculated, so cynical, you who have known me since I was that high.'

Surekha continued to look at her steadily. 'You still haven't answered my question.'

'Let's put it this way—even if I was perfectly miserable, surely I wouldn't burden all of you with my problems. So why don't we settle for happy?' Surekha shook her head. Swati switched the focus to her: 'And you?'

Surekha laughed, 'I'm an ordinary woman, who cares whether I'm happy or not? It doesn't interest anyone. But you're different—a famous lady. Everybody wants to know about you, your life.'

Swati leaned forward, 'Do you realize how evasive you are being? Come on—yes or no—are you or aren't you?'

'Hmmm. Let me think. I can't answer so easily. Nobody asks to interview me.' Swati waited. Finally, Surekha said, 'Maybe I am. Yes, I am. I'm married. I live in a comfortable house. I have a well-behaved daughter. A prosperous husband. What more do I need?'

'Nothing,' Swati answered quickly. 'I mean—if your happiness is defined by that, then you are lucky. You've got what you want.'

119

Both of them turned to see what was happening in the far corner where Noor was being fussed over. Swati got up, revealing her legs. She pulled down her short skirt and tossed back her long hair. She called out cheerfully, 'Hey Reema, when do we start our game—before lunch or after?'

Aparna answered before Reema could: 'Still playing your old tricks? What's the catch this time?'

Swati arched her eyebrows and cast a sidelong glance in Aparna's direction. 'Catch, honey? I don't know what you're talking about. I'm here for a friendly, relaxed lunch. Aren't you?'

Rashmi lit another cigarette nervously, 'I knew it. I knew this was going to be a mistake. I shouldn't have come.'

Reema bustled around pouring the champagne which was rapidly losing its bubbles. 'Girls, girls, girls, lunch will be on the table in ten minutes. I hope all of you have brought pictures. I've got my album ready. But before we start thinking about the past, let's ask our guest of honour to take the floor and tell us all about her fascinating adventures. I mean, she is the celebrity here. This lunch is for her. Let's not spoil it with silly fights.'

Aparna hid an ironic smile behind her sari pallav and said, 'Hear! Hear! We can always count on Reema to save a tricky situation just like she used to in school as the class monitor.'

Reema looked at her sharply to see if she was making fun of her. 'Stop it, Aparna. And anyway I may have been a monitor, but you were the one who beat me and became the house captain. Don't think I've forgotten.'

'I didn't expect you to,' Aparna said, throwing her head back and sticking her chin out.

Swati held up both her hands dramatically, her nails glistening as the spotlights in the false ceiling bounced off them. 'Party time, folks,' she said, as she bent down gracefully to pick up her flute of champagne. She raised her smooth arm high into the air: 'To us,' she sang out. Reema echoed her words. Noor wobbled to her feet unsteadily and lurched towards Swati. Rashmi was on the phone trying to say she'd be late for her rehearsal. Surekha was still seated where Swati had left her. She seemed to be lost in her own thoughts as she played with a bunch of keys at her waist. Reema clinked her glass with Swati's. 'It's been such a long, long, time. Welcome home, Swats. We envy you your success. But we are also proud of you. Very proud.'

Swati bowed her head modestly and stared straight into Aparna's eyes. 'You too, Aps? Are you really proud of me?' Aparna nodded imperceptibly and quickly turned away. 'Now I know I'm truly and completely forgiven.' Swati smiled a wide, happy smile as the catering duo brought out the chafing dishes and started serving lunch.

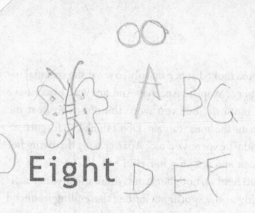

Eight

'I can't recognize myself here,' Reema said pointing to a pig-tailed teenager in shorts standing awkwardly behind a tall, bespectacled girl in a white divided skirt.

'That's me-e-e!' Aparna exclaimed in disbelief.

'And that ugly one in a corner in a crumpled uniform—guess who that is?' Surekha laughed.

The women were in Reema's bedroom sprawled out on her king-size, satin-covered bed. The lunch had been stylish but huge. All of them had happily overeaten, recalling the days they'd gorged themselves each afternoon in the vast lunch hall at school.

'I remember this picnic so clearly,' Noor sighed. 'It was the one where I broke my nose.'

'Yes, and bled over my shorts,' Rashmi added.

'Do you mind not puffing for a while, you'll survive,' Swati said digging a long fingernail into Rashmi's side.

'Stop bullying, *yaar*,' Rashmi countered. 'I can't relax without a beedi in my mouth, particularly after lunch.'

'Here's another picnic picture,' Reema said brightly. 'I look great in this one—look at my legs.'

'Yeah—just look at them here,' Aparna added, 'and look at them now.'

Reema pulled a face.

'Show, show,' the women chorused. 'Come on, we want to see.'

Reema protested: 'Don't be silly, they're all covered up. Why do you think I wear salwar-kameezes and not tiny minis like Swati?'

'Because you aren't in show business like her,' Rashmi pointed out.

'No, because I've grown fat and I hate my legs,' Reema admitted ruefully.

'Come on, be a sport, show them to us. We'll decide whether they're awful,' Swati urged.

Reema got up from the bed, 'Are you girls serious? Not that I mind too much. I waxed them last week.'

'Then hurry up and strip. What the fuck are you waiting for?'

Reema stared uncertainly, 'Really? What if someone comes in?'

'It's your bloody home, darling,' Swati reminded her, 'just lock the door.'

Reema made up her mind abruptly. 'OK, I'll do it. But Swati has to keep me company and show us something more.'

Everyone clapped. 'Wait a minute, where do I come into the picture? The legs under discussion do not belong to me. Unless you girls want to see my tits. Well, do you?'

Noor opened her mouth as if she was about to say something; Surekha looked at her and warned, 'Don't start your screaming business again—OK? Yes, Swati. Show us. We want to find out if they're original or plastic.'

Reema turned to Surekha sharply: 'Don't be mean, yaar. She didn't mean it.'

Aparna kept stealing furtive glances at Swati. Rashmi finally brought the topic back to Reema by saying, 'Let's forget the leg-show and get on with the story. Or let's have both—the legs and the story. But we're wasting too much time. I've got to go—I've got a kid to look after.'

Reema said, 'We all have kids to look after. Except Swati. And, of course, Aparna and . . . Noor. But they're different. Poor Swati. Must be awful to be childless. No?'

The women turned to look at Swati for her reaction. For a moment, her expression changed. It was almost as if she'd winced at the cruelty of the remark. But instantly assumed a familiar, blasé expression and shrugged, 'Me no like babies.'

'Why make such a big thing out of it?' Aparna stated flatly. 'I don't have brats. Don't miss them either. Neither does Noor. And I don't know about Swati. Let's not bring kids into this. Let's just stick to us.'

'Fine,' Swati said, stretching out her legs languorously. 'But before we switch topics, I want to know what happened to Reema's first boyfriend. And why she didn't marry him. What was his name? Raju or something.'

There was a stunned silence. Reema left the room mumbling something about fetching water for all of them. Swati finally spoke up: 'Did I say something I shouldn't have? Come on, girls. We aren't here to just chit-chat. I want to know everything about everybody from the time we left school. Every single dirty detail. What happened to all the old boyfriends? Where did the schoolgirl crushes go? And the breathless infatuations? Of course, I remember bits and pieces—but fill me in on the meat, someone. I've forgotten quite a few things. Something wrong about that?'

Aparna turned on her, 'You do have such a tremendous sense of delicacy and timing, don't you? Raju died. And before you ask Reema, let me tell you—he committed suicide.'

Reema walked in just then carrying an ugly acrylic tray covered with yellow chrysanthemums with uglier tumblers of iced water on it. 'I've made up my mind, girls,' she said to no one in particular. I want to do both—show you my legs and talk about everything. There was a picture I had in this album that I removed last night. It's right there,' Reema said indicating a chest of drawers along the side of the room.

'What picture?' Swati asked gently.

'Let me fish it out. It's a picture I haven't looked at since . . . since it happened,' Reema said tremulously.

'Are you sure you want to do this, babe?' Aparna asked.

'Yes,' Reema said, 'I do.' She walked to the drawer and unlocked it. 'I don't know why I've kept it. I should have torn it up long ago,' she said almost to herself.

The others watched as she reached into the drawer for something under a neat pile of bras and panties.

Rashmi eyed the lingerie and exclaimed, 'Wow, man! So many undies.'

Swati added, 'Sexy, black ones too.'

Noor piped in, 'I have some also. Black ones. Mummy got them for me from Paris. But I've never worn them.'

Reema retrieved an unmarked envelope yellowed around the edges. A dried rose fell out which Surekha picked up and held to her nose. Reema took it back from her roughly and replaced the envelope in the drawer. 'No. I can't do it. I'm sorry. It's impossible,' she said, her voice cracking.

Swati got up and went towards the door. 'Guess what? I'm going to get us some wine. Is that OK?'

'Get me a vodka-tonic,' Rashmi said quickly, 'wine gives me gas.'

Aparna added, 'And while you're at it, maybe a tequila for me. Or a Bloody Mary.'

Swati turned to Noor and Surekha, 'Ladies, and what may I fetch you? This is your friendly barmaid at your service.' They shook their heads. Swati refused to move. 'Hey, come on gals, nobody's watching. Nobody will know. There aren't husbands around to spoil our fun. Or fathers, lovers, boyfriends. No men for a change. What a bloody relief. Let's have a party. Remember how it used to be in school? Everybody joined in. You can't refuse. Leave it to me. I'm the expert. I'll fix something that won't leave a trace—no colour, no smell, no after-effects. Just a great high. Trust me. Mama Swati knows it all.'

Noor shook her head violently. 'No, Swats. Not for me. I've become religious these days. The Koran is so fascinating. I've become a believer since the riots and everything. Besides, my life has changed after Haj. I went last year. Please. I'm OK. Besides, Nawaz will find out immediately. You don't know him.'

Swati cocked an eyebrow, placed her hands on her hips and asked, 'Don't I? Well, darling, you'd be surprised.'

Noor flushed deeply and shook her head, while Aparna intervened swiftly. 'No ugly flashbacks, please. Let's get on with Reema's story.'

Once more, the women flopped on the bed, Swati holding a bottle of Bordeaux and offering frequent swigs to Rashmi, Surekha watching with a faintly disapproving smile and Aparna filing her nails busily. Only Noor gave the impression of being interested. Or perhaps she was thinking of Swati's remark about Nawaz. With Noor it had always been very hard to tell.

Reema stared at the yellowing black-and-white photograph in her lap. Raju looked so touchingly young and handsome in it. She looked rather sweet herself. Juhu. Juhu beach at noon—deserted and inviting. No camels. No ponies. No merry-go-rounds. No coconut-sellers. No hawkers. Just couples in love. Couples of all ages. Couples with nowhere else to go. Raju and Reema and so many others like them. Strange how much privacy there was in such a public place. It was because each couple was wrapped up in themselves, respecting the right of other couples to snatch a few moments of intimacy before the stray voyeur or policeman caught up with them.

Reema had dared to skip school that morning. Raju and she had taken a local train to the distant beach. For four hours they'd sat on the hot sand with nothing to protect them from the searing overhead sun. They'd felt neither hungry nor thirsty. Not even sweaty. Raju had caressed her body through her clothes, kissed her over and over again, using his tongue to pry her mouth open, and pressed her hand over his throbbing crotch. He'd pledged eternal love and promised to marry her, elope if they had to. Reema had believed it all and then as he'd led her to a comparatively shaded nook behind some rocks, she'd given herself to him quickly, blindly, willingly. It had been over within minutes, even before she'd realized that Raju had roughly penetrated her. It was when she felt hot, sticky semen trickling down her smooth thighs that she'd turned to him with stricken eyes and asked, 'Did you actually do it?' He'd laughed triumphantly and boasted, 'Of course. Wasn't it great?'

It was a moment Reema had never forgotten. Most women, she supposed, remembered their first time. It wasn't the physical act that had stayed with her for so many years, but the expression in Raju's eyes as he raised himself over her body like a conqueror. Every man behaved similarly, Reema had concluded. Her husband was no better. And these days their love-making had to be squeezed in between her watching *The Bold and the Beautiful* and his business calls. During the cricket season, she recalled at least three sexual encounters accomplished to the drone of Test Match commentary with her husband pausing mid-thrust to applaud a stylish sixer.

Staring at the faded snapshot so many years later, she felt a strange yearning—not for Raju, but her own lost passion. She'd turned into an unfeeling, mechanical woman with her sights fixed on the next big buy— piece of jewellery, a prized acre of farmland, gold in its most basic form. It was greed that kept her going. A greed that no longer excited her. She looked at the faces of her friends, their eyelids heavy with wine. 'Leg-show, ladies,' she announced, sounding far more animated than she was feeling. Everybody squealed, feigning an enthusiasm that was obviously at its lowest point. Wearily, Reema peeled off her voluminous pyjamas to a round of applause.

'Fleshy knees, sexy,' commented Rashmi, 'mine are knobbier than doorknobs.' 'Stand on the bed,' Surekha suggested, 'I can't see your calves properly.'

Reema started giggling. 'This is so silly. I'm feeling, I don't know, childish.'

Swati drawled, 'Wow, you would make it to the Follies with those. It's crazy to keep those assets covered up all the time. Why don't you switch to dresses, girl?'

Reema took in the compliments and stared at her reflection in the dressing table mirror. Her friends were right—she should show off her best features more often. Not as if those sweaty young studs at the health club didn't compliment her or anything. Or the other members she sometimes saunaed with. It was left to Noor to ask her the one question she was dreading: 'Tell me,' said Noor in her thin, quavering voice, 'does your husband appreciate your body? Does even notice it anymore?' She was saved from answering by Aparna who cut in sharply: 'That's a highly personal question, Noor, and Reema isn't obliged to answer it.' Reema shot her a grateful look and sat down heavily on the bed to climb back into her pyjamas.

'You know, girls, I haven't looked at these pictures for so many years. Life has been busy, what with changing our house and all that. Plus, my husband travels so much. And now that my daughter is a teenager, I have to be specially careful.'

'Careful about what, yaar?' Rashmi interrupted. 'Look, you are not her chastity belt, for God's sake. If she is going to fuck around, there's nothing you can do to stop her. I mean, could my mother stop me? It's all in the genes. Some girls are born that way. Some fuck. Some don't. Too much estrogen or something.'

Reema glared at her. 'Don't compare my baby with yourself. I don't mean to be insulting but Rashmi you were always *chaalu*. My daughter is different. Very innocent and pure.'

Swati laughed: 'Sure. Like *ganga-jal*. Or Perrier water,' then seeing Reema's stricken expression, she covered her mouth with her hands and said, 'Oops! Sorry. I didn't mean that. Just ignore my remarks, OK? I talk too much.'

'You always have,' Surekha noted dryly.

Reema stared at the photograph of Raju. 'Do all of you remember him?' she asked emotionally.

'Yes,' they chorused. 'How could we ever forget? You nearly got us thrown out of school,' Aparna added. 'Whatever happened to his crazy mother?'

Reema paused. It was obvious this wasn't easy for her. 'I need some water,' she said and left the room.

'You shouldn't have reminded her about Raju, *yaar*,' Rashmi said softly as they thought back to the time they'd first heard of him.

*

Reema was a buxom fourteen-year-old ('over-developed' as the nuns would comment). Her breasts were the focal point of her modest bosomed classmates, during her growing years—she was proud and embarrassed simultaneously when the other girls in her class commented on their size. Each week, her class would be taken to a nearby club for swimming lessons. Queues would form outside the wooden cabin to watch Reema change into a swimsuit. Flattered by the attention, Reema would take her time getting in and out of it. But soon fascination turned to taunts. 'Melon-boobs' became her unfortunate nickname. Reema started coming to school wearing the swimsuit under her uniform. This was not just horribly uncomfortable but unbearably hot during the muggy Bombay summers. After two seasons, Reema stopped swimming. But the teasing continued. That was the time Raju came on the scene. His father was the catering manager of the club. And Raju, an unemployed, uneducated dropout. The girls would spot him hanging around the pool, pretending to be shifting deck chairs and adjusting sun umbrellas, while the noisy class splashed around, often spraying water on him.

It was on the days Reema didn't swim, preferring to sit on the adjoining lawn, that Raju would sidle up to her and attempt a conversation, cleverly taking advantage of the nuns' preoccupation with the students in the pool. It began with Raju singing film songs as he dusted around her. It progressed to crudely written notes in Hindi that everybody giggled over later. Raju was not good-looking, but there was something about his swagger that drew people's attention to him. He wore his jeans tight at the crotch and the sleeves of his flashy shirts rolled up over well-muscled, tattooed arms. Raju was swarthily sexy with foxy eyes, a flashy hungry mouth and a don't-care-a-damn Romeo demeanour which gave sufficient cheap thrills to the girls. Their only contact with boys then was restricted to brothers and cousins. If Reema was attracted to Raju, she didn't tell anybody. Not even Swati, who was then her best friend (Swati was everybody's 'best friend' by turn). It was only when Reema began bunking school, or leaving the premises mysteriously during lunch hour that suspicions were aroused. The girls presumed she'd got involved with a boyfriend—perhaps a neighbour. No one even thought of Raju.

Not until he showed up at school one day and asked for Reema. The burly watchman stopped him at the narrow side gate and asked for identification. 'I'm her brother,' Raju lied, flexing his biceps menacingly.

Reema was summoned from the class by the vice principal and asked to go to the gate to verify the visitor's credentials. The sight of Raju standing there smoking a cigarette made her feel faint. She leaned against the stone wall and asked weakly, 'What are you doing here?'

Raju replied, 'I've been waiting for you at the club for three weeks. Why haven't you been coming? Are you trying to avoid me?'

Reema looked over her shoulder at the nun at her elbow and said, 'Please go away. I don't know who you are.'

Raju flicked the cigarette into a nearby gutter and laughed, 'Don't you? Let me remind you in that case. I'm the same boy you've been lying to your parents and teachers about. Shall I show them your letters?'

Reema's eyes widened with fear as she watched Raju reach for his back pocket. 'Raju, please, please don't. I'll meet you after school. Tomorrow. Please leave me alone now. Go away, I beg of you.'

The nun was pulling her back from the gate, her fingers causing welts in Reema's arm. 'Cheap girl. Sinner. Wait till Mother Superior hears about this.'

Reema was sent home in disgrace. And her parents were summoned for an urgent meeting. She was instructed to stay home for a week. And failed in her terminals. Swati and all the others agreed the punishment was too harsh. When Reema came back to school, they gathered around her and sympathized. Seeing that their attitude wasn't hostile she felt confident enough to tell them the truth. She was pregnant. It had happened in the back seat of a stolen car two months ago. And that was the reason she'd dropped out of the swimming classes and refused to see Raju.

'How was it?' Swati had asked, searching Reema's face. 'I mean, did his thing hurt?'

Reema had looked miserable as she narrated the episode.

Surekha had asked, 'Have you done it just once or many times?'

'About ten,' Reema had whispered.

Noor had interrupted, 'Was it nice?' but before Reema could reply, Rashmi had cut in, 'Of course it must've been nice, *yaar*. Why else would she do it ten times?'

Reema had sat with her head lowered, her fingers interlocked asking herself the same question—was it nice? Did she enjoy it? Why had she done it so many times?

The incident in the car had been particularly humiliating. They'd been caught mid-act by a bunch of local toughs, who'd plastered their faces against the windows of the battered-up black Fiat and pounded on the car aggressively. They'd also tried to unlock the car doors to drag the lovers out. Raju had taken the precaution of sealing the car—windows up, doors locked. He'd also acted with amazing speed, pulling on his pants, jumping into the front seat, putting the car into reverse gear and backing out of the narrow, dim-lit side-street along a garbage dump, before the toughs could react. Reema had been left to cover her nakedness with her hands. As he reversed the car at top speed, Reema had struggled into her abandoned clothes, tears streaming down her cheeks. Raju had been extra rough that evening, after they'd found a safer spot, bruising her young flesh with the pressure of his knees on her open thighs, the grip of his hard fingers over her firm breasts, the savagery of his brutal mouth as he attacked her lips, her ears, her throat, her neck, using his tongue like a sharp, pointed weapon designed to hurt not please. He'd come into her in thick, smelly, hot spurts, grunting at the release, sweating profusely, his eyes squeezed shut, his ugly mouth hanging open, dribbling saliva between her moist breasts. Reema had gone home and rushed to the bathroom to wash herself thoroughly and erase all traces. She'd sworn to herself that night—she wasn't going to see him again. She was determined to stick to her resolve. But when she didn't bleed the next month, her resolve had weakened. She hadn't dared think, even to herself, that the worst had happened. Scared, guilty, confused and ashamed she'd avoided Raju, afraid that her 'confession' would anger him, revolt him. But the days and then the weeks had gone by—and nothing had changed. It was the second month and she still hadn't bled. It was also time to get back to school.

Swati had been the first to offer help. 'Does he know? Do your parents know?'

Reema had broken down, shaking her head. 'I will be killed if my family finds out. My brothers will finish him off. I can't tell them. I can't tell anybody.' And then as an afterthought, she'd added: 'Maybe I should run away. And marry him.'

The girls had thought about it together. That was the way it was done in the movies. And in the romance books they read feverishly, stealthily, hiding in the school bathrooms. Again it was Swati who had asked, 'But does Raju want to marry you?' Reema hadn't considered the possibility that perhaps he might not want to. Swati had taken charge. 'I'll ask him next Tuesday when we go to the club.' And she had.

Raju had laughed heartlessly and said. 'Forget it. I didn't force her to do anything. She wanted so. She asked me to. She was the one who put my hand under her dress. She was the one who lay down first. She forced me to. She was hot, she would've even done it with a goat. And who knows who was responsible. Maybe it was me. But maybe it wasn't. Marriage? Are you crazy? I'm not even eighteen. We'll get arrested.'

Swati had blocked his way as he tried to swagger past. 'You have to do something. You must help her,' she'd said, 'because if you don't, I will tell your father.'

That had seemed to make all the difference. Raju had stopped dead in his tracks and turned on her fiercely. 'You will never go near my father, understand? OK. OK. I'll see what I can do. You just stay away.'

Swati had refused to move. 'Here is my phone number. You call me latest by tomorrow and give me your answer. Because if you don't, I'll call the club. My father knows the club secretary. I'll see to it that your father loses his job.'

Raju had taken the slip from her hand and rushed off. He didn't call.

The girls had got together and concluded there wouldn't be much of a point causing a scandal and exposing Reema. Swati had come up with an alternative plan. 'My aunt is a doctor. She delivers babies in a government hospital. She must also know how to get rid of them. I'll talk to her. Don't worry. She is very sweet. She won't tell anyone.'

Reema was examined by Dr Rai a week later. 'We can't wait,' she'd told Swati who'd accompanied her friend. Aparna had suggested a weekend at her place as an alibi was needed. Reema's parents were reluctant to let her go, but Swati had managed to convince them saying, 'We've all decided to study at Aparna's house. Our exams are less than a month away. She is going to teach us maths. Her father is a genius. He'll help.'

The procedure itself had taken no more than fifteen minutes but Reema could still recall each second vividly. The horror of it all hadn't diminished with the passing years. She could smell the antiseptic, feel the prick of the needle, the unnatural cooling of the skin under the tiny patch locally numbed by a brisk rub of spirit, the rough nursing home gown stiff with rice starch, the stubble of shaved pubic hair, the masked doctor (like a character from a particularly sinister sci-fi film), the impersonal nurses from Kerala gossiping over her head in garbled-sounding Malayalam, the cold feel of steel under her naked bottom and the final humiliating image, before blacking out, of her athletic legs being pushed apart roughly, strung up in stirrups. To this day, Reema detested hospitals and avoided going to them even to visit sick friends. Each time she got even a whiff of chloroform, her body stiffened at the memory, especially the moment when she had opened her eyes groggily in a shabby room adjoining the operation theatre and found all her friends there peering anxiously at her face which was as white as the sheet covering her body. 'Is it gone?' she had asked, her eyes swimming with tears. Swati had nodded. 'Everything's over. Don't worry. Nobody knows.' They had taken her over to Aparna's where her mother was told that Reema often felt weak when she had her periods. She had slept it off for ten straight hours, while the girls watched over protectively. It would've gone off without a hitch, and Reema's misadventure would have remained a secret, but someone squealed. It was never known who the culprit was but everybody suspected Swati. This despite her solicitousness and concern. The motive? Vindictiveness, pure and simple. Reema had been the teacher's pet that term, her grades had been better than Swati's. And worse . . . Reema had bagged the lead role in the annual school play—a role Swati had been determined to bag. There were far too many strikes against Reema in Swati's book—not the least of which was Reema refusing to give her a lift to school each day. What little evidence the girls had to go on, seemed to prove their theory. For instance, the carefully disguised handwriting on the anonymous note to Reema's parents had been too much like Swati's. Especially the circles over the 'i's in place of dots.

Raju, they were told, had left town. Jumped on a mining barge and gone off to Taiwan. It was four years before he had resurfaced in Bombay. By then Reema was in college. And her brothers very active in local politics. Nobody quite knew what happened, but Raju's body—a bloody, mangled mass, had been discovered near a sewage dump. The official version was that he'd killed himself. 'A clear case of suicide,' was how the police department put it. What nobody could explain was how any man could inflict such horrible injuries on himself. Raju's father, the catering manager had tried in vain to reopen the case by making several representations to the press. But who'd take the word of a drunk—particularly someone who'd been dismissed from his job for fudging accounts? So, one more mysterious death had got buried in government files. Reema had gone on to marry Ravi, the son of a prosperous businessman.

*

'Did you love Raju at least a little?' Swati asked Reema as they stared at the frayed black and white print.

She took her time to answer. 'Love him? No, I didn't love him. But I was attracted to him. Very attracted. He was the first male I took notice of physically. More attracted . . .' she trailed off while Rashmi completed the thought for her, 'More than you were to your husband or any other man. Right?' Reema nodded miserably.

Surekha folded her legs under her and said, 'I can't understand how any woman can be attracted to the man who raped her. How much trouble this fellow Raju caused! For all of us—have you girls forgotten?'

Noor joined in, fiddling nervously with the gift that was still in her clammy hands: 'He didn't cause me any trouble. I found him very sweet.'

Everybody turned to stare at her in surprise. 'You knew Raju?' Rashmi asked in disbelief.

'Yes, I did. And I also know that he didn't exactly rape Reema. She was more than willing. She just told you she felt attracted to him.'

Reema said heatedly, 'I was attracted. But that doesn't mean I seduced him.'

Aparna said evenly, 'Who said anything about seduction? Relax, girls. It was years ago. Let's talk about something else.'

Noor interrupted once more. 'Raju was a God-fearing fellow. I used to meet him on the way to the badminton court. He was willing to wait for Reema, marry her.

But she refused. Raju didn't have any money, not enough for Reema or her family.'

Reema snarled, 'Oh shut up, Noor, you've always had this awful habit of talking out of turn. You used to do it in school all the time. Remember, girls?'

Noor's eyes were flashing. 'I know you think I'm crazy and all that stuff. Maybe I am. But there are things that I know about all of you that nobody else does. That's why you people are scared of me. Admit it.'

Surekha took her arm and said soothingly, 'We don't think you are crazy or anything. But Raju—how can you defend him? He was a goonda.'

'No, he wasn't,' Noor said heatedly, 'he only looked like one. If you ask me, he was quite all right, better than. . . .'

Swati butted in, 'Better than Nawaz, darling? Anybody is better than that brother of yours.'

Surekha broke in to defuse what threatened to be an ugly row: 'Reema tell us about your husband, your life, your children, is this what you wanted for yourself when you were at school?'

Reema beamed: 'Could I ask for anything more?'

'You tell us, darling,' Swati said laconically, drinking deeply from the wine bottle.

Reema flipped the pages of her album to another section and stopped at her wedding picture. She giggled uncontrollably, 'Look at me here, *yaar*. I was so thin. And look at Ravi. He had all his hair then.'

Noor added, 'He still does. I saw him at a traffic light last month.'

Aparna turned to her, 'You seem to see a lot at traffic lights, don't you?'

Noor smiled sadly. 'I walk such a lot and I see so much.'

Reema was still staring at a laminated colour print of herself in a gaudy, ice-cream pink sharara encrusted with over-elaborate embroidery.

'Let's see your wedding jewellery now. Show us,' Surekha said snatching the album out of her hands.

'My mother gave me tons of it. Eldest daughter and all that,' Reema said smugly. 'Sorry, but I keep all of it in a bank locker. Bombay is so unsafe these days. Don't you read the newspapers? Full of murders. Mainly rich housewives.'

'Who's that stud-type in the background?' Rashmi asked interestedly, pointing to a cocky-looking, sharply-dressed young man standing behind Ravi.

'Oh him! No one. I mean he's just my brother-in-law. Ravi's younger brother. He lives in America.'

Rashmi studied the picture closely. 'Looks dishy.'

Swati grabbed it from her. 'Show. I'll decide. I'm the expert.'

'Says who?' Aparna asked.

It was Surekha who noticed Reema's expression. 'Why are you blushing?' she demanded, coming straight to the point.

Reema turned away. 'Who's blushing? What rubbish.'

All the girls gazed at her till Noor broke the spell: 'She's blushing because she has a crush on her brother-in-law. That's why.'

Reema whirled around. 'Stop it. Stop it all of you—you're talking crap.'

'Then why are you over-reacting?' Swati persisted. 'There's nothing unnatural about it. Come on, you can tell us. I believe it's the done thing in Delhi society to sleep with your husband's brother. Wow, Reema, maybe you'll start a similar trend in Bombay.'

*

Randhir was the one Reema had fallen for when she'd gone to Rangoli, the charming restaurant by the sea, to be surveyed by her future in-law's. She'd seen Randhir emerging from the loo and walking towards the neatly-laid-out table where his parents and elder brother were seated. Seeing Reema, looking flustered and pretty in a sky blue printed chiffon outfit, he'd smiled politely probably unaware that she was his brother's intended bride. She'd smiled back uncertainly, gripping her mother's hand tighter as they made their way self-consciously to where the Nath family was busy ordering mince samosas and cold coffee.

Ravi might have interested Reema had Randhir not been present that evening. Ravi was considered a prize catch in the community. Ravi had everything going for him as defined by the highly competitive marriage market—he was not particularly good-looking, but tall enough to qualify as well-built. Reema had noticed his greasy, lank hair and wondered idly about his choice of shampoo. She'd also noted the imminent beginnings of a paunch and thought to herself, 'If he has a belly in his early twenties, what will his body look like ten years from now?' Ravi was passable in a nondescript sort of way. The kind of man one wouldn't notice in an elevator even if nobody else was present. Randhir was different. Not good-looking, but rakish. Flamboyantly dressed. His eyes fringed with lashes half-an-inch in length and so thick they looked mascaraed. His physique was stockier than his brother's but devoid of flab. He resembled a sturdy bull with a thick neck and wide shoulders. Reema had scrutinized him minutely and noticed the thick matting of chest hairs with interest. She'd observed him observing her. The knowing, challenging, occasionally mocking expression in his eyes had made her uncomfortable in his presence. But that discomfort was better than the deadness of her reaction to his older, more successful brother. At that first encounter itself, Reema had mulled over their differences and had concluded that a violent flaming row with Randhir would be more sexually exciting than hours of mechanical, predictable love-making with Ravi. His family had made it clear they belonged to an enlightened society: no dowry for their trophy sons. Reema had tried hard to concentrate on the polite exchanges between the two families, but her entire being had been focussed on Randhir. She had found his eyes on her each time she glanced up. Ravi on the other hand had seemed indifferent, asking the standard questions—'Do you like music?' 'What do you hope to do now that you've finished college?' 'What are your hobbies?' When it was time to leave, Randhir had stood gallantly and offered to see Reema's family to the car. On the way, he had touched her arm lightly and said, 'I hope to hell bhaiya marries you. I'd love to have you in our family.' Reema's eyes were aglow and her cheeks aflame as she looked up at him gratefully, maintaining a discreet silence. He was the first curly-haired man she'd found attractive.

A week later, the formal acceptance had arrived. Once again, it was Randhir who had come by their home to convey it. Reema was dressed casually in jeans. 'You look real good today,' he'd commented looking her up and down appreciatively. She'd offered him a Thums Up which he refused. Spontaneously he'd said, 'Tell you what, let me take you for an ice-cream instead. How about it?' Seeing Reema's hesitation, he'd winked, 'I'm standing in for bhaiya. He's busy with some hot shot brokers tonight. But I'll have to submit a detailed report on you when I get back.'

Reema had jumped at the chance of being alone with Randhir though she told herself she was doing it for Ravi. In the lift going down to his car, she had asked him curiously, 'How old are you?'

'Older than you, I think, definitely older than you, dear bhabhi-to-be,' he'd answered tweaking her nose.

Reema had pulled back. 'Do you have a girlfriend in America?'

'Yes. But she isn't half as pretty as you,' Randhir had teased, as he escorted her to the waiting car. The smell of L'Homme had filled her nostrils and made her reel momentarily.

They'd driven to a popular ice-cream parlour on Marine Drive where Reema had slurped away happily on a chocolate cone. Randhir had stared at her deliberately before saying, 'Somehow I cannot imagine bhaiya and you licking ice-cream together like this.'

Reema had cocked her head to one side and asked, 'Why not? Doesn't your brother like ice-cream?'

Randhir had said, 'Forget it. That's not what I meant. Let's just say bhaiya and I are very different.'

Reema had noted the remark carefully. It prepared her a little for just how different from each other the two brothers were. It didn't lighten the disappointment or the regret, however.

Reema's affair with Randhir had started six months after her marriage. But on her wedding night itself she discovered she'd married the wrong man—or the wrong brother. A man who left her completely cold, physically and emotionally.

The wedding night had been orchestrated to duplicate countless such sequences from popular Hindi films. Reema's new bedroom had been filled with flowers. Rose petals were strewn everywhere. To this day, she continued to feel sickened by their fragrance. She couldn't stand the aroma of rose-ittar sprayed liberally on female guests at every possible 'auspicious occasion'. Roses themselves reminded her of that ghastly nuptial chamber, with its hideous synthetic carpets crackling with all the static generated by the polyester in the room. She remembered its green and purple geometric pattern which was echoed on the curtains. The air-conditioner leaked little puddles into a red plastic bucket placed on the carpet to catch the drip-drip. As she lay back against gigantic bolsters upholstered in yellow velvet, Reema closed her eyes and tried hard to heave her bosom to practise feigning passion. That's how the heroine did it in the movies. She'd wondered about the sequence to follow. Was she supposed to remove all her glittering gold jewellery by herself? The sets lovingly ordered by her mother from a particular jeweller in Delhi? Would Ravi help her with her hairpins—hundreds of them holding up an elaborate, hair-sprayed chignon that had taken the Chinese girls an hour to fix? Would it look rude if she told her brand-new husband she was dying to brush her teeth, wash her face, get the glue from the false eyelashes off her eyelids, before they *did* anything? Would he know how to undo the elaborate fastenings of her blouse? Unclasp the hook of her bra without fumbling? Remove her panties without getting his fingers caught in the waist band? And would she be expected to undress him as they did in Hollywood films? She had hoped not. Instead she'd prayed he'd keep his clothes on or undress in the bathroom. Or better still, that he'd spare both of them the impending ordeal and just go to sleep.

As it turned out, Ravi had been both gentle and patient. Reema ought to have been grateful. But she wasn't. He'd asked her whether she'd like to use the bathroom first. And he'd handed her a robe. While she climbed out of her bridal finery in the privacy of a reasonably clean and dry loo, she'd heard sounds of him changing outside. She'd stared at her painted up face in the mirror—the almost comic traditional make-up with dozens of dots forming patterns above her eyebrows. The lipstick was too shiny and too dark, the kohl in her eyes smudged and smeared after the stinging tears brought on by the smoke from the holy woodfire. Gold dust was evenly spread over her cheekbones giving her an unnatural, almost ghostly lustre. She hadn't liked what she saw in the mirror. If she looked ridiculous in her own eyes, how must she have looked to Ravi? Tiredly, she washed her face briskly with a freshly unwrapped imported soap and reached for her ice-cream pink robe with its white trim. She'd decided to keep her underwear on. When she emerged from the bathroom, she'd found Ravi on the flower-bedecked bed. He was reading the evening papers, his glasses perched on his nose. He'd looked up at her quickly and said, 'Nice. Sweet. Come, lie down. Do you want to watch TV or something? It's there in that corner. Here's the switch.' At that moment, Reema's heart had melted. She warmed to her mint-fresh husband and had snuggled up to him. He had continued to read for the next ten minutes, as she stroked his arm shyly. After finishing the comics, he had switched off the bedside light, pulled up the covers, patted her thigh companionably and said, 'Let's sleep tonight. We'll do it tomorrow. OK, darling? Don't mind, it's been a long day. I'm tired. Too much beer also.

Disappointed, Reema had moved to her side of the bed and started reading about Sridevi's love-life. Rather, the lack of it, and had instantly felt better. Even ravishing superstars suffered a sexless existence, Reema had comforted herself as she read the gossip magazine, timing each line with her husband's snores. She wasn't sure whether she felt a sense of relief or intense disappointment. Her entire body had been tense and receptive for whatever it was that would follow—clumsy coupling without arousal or a tender exploration. Passion wasn't even considered. But this—this was almost insulting. They'd slipped into duty-fucking without having fucked in the first place! She lay awake for hours beside her snoring husband. That night decided all the nights that followed. Nights that had an in-built pattern and rhythm without the slightest excitement or variation. Ravi discharged his husbandly obligation—literally. And expected Reema to be satisfied if not actually grateful. Sex was never discussed—only perpetrated on the other. Like a minor war. Nearly sixteen years after the event, she found herself sharing the memories with her friends. Sharing more than just the memories—for Reema, it was the first time she had actually confronted her unfulfilling relationship with Ravi—and the one with Randhir. And it required Swati to make it happen.

Her approach was direct. 'Let's take a short-cut, darlings,' she purred, as they flipped through more photographs. 'I'm sure there is just one thing all of us are dying to know—did Reema bed Randhir or not?'

Reema's colour changed at the brazenness of the question. Swati threw an affectionate arm round her, saying, 'Don't evade the question, girl. And don't lie. Sometimes it's better to reveal all. Believe me, baby. I've travelled the route. Besides, we don't have all day. Let's get to the bottom of it. My guess is that you did. And that you still do, whenever the dude shows up on these shores. Tell me if I'm wrong.'

Reema threw back her head defiantly. 'I was too young and inexperienced when I married Ravi. If I'd known how it would be with him, I'd have said no. But in our community these things don't happen. We marry the person we are told to marry. It's OK for you, Swati, to talk about my life. You had choices. I didn't.'

Swati corrected her. 'No, sweetheart, my circumstances weren't all that different from yours. I *made* my choices. And was willing to pay the price—that's what separates the women from the girls. But let's get back to you.'

*

The first time Reema found herself alone with Randhir was when Ravi had left town on an unscheduled assignment and Randhir flew in with some exporters. He called from a nondescript hotel at Kemp's Corner where he was staying. Reema's mother-in-law asked him to come over to dinner, adding that her brand new bahu would cook a meal for him. Reema felt her heart pounding at the thought of seeing him again, so soon, so unexpectedly.

Her mother-in-law came bustling into the kitchen to issue instructions. 'Randhir likes Continental food,' she said proudly, 'our cook cannot make it well. Why don't you prepare something different?' Reema blessed her mother for having insisted on her doing a holiday cooking course during her last vacation. Yes, she'd show Ravi and her mother-in-law what a great cook she was. In any case, the term 'Continental food' was used loosely for anything that didn't involve masalas and ghee. Reema wasn't a gourmet chef, but her repertoire included a few simple Italian and French dishes. Safe, unfussy cuisine no woman could seriously go wrong with. She planned an easy-to-make pasta dinner with a soufflé to follow. But more than anything else, she was worried about her appearance. Her sedentary lifestyle had added a few kilos to her frame. She'd gone along with her mother-in-law's taste in what a bride should wear for the first year or at least the first few months of her married life. Stealing a quick look at herself in the mirror, she shuddered at the reflection. As soon as she came out of her bath, Reema was expected to dress herself in expensive silks or chiffons, combined with matching jewellery. These made her look old and matronly. Gone was her girlish charm and casually smart appearance. Her wifely incarnation didn't please her at all.

After she'd organized a simple salad, she rushed into her newly-renovated bedroom to get ready for Randhir's arrival. Looking through her huge wardrobe, she could find nothing that would make her feel like her old self. In despair, she grabbed a cotton sari in lemon yellow and released her long hair from its restrictive nape bun. She kept her ten gold and diamond bangles on each arm but took off the three heavy chains from her neck and carefully removed her mother-in-law's favourite chandelier earrings, replacing them with discreet diamond ear-studs. She also tried—unsuccessfully—to remove as much of the messy sindhoor from the parting in her hair as possible. The door bell rang just as she'd finished spraying Wild Rose on herself. A quick appraisal assured her that she was looking fine ('Ripe and desirable,' as Randhir commented later).

Reema's mother-in-law monopolized her younger son all evening and the two of them barely got to exchange five sentences in all. But often, during pauses in the conversation, Randhir would look across the table at her and wink conspiratorially. And once, she started suddenly as she felt his foot (minus the shoe) searching for hers under the table.

Randhir commented loudly, 'I hate shoes and chappals, Mummy. Everybody in the world should be barefoot.' With that, his big toe jerked off Reema's sandals and soon his soft well-kept feet were caressing hers in deliberate, circular, sensuous motions. Reema tried to draw back, but gave up resisting when he caught one of her ankles between both his big toes, in a grip that was surprisingly firm. She soon found her own toe intertwining with her brother-in-law's, creating a rhythm pattern so suggestive and obvious, she was sure her mother-in-law could sense it, if not actually feel it. She felt his foot travelling up under her sari. Reema steadied herself by holding on to the dining table. His toes were on her knees, moving gently across the knee caps in fluid circles.

'Have some more souffle,' said Randhir holding out the bowl towards her.

She nearly gagged on what was already in her mouth and started to cough. Randhir laughed at her discomfiture as her mother-in-law looked on with concern and summoned a servant. 'Drink some water quickly,' she said, handing Reema a glass. By then Randhir's foot was on the inner silkiness of her warm, moist thigh and still climbing. Reema couldn't look up from her plate and meet her mother-in-law's eyes. She felt certain her cheeks were on fire. Her body was trembling as his big toe reached the target it sought. Randhir manoeuvred his foot till his big toe and the one next to it caught the edge of her panties and pushed it aside. Randhir didn't stop talking for even a minute while his toe explored Reema's wet softness seeking the spot that was most sensitive, most receptive. She wanted to slide under the table with this man who was driving her wild with desire. She shut her eyes briefly as his big toe stabbed her, opened her, played with her and tried to enter her. She felt the heel of his foot massaging her sensuously using just the right amount of pressure to bring her as close to orgasmic bliss as she'd ever known. Reema came again and again as Randhir discussed New York weather with his mother.

'I'm stealing your precious bahu for a while, Mummy.' Randhir announced after dinner. 'I know she loves ice-cream. And when I'm in India, I can't do without a paan after dinner.'

Reema shot a quick glance at her mother-in-law and started to protest: 'No, no, I have to clear up the dinner things and . . .'

'And-vand nothing,' Randhir said firmly. 'Surely I have some claim over bhaiya's wife?'

His mother smiled indulgently at him and said, 'Go on, you naughty boy. If I knew you craved for paan so much, I'd have arranged it for you.'

By then Randhir was halfway out of the entrance dragging Reema with him. Once the door shut on them he caught her by the shoulders, pressing himself against her. She brought her elbows up to keep her generous breasts from rubbing against his chest.

'Don't do that,' Randhir said roughly, removing the barrier and closing his hungry mouth over hers. Reema lost her balance as the heel of her sandal slipped from under her. Instinctively, her mouth opened and she found Randhir's eager tongue thrust into it. 'What are you doing?' she said, alarm in her voice.

'What you want me to,' he answered.

Once in the car they drove silently for a few minutes. Reema knew this wasn't going to be either a paan or an ice-cream outing. She wasn't surprised when Randhir pulled up at his hotel and told her to hop off while he parked. She stood self-consciously in the small, far-from-luxurious lobby, feeling every eye on her. Randhir took the few steps two at a time and joined her within minutes. Key in hand, they went up in the lift to his room, Reema's nervousness rising with each floor they passed. He squeezed her hand in a friendly manner. 'No problem,' he assured her. 'What are you worried about? Nobody will know. Besides, it's so convenient—you and I have the same surname. Who is to know you aren't my wife?'

Randhir didn't bother with preliminaries once they were in his room. The bed was unmade and his clothes were strewn untidily all over the place. Reema started to tidy up, making Randhir laugh. She turned around to see what was amusing him so much and gasped. He was stark naked and obviously raring to go. She gasped and covered her eyes with her sari. In two quick strides, Randhir had crossed the room and pinioned her on the springy bed.

'Stop behaving like a bloody wife. I've been waiting to eat you up since the day I saw you in Rangoli,' he said, unbuttoning her blouse. Reema held her breath. She lay immobilized as Randhir fiddled with the layers of her sari. 'You Indian women! Just how the hell is a horny man in a hurry supposed to get his hands on a female wearing yards and yards of stuff? Get these bloody things off, I can't wait,' he said impatiently.

Reema sat up on the bed to undo her buttons. She was glad she'd worn one of her sexy bras and that she'd waxed herself just the previous week. Randhir lay back against the bedpost and watched her. 'Please switch off the lights,' she pleaded.

'No, no, I'm enjoying this too much to deprive myself,' he answered with a light laugh. 'I'm an incorrigible voyeur and you, dear bhabhi, are the first Indian woman I've had. I find this exciting, very exciting. There's something so sexy about a sari being removed. Or maybe I've just got far too used to stockings and garters. This is a real treat. I don't want to miss a minute of it.' Reema gazed wordlessly at his lean, tanned body.

He entered her immediately. She was not really prepared to receive him. 'Shit,' he cursed, finding her tight and dry. 'Relax, woman, I'm not the first man to do it to you surely,' Randhir muttered still trying to manoeuvre himself roughly into her. Reema shut her eyes and tentatively put her arms around Randhir. The feel of his smooth bare back under her fingers made her tingle all over and she felt her body unwinding gradually. She moved her hips, shyly at first, and then with a rhythm that was aggressive and insistent. She arched herself to receive him better, her breasts straining to make contact with the rough hairs on his chest. Soon, their bodies were moving together perfectly synchronized and she could hear Randhir grunting in deep arousal as he drove himself harder, locked into a double embrace created by her arms and legs as she held him firmly, possessively, passionately to herself as if afraid of letting go.

And that formed the rather inelegant beginning to their ongoing affair. Reema was realistic enough to know she meant nothing to her brother-in-law, but she drew comfort from the fact that he continued to want her, telling herself he always came back for more when he could have sought and received sexual gratification from any other woman in this the country's premier city of eager, available, attractive women.

Reema was sure her husband didn't know about the affair. She half-suspected her shrewd mother-in-law did but said nothing in the interests of maintaining family peace. Sometimes she wondered whether her growing daughter sensed something when Randhir was at their home and being familiar with her. Within their community, his being single led to gossip and speculation about the possibility of an American girlfriend back in New York. But that didn't prevent parents of eligible daughters from thrusting girls at him. On each visit Reema's home got converted into a venue for many of these formal meetings. Randhir was obviously not in a hurry to settle down. With each rejection Reema sent up a prayer to her favourite deity—Santoshi Mata. It meant Ravi was still hers. All hers. At least while he was in Bombay. As he so crudely put it, 'Why look for meat elsewhere when there's a prime cut at home?' She'd reconciled herself to being nothing more than a fortnightly screw for Ravi years ago. She often asked herself whether she loved him. Or anybody else for that matter. The answer, unsurprisingly, was 'No'. She had quit complaining. Her husband wasn't the most exciting man around, but he was presentable enough and generous. If he had a sex-life outside their bedroom, she didn't particularly want to know about it. Their own was as listless and uninspiring as it had been since the early days of their marriage. She'd lie obediently beneath him, her mind on the following day's lunch party or some petty gossip she'd heard over the phone. He'd bury his face into the hollow in her shoulder, eyes tightly screwed, face contorted, a frown of concentration creasing his forehead. It was a routine that rarely varied—three minutes (by the clock) playing with her nipples, two minutes stroking her pubic hair, another two kissing her lips clumsily, his spit trickling down the sides of his open mouth, the muscles of his face moving spasmodically. Reema loathed their encounters and stared fixedly at the bedside clock timing her husband's foreplay, gritting her teeth the moment she felt him entering her and waiting impatiently for the whole business to finish so she could get on with her TV watching.

*

Aparna broke the spell by asking bluntly, 'What happens to you if Randhir walks away? Say, the guy gets married. Or tires of you. Or whatever. You seem to have invested your all into this crazy arrangement—I can't even call

it a relationship. But it can end tomorrow you know.
And he can end it. He has the power. You don't.'

Reema seemed surprisingly unperturbed as she smiled
and said indifferently, 'It's OK. I won't jump off my
balcony or anything. I have other interests in life. My
kitty club keeps me going. And besides, tell me, is sex
all that important? If I stop meeting Randhir, I'll probably
take up some other hobby.'

Everybody burst out laughing. Rashmi said, between
giggles, 'That's a very original description of an affair.
Is that what it's called these days? A hobby?'

Swati chipped in, 'Don't laugh girls. I can understand
what Reema means perfectly. Sex *is* a hobby. For some
it can be an all-consuming one. For others, a passing
fancy. Her world won't stop spinning because one
man—not a very likeable one at that—stops bedding
her. Right, Reema?'

Reema nodded. And switched off from the group.
She remembered the time Randhir had suggested a
'quickie' (as he bluntly put it) in the lift. Her lift. The
same lift that brought her husband up to their home.
And her daughter. And her.

'Don't be ridiculous,' she'd protested as he naughtily
pressed the button of the penthouse apartment of her
building.

'Thank God for automatic lifts. God bless Otis,'
he'd murmured before lifting her sari up and pulling
down her panties.

'Randhir—don't. I'm terrified.'

'Fear is the key,' he'd joked, unzipping his fly. 'The best sex is tension-sex,' he'd added before flattening her against the polished side of the smooth, silent, sleek and very slippery lift. He was inside her in seconds, parting her legs with his knees and propping her up precariously over his powerful thighs. Reema hadn't been able to take her eyes off the light panel—she'd watched with mounting fear as the lift moved up noiselessly—12 . . . 13 . . . 14 . . . 15 . . . 16 . . . Randhir's concentration was complete. A few swift thrusts and he'd been through. He'd stepped back from her with a triumphant smile.

'There,' he'd announced, tucking his shirt in and zipping up. 'That was easy.'

Reema had been frozen in a slightly ridiculous posture cruelly reflected in two full-length mirrors on either side of her—mirrors she generally used to check her lipstick and hair while leaving for a party. Never again would she be able to look at her reflection in them and not think about Randhir and their frenetic love-making that had climaxed on the twenty-second floor.

Noor's childlike voice broke into her reverie. She heard her say, 'I think it's immoral to sleep with your brother-in-law. I know it's pretty common. But that doesn't make it right.'

Swati patted her affectionately and said, 'Fine, fine, fine, fine. Now, let's take a look at what you've been hiding all afternoon. Come on open it up. What have you got there in that little parcel. Show us.'

Noor clutched it tighter and said, 'I couldn't find any old photographs so I brought this. I hope it's OK.' Surekha grabbed it, tore off the paper and opened the tiny, blue velvet box. She drew in her breath as she stared at the object inside. The others watched while Surekha turned it around so all of them could see it.

'Remember this girls?' she asked, her voice filled with awe.

'Of course we do. I do.' Swati said quickly taking it from her. With one swift move she slipped the gorgeous three-carat coloured diamond onto her finger. 'It was given to me years ago.'

Aparna lit a cigarette and asked slowly, 'Given? Really? I thought you'd stolen it.'

Noor knocked over a copper bowl noisily and everybody jumped. Swati looked up from the magnificent ring on her finger and spoke directly to Aparna. 'Stealing was never my speciality, Aps. Fortunately, I didn't have to stoop that low. Despite what you think. I don't pinch—not husbands and not stones. The ring was a present. A birthday present. But let Noor tell us all about it. If anybody knows—she does. Noor darling, why don't you set the record straight once and for all?'

Noor looked up at Swati and asked nervously, 'Should I? Do you think it's all right to? It's been years and I have forgotten so much.'

Swati nodded, adding, 'Don't worry. I've forgotten nothing. Nothing at all. It's all here,' she tapped her head. 'If you can't remember, I'll fill in for you. Go ahead, baby. We are among friends, after all.'

'Some friends,' Rashmi scoffed before leaving the room to make a call. Noor hesitated momentarily, but when she finally found her voice, it was strong and clear.

Nine

'Swati is telling the truth. She didn't steal it. She didn't steal the Cartier lighter either.'

The women watched Noor as she rose from her corner and began pacing the room, shutting her eyes occasionally, as if to look for something that wasn't there, or recollect an image that had faded.

Swati sat with her head bowed low. She looked cowed down, thought Aparna. Or maybe she was just tired. She'd removed the magnificent ring and put it on Reema's elaborate dresser carefully. Surekha picked it up to examine it, trying to push it on to her podgy fingers unsuccessfully. Noor was walking taller, shoulders pushed back, head held high. Like the others remembered her from school, when she'd won debates and walked away with the elocution prizes. Suddenly, she wasn't the vague, shabby person who'd walked into the apartment a couple of hours earlier. She was, instead, the privileged Noor, the daughter of an aristocratic if broke 'khaandani' family—cultured, pampered, decadent. The transformation was fascinating. Noor's voice had abandoned its quavery, uncertain edge. As she strode around, she seemed to gain her lost confidence with each step. And as her memories emerged, her fragility disappeared. Her friends couldn't quite make up their minds—was it a new Noor they were seeing? Or the old one—the one they'd all but forgotten.

*

It would be easy to dismiss Noor by her physical appearance alone as someone uninteresting but that would've been a mistake for more than most of them she had an astonishingly complex past. Her relationship with her brother Nawaz, for instance. The Begum had known about their unusual relationship for years. Naani had told her after she found them together in the large store-room which nobody ever entered, unless it was to look for the old, discarded accounts books required for 'tax purposes' (as the Nawab discreetly put it).

'How did you get in here, the two of you?' she'd demanded, taking in their dishevelled appearances.

Boldly, Nawaz had told her, 'I got a spare key made from the locksmith.'

Naani had been about to strike him—something she'd never done before—when Noor had thrown herself between them saying, 'It was my idea. Don't blame him.'

Naani had restrained herself but looked at the girl pityingly. 'Still protecting this no-good brother of yours. Why? What has he ever done for you but get you into trouble?' Nawaz had tucked his shirt into his pants, zipped up his fly and loped out of the room. Naani had taken Noor aside and tried to explain why what they were doing was wrong, but it had soon dawned on her that she was wasting her time. Noor had been genuinely perplexed at Naani's reaction.

'But he is my brother. And I love him. What is wrong with that?' Realizing that it was something quite beyond her, Naani had decided to inform their mother, telling herself, 'After all, they are her children, not mine.'

The Begum's reaction had been cool and distant. 'I'm sure it isn't anything like that. They are children after all. This is a part of growing up. Just curiosity and innocence. They must have been playing some game. Nothing more.' Naani had gone back to her quarters to wonder about her mistress' strange response. What she had seen, she'd never forget. But then she'd discharged her moral duty by informing the Begum. The rest was up to her.

*

It took Noor many years to realize that her relationship with her brother was unusual and considered abnormal. But even after that, she wasn't entirely convinced. She'd ask herself why it was wrong or bad. Wasn't it better with someone from your own family than with a stranger? The Begum never raised the subject—it was far too distasteful. The Nawab probably suspected something but preferred silence. So it was left to Nawaz and her to come to terms with their peculiar sexual equation. It seemed to suit Nawaz just fine. Almost every night he'd slide into Noor's large and airy bedroom and get under the sheets with her. She welcomed his arrival, moving over to make room for him under the light, soft mulmul razai she loved so much. She enjoyed his light touch, the assured groping and the final intimacy of his body becoming one with hers. It might have carried on this way right through school and perhaps into college had Swati not entered the picture.

Noor was referred to as Swati's Chief *Chamchi*— a diehard devotee. She was the one assigned to clean Swati's gym shoes and write her punishment lines for her. She was also the one who took the rap for Swati's misdeeds. Her puppy-like devotion was so obvious and consistent, everybody stopped paying attention to it, including Swati. She just took it for granted that Noor would be around, ready to jump at the snap of her fingers. She raided Noor's lunch box at will, often polishing off her delicious biryani and murg massalam within minutes before disappearing to play throwball. Noor considered it an honour to be the chosen one. Swati wasn't unkind to her. Underlying the bullying and teasing there was genuine affection. And, when they fought, a truce was quickly arrived at. Swati stood up for Noor when she had to and Noor appreciated that. Nobody was ever invited to Swati's home. Nobody except Noor, whose car took a great big detour each evening, so as to drop her friend home. If Swati was in a magnanimous mood, she'd call Noor in for a snack. It was an invitation Noor never turned down. She found Swati's home as lonely and cold as her own. Swati was the only child of mixed parentage—her father hailed from Kerala, and her mother was half-Assamese, half-Bengali. A prominent social worker and professor of anthropology, her mother had committed her life to the upliftment of the toiling masses and was rarely home. Swati's father was a civil engineer who spent most of his time on sites out of town. Her home was functional in an impersonal sort of way. Given her mother's perfectionistic standards, they could rarely retain servants. Swati was accustomed to a succession of indifferent ayahs assigned to take care of 'baby'. She'd inherited her nutmeg complexion from her Malayali father and rather exotic features with tip-tilted Oriental eyes from her mother. Swati was difficult to categorize physically. That was what made her unusual looks all the more captivating.

Noor preferred to spend evenings at Swati's Warden Road flat to going back to her own home. Perhaps, without even knowing it, she instinctively knew the consequences of what might happen if Nawaz and Swati were thrown together more than was unavoidable.

169

It might have remained that way if Swati hadn't stayed over one stormy monsoon night. 'There is no way you can go home now,' Noor said looking out at the water-levels rising steadily outside.

Swati wasn't particularly bothered. 'Great,' she said cheerfully, 'what's for din-din? I love the grub in your home.' Noor felt thrilled. Almost honoured. 'I'll tell the khansama to make something special. Whatever you like.'

Swati thought for a minute and then asked naughtily, 'What goes best with brandy?'

Noor shrieked, 'Brandy? What?'

Swati pointed to a bottle of Remy Martin on the sideboard. 'I want some of that—it's so cold. I might die of pneumonia.'

Noor looked around furtively. 'I can't, Swati, I'm not allowed to touch that. It's my father's.'

'Of course it is, silly. We'll just have a small sip each. Brandy on the rocks while it rains and rains outside. What fun. And then we can play some music and dance.'

Afraid that Swati would go away if she didn't do her bidding, Noor went to the sideboard to fetch a couple of snifters. 'Brandy glasses,' she announced.

'I know. I've seen them in movies,' Swati said helping herself to a generous shot.

'Don't take so much. Daddy will find out. He examines the bottle every morning just to see whether the cook's been drinking.'

'We'll top the bottle up with some water. He'll never know,' Swati assured her, sipping delicately. 'Cheers,' she said raising her glass. 'And now for a cigar.'

'Let me lock the door,' Noor whispered, bounding towards the heavy, carved, mahogany door that separated the study from the adjoining dining-room. She switched on a tape and the two of them started swaying to Diana Ross. Twenty minutes later, they heard a persistent knock on the door. Noor in a panic, left her glass on a side table, while Swati tried unsuccessfully to put out the cigar.

'Open up,' they heard Nawaz shouting. The next minute he was inside the room, sniffing the air and looking around suspiciously.

Noor pleaded, 'Please, don't tell Ammi.'

Nawaz sat down regally on an olive green velvet winged chair. 'Why shouldn't I? You've been wicked. Evil. You are drunk. I think I'll call the police.'

Noor began to cry, whimpering, 'I'll do anything, please.' But Swati strode up to him boldly and called his bluff. She pointed to the telephone and said clearly, 'There it is. Make the call. I dare you.'

Nawaz stared at her in disbelief. 'I'll really do it. Then don't come begging.'

'Do it,' she commanded.

Finally, Nawaz got up and moved to the balcony, 'You can't go home now,' he said casually to Swati. 'Do your parents know you are here?'

'I've informed them,' Swati answered.

'Well, wait till my parents find out what you've been up to. I'm going to tell them.'

Noor pleaded with him. Generously, he granted them some breathing time. 'I'll see you after dinner. I haven't made up my mind yet.' Noor thanked him profusely and went back to Swati.

'Don't worry,' Swati told her, 'I'll think of something.'

After dinner, Swati went to Nawaz's room. He was lying in bed with just his silk lungi on, arms behind his head, staring moodily at the ceiling. 'I've come to say sorry for what happened,' she said.

'Say it properly—with respect,' Nawaz replied. 'Kiss my feet first.'

Swati stared at him contemptuously, 'Are you mad? I'd rather die.'

Before she could finish her sentence, he'd pulled her down on the bed and torn her cotton shirt apart. 'I'll show you just how mad I am,' he snarled as he ripped off her clothes and straddled her roughly. 'Mad, mad, mad,' he repeated while crushing her mouth under his, one knee pushing her legs apart, one hand snaking its way up her thighs. Swati kept her eyes open and her mouth shut. She did not resist and she did not protest. She watched the animal astride her young body with cold, clinical interest, examining his expression, listening to his breath as it emerged in short gasps, looking at his slim, hairless torso with dark nipples, feeling his narrow, slim, smooth hips pushing against hers. Swati

172

didn't feel anything at all as Nawaz entered her expertly, his hands pinching her breasts till they hurt. It was over within minutes.

'Satisfied?' she asked, raising herself on her elbows. Nawaz was flat on his back, with the lungi covering his nakedness. She jerked it off his thighs, stared at his flaccid penis and laughed. It was a laugh so loud and so derisive, Nawaz's eyes flew open and the back of his hand brushed across Swati's cheeks. She caught it in time and said, 'Don't try your tricks with me. They may work with poor Noor. But I'm not frightened of you. If you touch me, I'll scream the place down and everybody will know what you just did to me. And what you've been doing to Noor too.'

Nawaz looked at her speechlessly, his mouth open, a driblet of saliva trickling down his chin. 'I hate you. You are no good. I'd warned my sister about you,' he said gathering up his lungi.

Swati sat down on the bed, close to him and stroked his face. 'Poor Nawaz. Such a bully, aren't you? Don't worry. This is going to be our secret. I quite enjoyed the experience. Maybe we can do it again. My way, next time, OK?' He wasn't sure whether she was making fun of him, as she quickly dressed and left the room.

*

Noor never discussed that night with Swati. It was only when things began disappearing from the house that she got worried. First, it was small objects—a silver paper knife, a pretty decanter, some cheap trinkets. Naani noticed their absence first and asked her about them. Noor told her what she suspected: 'Nawaz is taking them.'

Naani was puzzled. 'For what? To sell? He doesn't need money. Begum-sahiba gives him enough. As much as he wants.'

Noor looked away embarrassed. 'I think he's giving them as gifts to my friend Swati.'

Naani didn't need further explanation. She made up her mind to be more vigilant and began locking up the bric-à-brac. It was the simultaneous disappearance of the silver Cartier lighter and the priceless ring that set off alarm bells in the house. For once, the Begum bestirred herself sufficiently to emerge from her boudoir and create a fuss. The Nawab was livid, accusing all the servants of theft. It was Naani who suggested gently that the parents question Nawaz.

Swati returned the 'presents' without protest. She hadn't really liked them all that much any way. She was told by the Begum never to come to their home again. This suited her fine too. Swati had moved on. Nawaz's doggy-like devotion and sexual demands were beginning to get on her nerves in any case. Besides, the end of term was close. And Swati had other, far bigger plans. She wore the gorgeous ring in the privacy of her room for one last time before packing it up. As she stared at the flashes of fire within the stone, she vowed that one day she'd get one for herself—bigger, better and unquestionably her own.

*

The women turned to Swati to see her reactions. There were none. Swati's face remained impassive as she studiedly stared at her nails, refusing to meet anybody's eye.

Rashmi said aloud, 'Well?'

Swati looked up briefly. 'Well, what? I hope it has been established for all time to come that I didn't steal those bloody things. I am not a thief. Nawaz is the one. Even his precious mother knew he was pinching things. Everybody knew that, the servants too. I don't steal, period.'

'Really?' Aparna interjected. 'Does that include non-objects?'

Swati shot her a glance. 'I know what you're driving at. But that wasn't my fault. I told you before—I don't steal husbands. Boyfriends, yes. Not husbands. Ask *him* if you don't believe me. Go on, call and find out if you have the guts. Call now. I'll speak to him.'

Seeing the puzzled expressions all round, Aparna clarified briefly, 'A small, uncleared matter between the two of us. That's all.'

Reema commented, 'Doesn't seem all that small to me. I can guess though.'

Rashmi nodded knowingly, 'I remember some gossip I'd heard. Your little matter involves Rohit, doesn't it?'

Aparna winced at the sound of his name. Then she snapped in Rashmi's direction, 'Stop pretending, for Chrissake. You bloody well know the score.'

Swati got up. 'OK girls. I think I've had too much wine. Too much of everything as a matter of fact. Maybe it's time to split.'

Reema pulled her down on the bed. 'Come on, *yaar*, don't get so uptight. We're just talking informally. Nothing personal, as such. Besides, we're all old friends, aren't we?'

Swati tapped her foot theatrically, 'Yeah, sure. Of course we're friends. And of course there's nothing personal. But I still think I should leave the rest of you to shred me to pieces happily and in peace. I don't think I can stand much more of this.'

Surekha placed a motherly arm around her. 'What's happened is in the past. Nobody is holding anything against you. We are just remembering our childhood.'

Rashmi stood up abruptly, 'Hey! I don't have the time for nostalgia. I'm sure Swati doesn't either. This scene is getting a bit much. I'm through with bitching for the day.'

'Who's bitching?' they chorused collectively. 'Nobody is being bitchy—just honest.'

Swati started rummaging around in her smart handbag for her Raybans and hair brush. Suddenly she exclaimed, 'Hey, girls—here it is. How could I forget?'

'Not another photograph or album,' Rashmi groaned.

'No, it's something far more fun. It's a video.'

'Don't bother to show it unless it's hard-core and features you,' Aparna said, taking a large gulp of her semi-warm wine.

Swati refused to be baited. 'I'll leave you to enjoy it, while Rashmi and I take a short breather. I need to get out of this place. Get some fresh air. Clear my head. Have I really knocked back all that much wine?' she asked pointing to the bottle.

Reema smiled sweetly: 'You must be used to drinking daily living abroad and all that.' Surekha looked on smugly, lips pressed together, suppressing a smile. 'Her life is different, baba,' she said. 'We are all ordinary people. She is a big-shot. A *maha* celebrity. Right, Swati?'

'Right,' Swati confirmed before sailing out.

Once in the compound of the apartment complex, she held on to Rashmi. 'Jeez. I wasn't expecting anything like this. I'd thought we'd have a friendly lunch, gab about the old days, that's all. This turned out to be bizarre. Like one of those dense film-noirs.' Rashmi's eyes were searching the street for taxis. Swati said, 'Did you hear me, baby? I was trying to make a significant statement.'

Rashmi turned to her distractedly. 'Fuck you, Swati. You are so full of yourself. So full of shit. I can't stand it. Besides, don't give me all that crap about your innocent little idea for an innocent little afternoon with innocent schoolfriends. Balls! Every bit of this was planned by you for some weird reason of your own. Nothing you say or do is without some advantage to yourself. So let's hear it. What did your devilish mind want this time? Why did you pick Reema and not Aparna? Why the specific names? What the fuck do you have in common with Surekha? Why was she included?'

Swati's hired Contessa rolled up. 'Let's go for a drive,' she suggested like she hadn't heard a word.

'Let's not. I have a kid waiting for me. Unlike you, madam, the rest of us have responsibilities.'

'Sure you do, Rush,' said Swati using Rashmi's old pet name, 'and I know exactly how I must appear to you, to all of you. But try and forget it if you can. I'm here after years and only for a day. You have your kid for life. Surely you can sacrifice momhood or at least postpone it, for a couple of hours? Come on—I'm thirsty. I'll buy you a drink somewhere—any suggestions?

Wearily, Rashmi got into the car, sliding in after Swati. As she bent low to get in, her sari pallav dropped revealing a deep, high cleavage. Swati stared blatantly. 'Some tits you have there,' she said as the car moved away, 'I've always been jealous of your body. Bet you didn't know that?'

Rashmi looked at her with surprise: 'You don't have a bad one yourself.'

Swati patted her thighs. 'Look at these. Firm maybe, but still thick. As for my boobs—I'm swearing you to secrecy—but I've had them augmented.'

Rashmi looked at Swati's bust with new interest and asked, 'You mean—silicone implants? But isn't that kind of dangerous?'

Swati told the chauffeur to head for the Lancer's Bar at the Oberoi, then turned to Rashmi. 'I didn't know that when I went in for the operation. But then, I didn't have much of a choice either. It was either getting myself a new pair of boobs or losing out on a role I badly needed. You remember that vampy bit I did on the never-ending serial called *Legacy*? The casting director took one look at me and advised, "Fix your boobs . . . then we'll talk." My agent thought it was a good idea. An investment actually. It was. I got all my breaks subsequently.'

Rashmi nodded moodily, 'And all your screws too, I suppose.'

Swati laughed. 'You really think I'm no better than a common tuppeny whore, huh? I bet I don't fuck around any more than you do, probably less. So, what's your problem? This topic was about breasts. Yours and mine. You are lucky enough to be born with yours. I had to buy mine.'

Rashmi touched hers protectively. 'Well, they haven't got me anywhere, have they? I mean compared to you and your plastic jobs. . . I'd like to touch them, see them. How do they feel? Light or heavy?'

Swati looked at Rashmi in the low afternoon light and thought how sultry she looked in a wild, unkempt way. The sort of woman who didn't bother about unshaved armpits or grey pubic hair. Very quietly she asked, 'Where did you want to go? I'm sure you would've made it if you'd tried. You were certainly smarter at studies than I was. You were better at dramatics. And debate. You walked away with all the major prizes. Bloody hell, you were even good at gymnastics. We used to call you the 'best all rounder'—didn't you get the cup for that in the tenth?'

Rashmi smiled bitterly at the collection. 'Sure. I was an "all rounder". What happened then?'

Swati told the chauffeur to wait for them in the parking lot. 'You tell me. I'm all ears. But let's talk over something tall and cold and potent.'

The two women turned a lot of heads as they crossed the granite floor of the hotel lobby. Rashmi's walk hadn't changed since those early days when she would thrust her breasts out and sashay around the tennis courts, her school uniform a good three inches shorter than was permissible. It was the natural earthiness that made people look twice and thrice at her torso which had an entirely different rhythm to her hips. Swati had altered her gait. She held herself differently—more stiffly. She walked with her head, rather than the shoulders, thrown back. Her hips had a suggestion of a swivel. The effect was provocative and deliberate.

Swati giggled as they sipped cold beers in the dark, wood-panelled bar with tall, strapping waiters dressed in the magnificent livery of the Bengal Lancer's. 'Do you remember showing off your breasts in the ninth standard? We were both in the loo and you lifted up your tunic saying, "Look, look, aren't I big? I bet I'm bigger than you—than all the other girls." You conveniently forgot Reema, of course. I bet you were jealous of her boobs—admit it. Only she hadn't shown them to us—right? We'd only imagined their size. Anyway, I couldn't take my eyes off your tits—they were huge even then. You weren't wearing a bra—in fact, you didn't start wearing one till much after the rest of us did—and we had tiny little lemons floating around inside our bra cups. I kept staring. We turned to look into those filthy broken mirrors over the wash basins. And you touched your nipples. I found that so erotic. Your nipples became erect as you continued to fondle yourself. You'd forgotten I was there. Or pretended to. Suddenly, you asked me to lift up my tunic. I refused. The bell rang. Guiltily, we rushed out before the rest came storming in.'

Rashmi was smiling happily at Swati's recollections. 'How strange,' she said, 'I don't remember a thing, not a frigging thing. Are you sure you aren't making all this up?'

'Why should I bother?' Swati asked, opening her bag and fiddling around with what looked like a compact.

Rashmi looked around the bar interestedly. 'Where are the fucking men in this joint?'

Swati stared around her. Two Japanese businessmen were shuffling papers. A black in gaily patterned Bermudas strolled in and strolled out, and in a corner, an Indian resident nursed a hangover. 'I'm perfectly happy talking to you, sweetie,' she said, resting her face on her hand and looking into Rashmi's eyes.

'Yeah, well, I'm surprised. I don't make such great company these days. Not since . . . not since. You know.'

Swati shook her head, 'No, I don't know. Tell me . . .'

*

'Stop that, stop that, stop that,' the man clad in navy blue underpants banged his hand on the bedside table.

Rashmi looked at him contemptuously. 'What's the matter—never seen a woman waxing her legs before? Stick around. I'll be doing my underarms soon. I might need your help for those.'

He turned away disgustedly and began searching for cigarettes, under a pile of discarded clothes. 'Why must you do all this in front of me? Why not in the bathroom? Or better still, couldn't you have waited till I'd gone?'

Rashmi continued applying a layer of wax over her skin, taking care to blow on the knife to cool the hot, messy, sticky mixture of sugar and lime juice. She reached for a fresh strip of cloth and pressed it carefully over her leg. With one jerky move, she tugged the cloth against the direction of the hair growth. With a satisfied smile she examined the stained strip in her hand where hundreds of hairs pulled out from their roots had stuck to the wax.

'It makes me sick,' the man commented, blowing billows of smoke in her direction.

'Lots of things about you make me sick too,' she responded cheerfully. 'So, big deal.'

'Such as what?' he asked, averting his eyes as she spread fresh wax over her thighs.

'Like your clearing your throat noisily after brushing your teeth. Yeah, that makes me want to throw up.'

'How come you aren't used to it?' he asked, watching her reflection in the mirror as she repeated the process.

'Same way you aren't used to watching me wax myself,' Rashmi replied.

'This is different—it is painful to see. Each time you pull that bloody piece of cloth, I get a pain in my groin . . . and . . . and . . . whoever it was who told you that men liked bald pussies was a fucking liar. I happen to love a bushy pussy.'

Rashmi continued with her waxing, pretending she hadn't heard. When she was through with her legs, she climbed out of her bikini panties and walked up to the dressing table mirror. 'Maybe I should leave my pussy alone this time,' she said thoughtfully. 'It's looking rather sweet with its fifteen-day stubble. What do you think?' She parted her legs and raised one up.

'What the fuck are you up to now? Stop behaving like a fucking whore.'

Rashmi turned to him. 'I'm looking at myself, damn you. Why can't I do that? You watch your stupid little tool all the time. I've seen you. You think I'm not looking. But I know each time we make love, your attention is on your prick—not on me. I see it in your eyes as you admire its dimensions before you reluctantly enter me. Almost like you can't bear to lose sight of it. If you could, you'd end up screwing yourself. Confess.'

'You're such a fucked-up bitch, has anyone told you that?'

Rashmi walked around naked, looking down at her body, a pleased smile on her face. 'What are you doing here in that case?' she asked him.

'Looking for an easy screw. Like all the others sniffing around. Hey, do me a favour—leave your bush alone. It looks great the way it is. You still haven't told me when and why you started to clean up down there.'

Rashmi came and sat in his lap. 'Some air-hostesses I knew told me it was what they did. They said it turned guys on. I believed them. Makes pussy easier to eat. Tastier too. They were more adventurous, more experienced. After the first time—it felt so smooth and silky, I liked the feel of it myself—you know? Besides, when we used to go swimming, I'd always stare at my friends' crotches, looking for stray pubic hair sticking out of the bathing suits.'

He laughed. 'I still do. I find it very sexy. You girls are really dumb. Or you read too much of that junky *Cosmo* stuff and get sold on bikini lines and other trashy ads.'

Rashmi sat astride him and asked, 'What makes me different? You must've fucked dozens of girls. But you've told me I'm the best—or at least, one of the best. Come on, tell me, how am I better than the others?'

He put his arms around her slim waist and caressed her back gently. 'There are times I can't stand the sight of you—and yet, I keep wanting more. I've asked myself why. Yes, you are sexy but so are so many others. I think I know. You are one of the few women who gives the impression that you actually enjoy screwing, being screwed, that you don't just grit your teeth and go through with the act—that dear girl, is the real turn-on, if you must know.'

Rashmi leaned over and kissed him passionately. 'I love sex like I love food. It's the same sort of hunger—and I knew it when I was eight or ten and used to get my neighbour's kid to touch me. But it scared me then. It doesn't scare me now.'

He raised himself up enough to strip off his underpants. 'Take me in,' he told Rashmi, 'and keep me there till I tell you.'

*

'Who was he? Or doesn't it matter?' Swati asked her reflectively.

'Oh, I don't mind telling you. He was a broke actor from Amritsar. Very big—you know. Very crude. I had this little place and he had nowhere to go. I think he really liked me though.'

'Did he come to Bombay to join films?' Swati asked.

'Everybody comes to Bombay to join films,' Rashmi laughed. 'His name was Anupam and he was one of many. I mean he wasn't my boyfriend or anything. Just one of the guys I was sleeping with.'

Swati shook her head disbelievingly. 'Has anyone called you a nympho before?'

Rashmi threw back her head and gave a throaty laugh.

'Sweetheart, you can say it's my middle name.'

'Doesn't it bother you? Embarrass you? I mean, what about your kid. He's young now. But he will grow up soon enough.'

'Oh Pips? He's not like other kids. Never was. I've raised him differently. Kids love their mother—even if they're nymphos. Sometimes, I feel worried about him, for him. But he'll be OK. If either of us was to

186

be destroyed, it would've happened when that bastard—his father—walked out. I survived. Pips survived.' Rashmi watched as two local executives walked in. 'Yuppie types. Rather Puppy types. I bet they'll try and chat us up,' she commented laconically.

'They always do. Come on, let's time them.' Rashmi sipped her beer silently. Swati took out a tiny mirror and checked her lipstick. Old Rose by Guerlain. The men were staring interestedly in their direction. Ten minutes later, Swati said tiredly, 'I give up. I was wrong. Maybe the guys have changed. Maybe we don't send out the sort of signals we once did.'

Rashmi looked past her shoulder and at them. 'Look carefully. These chaps are *bachchas*. I'd say in their early twenties. Why should they bother with us? They've probably cancelled us out as hag-bags *buddhis*.'

'Wait a minute, speak for yourself,' Swati protested. 'I can still get 'em all—any man, any age, any colour.'

Rashmi clapped deliberately. 'Bravo! Still the same gal, huh? Bragging about conquests. Remember when I came to London, when Pips was little.' Swati swiftly interrupted, 'Now, now, let's not bring that up. I was in no position to help. And you put me in one hell of a position. That wasn't fair at all.'

Rashmi asked for a fresh beer and lit a cigarette. 'Don't bullshit me, darling. If anybody could've helped me then, it was you. I was counting on you.'

187

'That's your problem always, thinking of yourself. Did it occur to you that I could've been having problems of my own? I was in the middle of a bloody crisis. You caught me in the thick of a bloody scandal when I thought my life was coming apart at the seams. But you, you couldn't think beyond your nose, your crisis, your kid.'

Rashmi stared into her drink. 'You're excusing yourself too easily, Swati my girl. You always have. Even in school. Have you ever owned up to anything? Taken the blame? The rap? Never. There were always scapegoats around. And all those silly *chamchis* of yours ready to cover up for you.'

Swati excused herself to go to the loo. On her way back, she decided to stop at the florist and pick up a few lilies for Rashmi. And maybe a box of chocolates for her little boy. While waiting for the cashier to make up the bill, she heard a familiar voice at the next counter asking the price of carnations. No. There was no mistaking the baritone. She listened to its velvety richness for a few seconds before turning around.

'Swati!' Balbir exclaimed as he grabbed her in a bear hug. 'What are you doing here?'

She pulled his flowing beard and teased, 'I could ask you the same question, Mr Big Boots.' Balbir was dressed in fashionably fitted jeans. He was bigger and hairier than she remembered him from London. 'Still in the music business?' she enquired, taking the cellophane wrapped lilies from the sales girl. He was staring at her in the sort of blatant way that made it obvious they'd slept together. She continued, 'You'll never guess who these flowers are for——and the person is waiting in the bar right this minute even as we are talking.'

Balbir didn't seem at all interested. 'I don't care, I really don't. It's you I can't take my eyes off. It's great meeting you like this, just great. Why don't you forget this other person and let's go grab a drink somewhere? How about my room? I'm staying here in the new wing . . . .' Balbir's voice trailed off, his eyes still surveying her appreciatively.

Swati smiled. 'Tell you what——I'm game if my friend is game. It's a woman, so don't pull a face. A verr-r-y attractive woman, I might add. You know her . . . ahem . . . intimately . . . but I'm not telling. Let's make it a threesome. Come on Big Boy, you're on.'

Balbir carelessly waved the carnations he'd been about to buy away and followed Swati out of the shop. 'You've got me curious now,' he kept repeating. 'Who is this woman?'

'You'll find out soon enough.'

*

When they reached the bar, Rashmi had disappeared. Thinking she'd probably gone to the ladies' room, the two of them settled down and Balbir ordered a gin

189

and tonic. Ten minutes later, Swati felt uneasy enough to summon the waiter. He shrugged stupidly as if to say, 'How do you expect me to keep track of every boozed up broad going in and out of the place?'

'I'll go look around,' she told Balbir.

He grabbed her arm and pulled her back. 'Forget it, man. You haven't even told me who she is. Frankly, I'd rather catch up with you.'

'Plenty of time for that,' Swati replied, pushing her skirt down and slapping his hairy hand off her thigh. 'I'm a little worried. You'd be too if I told you her identity.'

Balbir stood upon hearing that. And gulped down his drink swiftly. 'OK. Let's settle the bill and get out of this joint. But first—tell me.'

'Rashmi,' Swati answered shortly, not bothering to look at his face.

He let out a long low whistle. 'Shit man! Rashmi, after so many years. How come? What is she doing here?'

'Having a drink with me—do you mind?'

Balbir walked slowly behind Swati as she negotiated her way down the gleaming lobby and summoned her car over the intercom. It wasn't there. She thought the Sardar at the mike had got the number wrong and repeated it for him. Another liveried doorman turned up to say that the car had already been paged by some woman twenty minutes earlier. 'Madam, it's gone,' he informed the two of them as Swati stamped her foot angrily and swore.

'No sweat,' Balbir said, 'I've got wheels. Let me drop you off.'

Swati leaned back and shut her eyes. Balbir was pulling out of the driveway and into the rush of traffic on Marine Drive, heading north, beyond the neat residential buildings, restaurants and discotheques lining Bombay's famous Queen's Necklace. Within seconds Swati felt Balbir's large, warm hand on her thigh. She didn't move. And she kept her eyes shut. Balbir started to stroke the length of her leg, lingering behind her knee. It took Swati no more than a few moments to decide that the sensation she was experiencing wasn't in the least bit unpleasant. With a quick, subtle movement, she parted her knees, just wide enough for Balbir's hand to move between her legs. She felt his fingers searching, probing through the flimsy silk of her underwear. Though her eyes were shut, she knew when the car was approaching a traffic light—Balbir would hastily withdraw his hand and slow down, leaving Swati feeling restless and impatient. The car stereo was playing bhangra rap and Balbir's fingers kept up the beat. Swati was tempted to tell him to pull into a deserted lane and finish what he had begun. Instead, she held her breath and concentrated on the circular rhythmic patterns being made by his powerful, experienced thumb. She'd lost track of where the car might be headed or the time they had been in it. All she could think of was the interrupted, intense pleasure she was feeling. Now they

appeared to have left all the traffic signals behind—
Balbir was speeding along at a smooth pace. And he
hadn't removed his hand. He couldn't. Swati had locked
it in tightly between her thighs and was moving against
it energetically, her hips off the seat of the car, her
hands clutching the sides. It was only when she relaxed
her muscles and started breathing normally that Balbir
gently retrieved his fingers.

After giving Swati a few minutes to recover, Balbir
turned to her jauntily. 'Where to?' he asked, as if nothing
had transpired between them.

Swati sat up, looked around groggily and realized
that they were at the far end of Worli Sea Face. 'Turn
around and head back,' she said.

Sometime later they were travelling up Peddar
Road silently. Swati was lost in some distant world
while Balbir hummed along with the bhangra rap
singer. 'Which way?' he asked when they arrived at
crossroads—one way went up Malabar Hill, the other
led to Kemp's Corner. The street lights were on and
Balbir's Gypsy was caught in the commuter rush that
regularly snarled up this narrow artery—the lone one
in and out of South Bombay.

'Reema's place,' Swati told him.

'Who's Reema?' Balbir asked, his eyes fixed on the
car in front of him.

'Our schoolfriend—you know Reema. Rashmi's
friend too. We were all at school together. That's

how all of us met today. A belated get-together. It was my idea. Shit! I wish I hadn't suggested it. I'm beginning to feel fucked. I don't know what I'd expected.

Balbir said, 'The address—do you mind?'

Swati gave it to him and turned to gaze out of the window.

Balbir said slowly, 'Whatever happened between Rashmi and me was a long time ago. She was always a little crazy. I don't have to tell you that—you know it. Anyway, it wasn't my fault.'

Swati turned to him sharply. 'Who said anything about fault? I wasn't even thinking about the two of you, I was thinking about us—you and me.'

Balbir narrowly missed scraping the side of his Gypsy against a BEST bus careering down from the opposite direction. 'That wasn't my fault either—sorry—I shouldn't have said that.'

'It's OK,' Swati said, 'but it does seem so strange somehow. How many years ago was it?

'Ten? Eight? Twelve? I can't remember.'

'I was trying to get a break on that idiotic Asian Channel and so were you—remember? Social issues or some such nonsense.'

Balbir protested: 'Don't call it nonsense. It was new then and it did become a rage. I had a bigger fan following as the sexiest anchor on the tube at that point than you did.'

'That's true,' Swati giggled, 'and then you became some sort of an Asian rock star. What were you called? The Turbo Turban or something, wasn't it?'

Balbir laughed heartily at the memory. 'From Patiala to Perth I've travelled quite a distance, wouldn't you say? Two marriages, six albums, enough money and now an independent record producer signing on big names. Not bad at all.'

Swati agreed. 'Not bad, not bad.'

Balbir turned to her curiously. 'Did you sleep with me because you thought I'd give you a break on my show or was it to get even with Rashmi? Wow! Imagine the two of you, fighting over me! ME!! Come on—the truth.'

Swati didn't answer. Instead, she said: 'Take a left here. We're nearly there.'

Balbir freed one strong hand and caught her wrist. 'Don't play Miss High-and-Mighty with me. I know all your games, all your tricks. I saw through you the first afternoon you came to my dressing room pretending you'd lost your watch. I knew exactly why you were there and what you wanted. I can still recall your smell. Has any other man told you that you exude a very special, very sexy smell that lingers and lingers hours after you've been had? It must be hormonal. But it has stayed with me all these years.' Balbir thought he caught Swati blushing.

'Balls, Balbir! Is that some new line you've invented these days?' she snapped, checking her watch. She directed him into Reema's compound and scanned the parking lot for her own car. Swati was worried about Rashmi. Impetuous as she was, her disappearance from the bar with the car had upset Swati.

As Balbir and she waited for Reema to open the door, she wondered whether the others were still there. Probably not, she reasoned. It was more than two hours since she'd walked out with Rashmi. The servant who answered the urgent ringing of the bell, looked surprised to see them.

'Memsaab at home?' Swati asked, her words slurring just a little. They were escorted into the living-room which had been tidied up. A quick glance at the dining area showed that Reema's efficient staff had been hard at work—not a trace of the afternoon's feasting was visible. All the glasses and bottles had been removed and the apartment restored to its pristine, pre-party order. A young girl emerged from one of the rooms and greeted them uncertainly. 'Mini Reema,' Swati whispered to Balbir. 'Is your mummy home?' Swati asked Reema's daughter. She nodded her head in the direction of her mother's room, and indicated that she was sleeping. 'Weird time to sleep, don't you think?' Swati said to Balbir.

'Probably bombed,' he replied, staring interestedly around.

The young girl came back into the room to say, 'Oh, there's one aunty sleeping in the guest room.

No, two, one came later.' Swati raised her eyebrows quizzically and whispered, 'What's going on?'

Balbir held up his hands. I'm out of here. This is getting bizarre.'

Swati held his hand tightly and hissed: 'Don't be mad. The fun is just beginning. Stick around. I'll go find out more.'

She followed Reema's daughter into the beige and brown guest room and found Rashmi and Noor asleep on the twin beds. The curtains were drawn and the place was smelling of perfume, roses and fresh paint. Swati touched the wall near the switches and pulled back her hand. 'Jesus! Don't tell me she had her apartment painted this morning especially for our fucking lunch! The lengths people go to. . . .'

Balbir was staring at Rashmi, his eyes travelling over her sleeping figure. 'Still looks good. Looks great,' he said, standing with his arms folded across his chest, barely two feet away from her.

Swati laughed softly. 'Let me pass you some Kleenex to wipe off all that dribble. Behave yourself, you're drooling.'

Balbir hadn't taken his eyes off Rashmi, whose sari pallav had fallen to a side, revealing her slim midriff with its deep, round belly button. Her breasts were partially visible through the neckline of her knotted blouse. 'What did you tell me in the car? Didn't you say she was single? A single mother? Why did the guy leave her?'

Swati shrugged before saying, 'Fatigue perhaps. I heard she devours her men. She was quite a sexy thing in school.'

Balbir tore his eyes away reluctantly to stare at Noor. 'And who is this creature? She looks kind of shrivelled up—like a dehydrated pea pod.'

'Don't be mean. That's Noor—another schoolfriend. Very sweet but flaky.'

'Shall we wake them up? And our hostess?'

Swati brightened up at the prospect. 'Why don't you get into bed with Rashmi? I'll take pictures. Who knows, she might feel nostalgic and then anything can happen. That should be fun.'

Balbir considered it. 'Why not?' he said, adding, 'With clothes, or without?'

'Let's try it with for starters. She might die of shock if she finds a big, hairy, naked man in bed with her.'

Balbir winked. 'I'm not too sure—maybe she's used to it.'

Swati noticed Noor stirring and shushed him. 'Let's not wake everybody up.' She pulled out a small camera from her bag and announced, 'I'm ready. Let's have some action.'

Just as Balbir gingerly climbed into the tiny bed, the door of the room flew open and Aparna stood framed against the bright light of the chandelier. She took in the scene wordlessly. It was as if a cinematographer had frozen the picture momentarily.

Nobody spoke. Nobody moved. Aparna herself broke the silence. 'Excuse me,' she said sharply, 'I came back to collect my glasses. Blind as a bat without them at night. Thought I'd forgotten them in this loo.' She strode past them briskly and went into the bathroom. Rashmi sat up in bed, rubbing her sleepy eyes, her sari still off her shoulders. 'What's going on, where am I?' she asked drowsily. Noor opened her eyes and lay very still, blinking into the bright light that was flooding the room from the chandelier.

Swati sat down next to Rashmi and affectionately put an arm around her. 'Hey, wake up. Look who's here. I have a surprise for you. Remember Balbir?'

Rashmi squinted at him before straightening up. 'Bastard!' she spat out. 'What the fuck are you doing here?'

Balbir grinned sheepishly. 'Swati asked me to come along. I was just passing through, you know.'

'No, I don't know. And I don't want to know. I didn't think I'd ever set eyes on you again. How dare you—really—how dare you!'

Aparna emerged saying, 'They aren't here. Damn! Wonder where I left them.'

Swati held out her arm and purred,' A-pa-r-n-a darling. Don't disappear. We hardly got to talk.'

Aparna ignored her and asked Rashmi, 'Seen Reema? Is she OK?'

Swati interrupted her, 'Something happen to her while we were gone?'

Noor sat up in bed and said in a high-pitched voice, 'Why is the man staring at me? Who is he? Please call Nawaz. I want to go home.'

Swati stood up. 'Calm down everybody. The party's over. It's time for all of us to go home. I want to know what you girls thought of the video film I left behind. Aps baby—did you see it? Was it any good? I mean you are the communications expert. What do you think? Am I any good? Will I make it?'

Aparna snorted. 'Come off it, Swati. You didn't show it to us because you wanted our opinion. You were just showing off as usual. Dazzling us or trying to. I stopped getting impressed by such cheap stunts a long time ago. But since you want to know, let me tell you. The thing stinks. You need to hire a better dress designer and a more competent choreographer. You also need to work much harder on your act. What's the demo tape for, anyway? Vaudeville? Or a porn show?'

Swati smiled. 'Still the same. Still running me down. When will you stop competing, Aparna? Is it so hard to accept that I am the one who has made it and not you?'

Ten

Reema had been keen to see the tape but not the others, least of all Surekha who spoke for all of them when she announced, 'Forget it. I've come here to relax, eat, talk and meet everyone. Not sit through Swati's shows. If she's so keen on our seeing whatever it is on this tape, she should've brought enough copies and left them with us.'

'Quite right,' Noor added, without being very sure what the topic was.

Reema slipped it into the VCR anyway saying, 'Let's keep it on without the volume. That way we can watch *and* gossip.'

Aparna kicked off her low heels and put her feet up. 'If we are to torture ourselves, let's do it comfortably,' she'd said in a resigned voice.

Aparna was curious. Very curious. But she didn't want the others to know. Swati was definitely up to something and Aparna still hadn't figured out what.

Maybe she just wanted to impress her old friends. Prove to them that she—yes, she—had made it and made it big. Abroad. Which was where it counted. At least in India. Make it there and you were made everywhere. There was no escaping the glamour of a foreign tag. Recognition overseas ensured adulation back home. That's what Swati craved—she wanted the folks she'd left behind to know she'd done it. Aparna suppressed a smile. How depressing that it still seemed to matter so much—the all-important 'recognition' from the West. But it did. Not only to Swati but to everybody else.

The tape began with a tight close-up of Swati's face. So tight that you could only see her lips mouthing some words. A song? 'Put the volume up,' Aparna said in her office voice momentarily forgetting that she was in a friend's home and not in a darkened conference room watching an audio-visual presentation for a prospective client. No, Swati wasn't singing. She was talking—very intimately—to nobody in particular and to every single person watching her. The words, whispered throatily, were sexy without being obvious. It was such a come-on, Aparna found herself turning away in embarrassment. Swati was enjoying herself as she spoke. The camera moved back to reveal more of her. Aparna took in the shocking pink sari draped seductively over Swati's bare shoulders. No blouse. Not even a slip underneath. Just six yards of delicately embroidered chiffon glittering over Swati's high-gloss skin. Her face was made up to look exotic, almost bridal, with sandalwood paste filigree arranged over the eyebrows. Swati's dark, tip-tilted, Oriental eyes had layers of shadow deepening them further, accentuating their unique shape with thick kohl on the lower lid. Swati's lips, her best feature, were painted a pale gold, and outlined with a pink that matched her sari. Gold highlights over her angular cheekbones and gold dust over her shoulders made her resemble a calendar goddess. Swati wasn't singing so much as speaking the words. The music in the background was provided by the tinkling strains of the santoor with a percussion accompaniment that sounded like bongo drums from the African wilds. Her song writer (if the person could be thus described) had restricted the lyrics to just two words 'Kama Sutra'. Swati writhed suggestively on a bed of roses mouthing 'Kama Sutra . . . . Kama Sutra' over and over again, sometimes whispering throatily, at other times miming sensuously.

Surekha, clearly uncomfortable, said in a voice that registered her outrage, 'What is all this nonsense? Why are we wasting our time watching a blue film?'

'Not blue, pink,' Aparna corrected. The rest of the video had Swati doing an Indian Madonna routine, clad in a bra-like choli with a form-hugging dhoti worn round her shapely legs. It was obvious that she wasn't wearing undergarments and her nipples could be clearly seen straining against the wispy fabric binding her breasts.

Swati sang, danced, even acted. There were clips from her soaps—dramatic moments during which Swati was shown defending herself while an irate English boyfriend railed at her. 'Adulterous bitch!' spat out the wispy-haired hero, while Swati took long drags of her cigarette and studied her nails. This was followed by an eye-contact monologue where she accused him and all the other Brits of being racist. 'You dare to treat me this way because I'm coloured,' said Swati, eyes afire, sari carelessly leaving her moulded breasts bare.

The next shot had her on a talk show answering loaded questions provocatively, not allowing the snide interviewer to get the better of her. Then there was Swati at one of her weddings clad in a magnificent wedding gown which was so cleverly designed, it could've passed for a crooner's costume. There was Swati in a shower of confetti, tossing a bouquet at a black friend, throwing her head back to receive a passionate, full-blooded kiss from her husband, incongruously dressed in an Indian sherwani and turban. 'Reversal of roles,' giggled Swati at the cameraman pulling off the bridegroom's turban and placing her flowered veil over his blond head.

'So foolish,' Reema sniffed reaching for her wine.

'Still acting like a kindergarten kid,' Surekha added, with Noor laughing uncertainly and saying, 'What?'

The twenty-five minute tape ended with Swati winking at the viewers and saying, 'Call me,' making it sound like an invitation to a fellatio party.

Aparna broke the puzzled silence by saying laconically, 'I wonder what that was about? None of us can get her any bookings.'

To which Reema replied: 'My God! The stories I've heard. I didn't want to believe them. I told these people, "Never! It can't be true. I've known Swati from school. She isn't like that at all. She's such a sweet person."'

'What stories?' Surekha asked, excitement in her voice, 'Tell us. After all, we aren't going to repeat them or anything. What is there? There are no secrets between us. We're friends, *na*?'

Aparna snorted noisily.

Noor said, 'What?'

Reema widened her eyes and lowered her voice, 'Let me tell the servants not to disturb us. The phone doesn't stop ringing at this time. Friends, you know. Just women, don't worry. One wants to go to the club. Another to dancercises. Third to buy shoes. No peace in this house.' Aparna looked at her watch. 'Really, I'd have loved to stay for the dirt. But I've got to run. I have a brain-storming session. I'm already late.'

Reema tried to pull her down on the bed. 'Don't be such a bore. We know you're a very busy lady running an ad agency and all that. We are impressed, *yaar*. But we hardly see each other. Stay. Besides, you're never going to believe what I'm going to tell you. Never.'

Aparna firmly shook herself free and said, 'Maybe I don't really want to hear anything. Swati is coming out of my ears. You girls enjoy yourselves. I'll talk to you soon. Must do this again. Let's not wait for Swati to show up next time.'

Reema pulled a face. 'Such a spoilsport. I don't believe you're all that busy. In any case, it's your own office, right? You are the boss. You can call and tell them you aren't coming. That is if you're really rushing back to the office right now.'

Aparna stopped near the bedroom door, crossed her arms and asked testily, 'And what is that supposed to mean?'

Surekha nudged Reema, who broke into uncontrollable giggles. 'Mean? It means what it sounds like, what else? I've heard you have a new boyfriend. I'm told his wife had a nervous breakdown because of you. She was telling all the women at the Khanna's anniversary party last month that you'd ruined her marriage.'

Aparna's eyes were blazing as she said in an icy tone, 'It's a load of rubbish. Prem is a colleague, that's it. If his wife feels so bloody insecure about her husband she should keep him at home tied to her sari.'

Surekha butted in: 'Prem who?'

Reema added, 'Prem Nobody. He's no one. Just an ad fellow who chucked up his fabulous job in Delhi to come and work for Aparna for peanuts. I'm not saying anything, but it does seem a little funny. His wife said Aparna is paying him half of what he was getting in his old job.'

'That's not true,' Aparna protested, rapidly losing her cool. 'I got him here on great terms—better than any he'd have got elsewhere. I've given him a big break. Within a year, he had made it—made a name for himself. I got him an apartment, a car, other perks. Did his wife tell you that? I'm sure she didn't.'

Surekha said smoothly, 'But why are you getting so worked up, Aparna? These things always happen to single women. Lady bosses. Haven't you read that Jackie Collins book? If you ask me, you should get married again. So what if Rohit left you for some other woman? Men are like that. Not all men, mind you. But for career women it is important to have a man to back them up. Nobody takes them seriously otherwise. Everybody will say, "She's sleeping with this one and that one." My husband, for instance, won't look at another woman.'

Aparna gave her a withering look. 'Oh, you lucky thing,' she said flatly, 'but no thank you. I won't make that mistake again.' Then turning to Reema she said in a voice that was firm and strong. 'And you can tell your wonderful friends not to worry about Prem's marriage. If it's on shaky grounds, it's certainly not on account of me. Sorry, we aren't having an affair. Believe it or don't. I couldn't care less.' She walked out quickly leaving Reema with a knowing smile on her face.

'They all say the same thing. It's easy to deny, but I know the facts. Aparna is lying. Why should she lie to us? We aren't going to spread stories about her or anything. Kittu was telling me where they meet—in Prem's friend's empty flat.'

Surekha hugged a cushion to herself. 'Really? What does he tell his wife?'

Reema continued: 'Don't be dumb. They meet in the afternoons. He probably says they're going to see a client or something. Renu—Prem's wife—is such a sweet girl. Very pretty also. Not like Aparna at all. She designs pottery. Lovely stuff—see that vase there with the golden pattern? That's one of Renu's. She was telling one of the women at the last party that Aparna also rings him at home. That's bad, OK. If you're having an affair with somebody's husband, at least have the decency not to phone when the wife is there, no?'

Surekha nodded. Noor spoke up unexpectedly, 'Maybe she rings him for work. To discuss some office matter.'

Both the women laughed loudly. 'You are so childish, Noor,' Reema said, using the tone she usually adopted towards her daughter.

Surekha added, 'Poor thing, she lives in a world of her own. So sweet! Office work? Ha! No woman ever phones my home for office work, I can tell you that.'

Noor withdrew into a corner and curled up, drawing a quilt over her face. Reema continued, 'Anyway, I was going to tell you about Swati. You have time?'

Surekha looked at her cheap watch guiltily. 'Maybe I should phone my mother-in-law. She must be worried.'

Reema scoffed, 'Don't be mad. Why give her so much importance? That is how you women spoil them. I used to be like that—worrying constantly about what she'll think and what she'll say. Then I told myself, you are acting like a fool. You are an adult. Just because you've married her son doesn't mean she owns your life. Forget it. Surekha, take my advice—tell your husband to either move her out or move your family out. This rubbishy joint family system does not work. Ask me. I'm so much happier in my own home.'

Surekha shook her head. 'He'll never agree. Never. I know him. He'd rather leave me.'

'Don't underestimate yourself. Why should he leave you? He *needs* you, damn it. Look at my husband. He'll be lost if I go away. Even if I tell him I'm going for a weekend to my mother's place, he gets jittery. Can anybody else run this house the way I do? No way. My husband is lost without me—can't find a thing for himself. You just have to assert yourself once. Once your husband becomes a hundred per cent dependent on you, he won't look elsewhere. Men like their comforts. And men are spoilt lazy babies. Feed them well. Fuck them regularly and sit tight. That's the way to keep them. Control them. The rest is easy. Believe me—I was in your shoes not so long ago.'

Surekha looked around longingly. 'I'd love to have a place like this. Maybe not as grand. But just a room to call my own without that woman watching me all the time. It's really horrible. I can't do anything, anything at all, without her knowing about it. I'm surprised she leaves the two of us alone at night.'

Reema looked at her slyly. 'How is it? I mean, you've been married for nearly fifteen years, right? Do the two of you still do it regularly?'

Surekha blushed. 'I feel very funny talking about all that. Let's change the topic'

Reema sidled up to her. 'You can tell me. I don't mind telling you. We hardly do. That too when he is slightly high. And then for a man it doesn't really matter who you're doing it with. It becomes a habit. But you . . . look at you blushing like a bride! I bet he's the only man you've ever known. Right?' Surekha looked down and nodded. 'How boring!' Reema exclaimed. 'Imagine not knowing any other body, any other feeling, any other sensation. Forever. Sounds terrible. Like eating dal-chaval day in and day out.'

Noor pulled down her quilt to say, 'And what about me? Think of me.'

Reema laughed. 'I thought you weren't listening.'

Noor balanced herself on her elbows. 'I hear everything. People just think I've not heard, that's all.'

Surekha smiled. 'Dangerous woman—quiet and deep.' Reema began climbing out of her clothes. 'What are you doing?' Surekha asked looking alarmed.

'Nothing. Relax. Just changing out of this fancy outfit into a kaftan. What do you think—I am a lesbian or something?'

209

Noor piped up, 'Wasn't Surekha going around with Dolly? I remember catching them in the loo one afternoon. They had their hands up each other's uniforms. And they were kissing on the lips. Surekha—do you still meet Dolly?'

Surekha stood up abruptly and raised her voice, 'This woman talks such nonsense. You were half-mad in school and you're totally mad now. Why don't you shut up? Your mother was right when she told our teacher that she didn't know what to do with a crazy daughter. *I'm* not saying it—*she* said it. She said you were constantly making up stories.'

Noor took off her glasses and said quietly, 'My mother had to say all that or else my father would've killed her. She told everybody I was mad just to protect herself. I was the only one who knew what she was up to. I was the person she was scared of. She still is. I know all her secrets. I know everybody's secrets. I know the names of all her lovers. If I pass them on to my father, he will pick up one of his shikar guns and shoot her. She deserves it in any case.'

Reema pulled out a black and while ikat kaftan from her cupboard and slipped it on, taking her time over it, making sure the two women had ample opportunity to look at her body clad in cotton panties and a pretty bra. Surekha kept her eyes fixed on the carpet while Noor stared openly.

'Wow! Your body isn't bad, Reema. Nice and fat. Men find that sexy. I know that—Nawaz always

210

says he finds plump women juicier than thin, bony fashion models.'

Reema twirled in front of them, obviously pleased with herself. 'My husband likes it this way. But my daughter keeps telling me to reduce. I don't know whom to keep happy.'

Surekha butted in, 'What about your brother-in-law? What kind of a woman does he like?'

Reema pretended she hadn't heard. Instead, she asked sweetly, 'Dolly lives somewhere near your place, doesn't she?'

Noor added, 'Next building. And she hasn't married anyone. Maybe she's still waiting for Surekha.'

Reema giggled. 'Come on Surekha, tell us. How often do you and Dolly meet? Does your husband know about her?'

'It's nothing like that. What is there to know? We are still friendly, what's wrong? Can't two women be friends?'

'Sure they can,' Reema said, 'I have so many girlfriends. But I'm not emotionally involved with them as such.'

Surekha burst out: 'What do you mean? I'm not involved with Dolly either. It's just that we share a very close relationship. She's my best friend, that's all.'

'That's all,' mimicked Noor. 'Let me tell you that's not all. And that's not what Dolly's family thinks. They blame you for Dolly being unmarried. They say you broke up all her relationships.'

Surekha's face looked puffy as she fidgeted with her hair. 'They are blaming me for nothing. Dolly didn't like any of those men—that's not my fault.'

Noor continued, 'But isn't it true that she comes over for afternoon naps very often and your mother-in-law throws fits?'

Reema smiled. 'My! My! Noor, I'm really impressed. How do you keep track of everybody's lives? It's amazing.'

Noor took out a pair of tweezers and a small mirror from her bag and began pulling at hairs on her upper lip with total concentration. 'When a person is as lonely as I am, it's easy to keep track of other people's lives, especially other lonely people, like Dolly. I meet her in the library sometimes. Or at a bus-stop. We've gone for a coffee once or twice.'

Surekha looked up sharply, 'Funny, she didn't tell me. Normally she tells me everything.'

Noor smiled fiendishly. 'That's what you think. But I'm sure I know many things about Dolly's life that you don't. Jealous?'

'Like what?' Surekha challenged.

'Like the fact she thought she had a lump in her breast two years ago. Dolly was sure she was dying but she was too scared to tell you. Why do you terrorize her so much?'

'Dying? Cancer? You're making it all up.'

'Why should I?' Noor asked, carefully tweezing out a stray hair. 'She tells me all the things she dares not

212

tell you. I also know you stopped her from joining that German bank in Singapore. You did, didn't you?'

Surekha seemed flustered. 'I did it for her. She would've been most unhappy. And completely alone. She isn't used to living like that. She doesn't know anybody in Singapore.'

'That's not her story,' Noor continued. 'She told me everything was fixed up. She'd got her ticket. The bank had got her a place to stay. She'd even found a friend. That's what bothered you. It was her one chance to escape from you and your clutches. To make a new independent life for herself. Dolly was so hurt. So angry. She nearly broke off with you then. Ask her if you don't believe me.'

Surekha was thoughtful. 'She should've told me in that case. I thought she wasn't keen on going. What if she'd fallen sick there? Who would've looked after her? She wouldn't have been able to cope with the job pressure. Her health isn't all that good.'

Reema, who had been silent all this while, butted in, 'But you can't take on her responsibility for the rest of your life. What is she to you?'

Surekha said softly, 'It isn't what you people are thinking. Nobody will understand our relationship. It is . . . it is . . . spiritual. We must have had some connection in our last lives.'

Noor laughed out loud, while Reema suppressed a smile saying, 'It's OK, whatever it is. Actually, it isn't any of our business. As long as you're happy, what does it matter? People will always talk. Just because Dolly is unmarried they'll label her a lesbian. You have a good camouflage. You can hide behind your marriage. But for Dolly it must be very difficult. Anyway, we seek our happiness whichever way we can. Why criticize?'

Surekha reached for her handbag and pulled out the bottle of muramba. 'I'd brought this for Swati. Give it to her in case she sees you before leaving. I remember she used to love it in school.'

Noor asked, 'Does Dolly still hate her?'

Surekha shook her head. 'No. Not really. She has found someone new to hate now. Herself.'

*

Dolly had adored Swati long before she'd switched to Surekha. It wasn't easy adoring Swati and yet almost everybody who came into contact with her ended up doing just that, at least temporarily. Dolly had grown up in a large, untidy Parsi family living on Sleater Road in Central Bombay. 'Downmarket Bawajis' as they were called. Her father was an accountant in a mill of moderate size. Dolly's mother, Zerbanoo, was the neighbourhood seamstress. She specialized in sewing Navjote frocks for little girls. She was renowned in her community for creating frothy, lacy, pink and white confections that made every child resemble a fairy-tale princess for the most important evening in her young life. Zerbanoo was a formidable woman, ill-tempered and fierce. Dolly lived in abject terror of her overworked mother. And she never forgave Zerbanoo for not sewing a Navjote dress for her. Zerbanoo had too many pricey outside orders to bother with her daughter's dress. Dolly was a far from attractive child—too dark, too scrawny and too gawky. 'She doesn't even look like a Parsi,' neighbours would comment staring critically at her. When she grew into adolescence and fell hopelessly in love with Swati, Dolly began identifying with Swati's family thereby further alienating herself from her own people. *'Khodai!* She's dressing like a Hindu,' they'd exclaim as Dolly left her shabby home clad in an ill-fitting salwar-kameez with a bindi stuck defiantly on her forehead.

She might have gone on loving Swati if Swati had permitted her to. Dolly continued to worship Swati even after her public humiliation and rejection. It was then that Surekha stood by her—the only one from the large class to do so. And to think the whole thing was triggered off by the race to score 'house points'. How vitally important they had seemed. How crucial each hard-won point. The shield for the 'Best House' had been won by the Red House for the past five years. And Swati as aspiring house captain wasn't about to yield it that year to the rival Green House (with Aparna heading it). Swati demanded, and got, absolute loyalty from juniors and contemporaries alike. She'd put Dolly in charge of choir practice and dramatics. 'Crack the whip,' she'd told her, 'be ruthless if you have to. We have to win. And I must be the captain.' She'd also instructed Dolly to sabotage the Green House efforts by spying on their practices, finding out about their chosen songs and discovering the plays they were planning. 'Make sure they don't succeed,' she'd hissed. Dolly, carried away by the assignment given to her, had exceeded her brief. Not only was she caught eavesdropping at the rehearsal but it was established later that on the day of the Dramatics Competition she had made sure that the talented young girl playing Eliza Doolittle for the Green House production of *Pygmalion* was rendered out of action. Dolly had ground twenty laxatives into her soft drink. She'd also ripped two of her elaborate costumes. Priya hadn't been able to get out of her bed that morning. Her overwrought parents, fearing dehydration had had to eventually rush her to a nursing home to have her put on the drip. Someone who had spotted Dolly fixing the drink had finally squealed. Tearfully, Dolly had admitted her guilt, adding in her confession that she'd done it for Swati.

There were many who believed it to be Swati's brainchild since Dolly wasn't ingenious enough to come up with something so devilish all on her own. Confronted with the rap, Swati had denounced Dolly in the harshest of terms and denied any involvement in the sordid mess.

There were rumours that Dolly faced rustication. In any case, she'd been punished sufficiently. Not a single girl was willing to talk to her for weeks after the incident.

Except Surekha. Dolly had never forgotten her kindness as she comforted her in the empty gym. 'We all know what sort of a person Swati is,' Surekha had said, cradling a copiously weeping Dolly in her arms. 'People are scared of her—but not I. I know the truth. She made you do it.' Whimpering noisily, Dolly had stayed in Surekha's warm embrace for half an hour. Later, Surekha had washed her face, dried it, kissed her softly and led her back into the hostile classroom. Surekha could still recall the expression on Swati's face—a mixture of contempt and rage—as the two girls took their seats. They'd been inseparable since then.

When Surekha's family decided it was time for her to get married, Dolly had swallowed insecticide. Not too many people had made the connection between the two events. Dolly was regarded as an eccentric, a misfit, someone who lived on the fragile edge of sanity.

She'd moved out of her Sleater Road residence while at college. For all her imbalance, she had turned out to be an enterprising girl at a very young age, showing remarkable entrepreneurial skills. She had no qualms about the jobs she undertook so long as they fetched her money. She worked hard and long at all sorts of things—selling children's books, acting as a share broker,

an insurance agent, even helping out at a business service
centre during the last shift. She'd successfully done
several correspondence courses and become a fairly
competent secretary with a shorthand speed of over
sixty. Later, she'd bridged the computer age by going
in for an eight week summer course. Dolly managed
to earn enough to keep herself going independently.
After negotiating a small loan, she'd managed to acquire
a flat, helping out with the building society's clerical
work on the side. Surekha and she remained close.

They spoke to each other frequently, as often as
Surekha could escape her mother-in-law's eagle eyes.
There was little they didn't know about one another:
menstrual cycles, pre-menstrual headaches, anxieties
big and small. Surekha did most of the talking, using
Dolly to pour out her daily frustrations, minor bickerings
with her mother-in-law, major fights with her husband,
arguments with her child's class teacher, defiance from
old servants, even dissatisfaction with her sex life.
Surprisingly, Dolly was not jealous. She didn't consider
Surekha's husband a rival. He was merely the man who
paid all the bills and demanded his conjugal rights
periodically. She knew Surekha hated having sex with
him—detested every coupling. But both of them were
practical enough to realize that that was the ticket to
keeping the marriage going. Besides, as Surekha often
told her, 'What is there? It doesn't cost me anything.
I open my legs mechanically and stare at the clock on

the wall across the bed. It's all over in about six to eight minutes.'

Dolly's dependence on Surekha was more profound. Surekha was her crutch, her sanity, her love. There was nothing she wouldn't do to make Surekha happy. And Dolly undertook her little tasks unhesitatingly, ungrudgingly, unreservedly. There was little in life for her beyond Surekha.

Over the years, their relationship had evolved into an intense, mutually-dependent camaraderie. Surekha's family didn't suspect their relationship since it was beyond their imagination to do so. Besides, Dolly had made herself virtually indispensable to their lives. If Surekha's mother-in-law needed to be escorted to a pathology lab for a blood test, Dolly was there to take her. If Surekha's husband needed someone to go through his tax papers for free, he could count on Dolly. If their daughter's fees had to be paid or a dress organized for her school concert—Dolly would oblige. And, of course, if Surekha herself required any assistance there was no one else she even thought of turning to. 'I am so lucky to have such a friend,' she'd tell curious neighbours. Dolly had become the family driver, accountant, bill collector and general adviser. Surekha and her family couldn't do without her. As for Dolly, she'd committed herself to looking after Surekha's eternal well-being a long, long time ago. It was the only real commitment in her life. The one thing that kept her going. Surekha too couldn't imagine life without Dolly. Their lives had become inextricably intertwined. Dolly and Surekha were like a well-adjusted, happily married couple. There was no passion to deal with any longer. Just enough physical familiarity to provide regular comfort. It would have gone on in this placid, even manner had Swati's visit not upset the balance.

Just the mention of that dreaded name was enough to send Dolly into a violent tailspin. The day Surekha received Reema's invitation she debated with herself whether or not to mention it to Dolly. But since secrets were not a part of their pact, she had brought it up casually when Dolly phoned that day. She had been totally unprepared for the violence of Dolly's reaction. 'How can you even *think* of accepting?' Dolly had shouted into the phone. 'That female nearly destroyed me. I haven't forgiven her. And never will. But you. . . why? Why do you want to go? What will you get out of this stupid lunch? Have you asked yourself one question . . . no, I'm sure not. The only reason Swati has asked you is to hurt me. What else? You have nothing in common with her. Nothing at all.' And then with perfect timing, Dolly had spat out the words she knew would hurt the most: 'Besides, Swati always made so much fun of you: called you fatso, criticized your clothes, teased you about your funny accent. Forgotten? She made you feel so ashamed of yourself and your family.'

Dolly had slammed the phone down, abruptly cutting off the noisy weeping that had accompanied the outburst. Surekha knew it would take her a few days to cool off. And then she'd be back, shopping bag in hand, ready to travel to Crawford Market and lug back Surekha's weekly supply of fruit and vegetables. Surekha waited by the phone till she was sure her mother-in-law had withdrawn into the kitchen—there to attack ten, fat, soaked potatoes. It was only when Surekha heard the harsh scraping sound of the peeler that she emerged to water the hibiscus bush in the balcony. She noted delightedly that three new blossoms had bloomed since the previous evening.

Eleven

'Where's your husband?' Swati asked Reema casually. One of the servants had produced tea for everybody. Reema had a particularly resentful look in her eyes as she sank into a roomy chair, her make-up streaked across her face, her hair mussed up untidily, her hands fidgeting incessantly with a napkin. 'Please ask this man to leave my house, Swati. It will be most embarrassing if my husband finds him here with me dressed like this. And all you girls. . . .'

Swati winked at Balbir and purred, 'Be an absolute poppet and run along, darling. This isn't exactly your scene. Now that you've seen good old Rush and found out just how warmly she feels towards you, I think it might be wiser to beat it.'

Aparna twirled her car keys impatiently and said to Balbir, 'Haven't I seen you before somewhere? Yes—I remember, we met at an Ad Congress in Singapore. You've put on a great deal of weight since then.'

Balbir looked at her interestedly. 'Baby, I'd have remembered you. I think you have the wrong man.'

Aparna repeated firmly, 'No, I don't think so. You were the stud every woman within a three-mile radius was panting after. And there was that famous little incident when you went down on somebody's wife in the loo and the guy walked in.'

Balbir shook his head stubbornly repeating, 'Not me, not me.'

Aparna leaned against the wall, threw back her head, narrowed her eyes, wagged a finger in his direction like a starchy schoolteacher and repeated, 'Yes, you. Yes, you. I don't forget faces. Also, I recall a memorable discussion led by you. It was all about your ridiculous theory on women's sexuality. You said each time a woman screwed a man it was to try and trap him into making her pregnant.'

Balbir sat back, his legs stretched out in front of him, his fingers tapping the side table. 'Now I remember. You were the bitch who strained her vocal chords so much, you went hoarse—and finally your larynx just packed up. Right? I still believe in that theory, by the way.'

Aparna sneered, 'You would. People with your sort of limitations aren't capable of moving forward.'

Balbir turned to the other women and shrugged, assuming his best little boy expression. 'Tell me, girls. Am I wrong? Be honest with yourselves. Do you fuck because you enjoy fucking? Or is it power-play? Haven't you ever told a man screwing you, "I want to carry your child?" It's the world's biggest con line. The moment I hear it, I shrink, jump off the bed, zip up and leave town.'

Swati laughed aloud, clapping rhythmically. 'This is better than any talk show. I love it. Let's have more. Rashmi—what are your views? Have you used that line on anyone? Did you use it on Pips? Is that how Pips Jr got made?'

Rashmi tossed back her hair and stared fixedly at a print of wild orchids framed in non-reflecting glass, which for some peculiar reason was hung amidst family portraits. 'Basically, I think all men are bastards,' she announced stonily.

'But that doesn't answer my question,' Swati persisted.

Rashmi turned to Balbir. 'And this man is the biggest bastard of them all. Yes, he screwed me good and proper. Want to know where? In a lift! Can you imagine that? A lift.'

Reema was suddenly awake and very interested. 'But how did you do it? Weren't there other people? Which lift? When?'

Rashmi pulled up her legs and tucked them under her bottom. 'It was a few years ago. I was on my way to see some ad guy at Nariman Point. I needed sponsorship desperately for a play we were trying to put on. It was an automatic lift, no attendant, after office hours. Balbir had offered to introduce me to this chap—I think he used to handle a cigarette account or something. Suddenly, he pounced on me when the lift door shut. I screamed, but of course, nobody could hear me. He pushed his hand under my sari and between my legs. He was pretty tough even in those days. The office was on the twenty-third floor. With one hand Balbir pressed against the 'Doors Closed' button, he ripped my panties off and stuck his fingers inside roughly. We were in the lift only for ten minutes—but it seemed so much longer. The lift kept going up and down. And there was this animal sticking it up my throat.'

Balbir listened unperturbed. As soon as there was a pause, he added nonchalantly, 'Hey, baby! Haven't you forgotten something? *You* wanted it. Not I. I prefer beds. Comfort. That fucking elevator was smelly. Stench of polyester, sweat and garlic farts. You attacked me, remember and begged, "Do it. I've never done it before in a lift." I was only being gallant. I didn't want to disappoint you.'

Rashmi fiddled with her sari pallav and stared moodily away. 'That's your version. I prefer mine. In any case, there's no uglier sight in the world than that of a man with an erection. You guys believe it turns us women on. But let me tell you, the male organ is grotesque. Hideous. Threatening. Especially when it is swollen. It resembles a weapon. The only person it turns on is the guy himself.'

Balbir turned to Swati. 'Is that right, sweetheart? Jesus! This is turning out to be one hell of an evening. I'm learning so much. I always thought women turned to jelly at the sight of a ready-for-action cock.'

'Bull!' snorted Aparna. 'It's a favourite male myth—another stupid stud fantasy, that's all. The truth is women don't need men at all—there are ways and ways of seeking satisfaction.'

Balbir laughed uproariously. 'Hey! I didn't know you'd become a dildo-baby. This is the age of hi-tech sex. I love it. But you are only reconfirming what I said earlier. Women screw men for babies.'

Aparna paced the room restlessly. 'Look, this is a ridiculous discussion. I disagree completely. Women are so self-sufficient, men can't bear it. That's what gets them. Nobody is a cock-slave. No woman gets turned on looking at male nudes. All those ghastly frontals are designed for other men—sick men.'

Swati interrupted her abruptly: 'Are you calling gays sick? If so, be prepared to wage war. Some of my best friends are gay. And frankly, darling, I'd thought you'd switched long ago. Way back when—you know what I'm talking about.'

'Don't be ridiculous. Just because a woman happens to be principled and doesn't screw around like a randy little whore, doesn't mean she's gay.'

Swati got up and adjusted her stockings, taking her time to bend low enough for Balbir to glimpse her panties. 'I don't know why you are denying an area of your life so strenuously. There's nothing to be ashamed of. We've all had our girlie affairs. So what? And we've survived heartbreaks too. Just because one son-of-a-bitch walked out on you doesn't have to turn you into a man-hater. You were discussing cocks—I happen to like them.'

Reema said, a little too loudly, 'Can we please change the subject? I have a young daughter in the house. I don't want her to hear such disgusting, filthy talk.'

'Sex isn't filthy,' Swati commented, 'our minds make it so. Look at Khajuraho, Konarak . . . have any of you studied the *Kama Sutra?* Fascinating. It's a pity we got brainwashed by some frustrated, repressed idiots. I think sex is a celebration—the highest form of religion. I'm a cock-worshipper and I don't mind admitting it.'

Rashmi giggled. 'You aren't a worshipper, you are a user. It's nothing more than a consumer durable to you. Don't lie. You screw because you want something, you don't do it for pleasure. Admit it.' Swati smiled a self-satisfied smile. At that point Aparna thought she could almost see her glow with a smug radiance. She'd never hated Swati more. Or been as repelled.

Swati went and sat on Balbir's lap. 'Here's a man who knows what he wants. If he is hungry for pussy—he goes after it and gets it. I'm a lot like that myself. The difference between the two of us and all of you is that we rejoice in our sexuality. We don't suppress it. We don't dismiss it. We don't find it dirty. Sex doesn't threaten us. I'm not afraid to fuck. I feel sorry for all you women hanging on so desperately to outdated ideas of purity, morality, chastity. It's pathetic.'

Balbir butted in: 'I'm with you, baby. But unfortunately a nasty four-letter-word has come along and ruined the pleasure of the other four-letter word.'

Rashmi sprang up. 'If you are talking about AIDS, please be careful. I'm very involved with street theatre these days and spreading AIDS-awareness is our biggest challenge. We've been performing in all the red-light areas. The response has been fantastic.'

Aparna asked for another cup of tea and looked anxiously at Reema. 'Listen, tell us to scram in case your husband is expected and will mind. When does he get home?'

'Never before nine, sometimes ten. We eat our dinner at eleven, horrible. But he's so busy. He works very hard, poor chap.'

'Does that suit you or not?' Noor asked quietly.

It was the first time in close to an hour that anybody had heard her voice.

'Noor you surprise us all by piping up like that,' Aparna scolded.

'But did I ask something wrong?' Noor enquired.

'No, no. Forget it,' Reema said quickly, 'I don't mind telling. Yes, it rather suits me. We've hardly anything as such to talk about. This way I have the whole day free for myself. I go to the Priyadarshini park every evening for a long walk. Then I come home and chat on the phone. We plan our kitty lunches, shopping trips for the next day. What to make for dinner. Holiday plans. It's much better this way. He's so tired at night, he finishes his dinner in ten minutes and goes to sleep. On days when I want to watch a movie or read, I sleep in the guest room.'

'You've got it all worked out, haven't you?' Rashmi marvelled. 'Boy! I've never had it this good. All my men have been slave drivers demanding this, demanding that. Expecting me to be perfect all the time. And yet I can't do without them. I must be mad.'

Balbir exploded into loud laughter. 'Of course you are. That's what makes you so interesting, so much fun. Believe me, had any other broad wanted me to screw her in a stinking elevator, I would've said fuck off. Women are always suggesting crazy things. Maybe they like the danger. Maybe fear and tension are the ultimate turn-ons. The best screws I've had are with depressed women. They want it so badly, it's great. Therapy for them. A roller-coaster ride for me.'

Twelve

Balbir had enjoyed a more than privileged childhood materially. His father, a strapping six-foot-two army man was a much-decorated brigadier when Balbir went off to a public school. His mother, Amrita, was palely beautiful and determinedly anorexic when all the other army wives took pride in their prosperous, generous, ghee-soaked waistlines. Amrita remained isolated, preferring to spend her time gardening or listening to Pakistani ghazal singers. Clad in salwar-kameez suits that completely ignored contemporary fashions and reminded everyone of a bygone Lahore, Amrita put in rare appearances at the Delhi Gym to a surprised chorus of 'Helloji, hawryouji?'

Balbir was their only child, but it had been decided very early in his young life that he was not to be 'spoilt'. That he was to receive no special attention or favours. This was about the only thing the husband and wife had ever agreed on. Papa Jasjit wanted his son to be brought up in a rigidly disciplined manner so that one day he too would become a soldier.

Amrita went along with her husband's dreams not because she believed in them but because anything else confused her. They'd been married when she was just sixteen. Balbir was born two years later. His father had reacted with subdued jubilation and treated his arrival as a tactical victory, a war manoeuvre.

'This is the way I'd planned it,' he'd announced at the Mess the next evening as he bought everybody a round of rum. Amrita had stared at the fat little baby and thought of the pain he'd put her frail body through. She'd vowed she wouldn't go through with it again. Besides, she'd reasoned, there really wouldn't be any need to. Her husband had got the child of the desired sex and thereby liberated her from further obligation.

*

Balbir was brought up in assorted cantonments all over India and raised by a succession of subedars and orderlies. He rarely saw his parents and rarely missed them. He was big and strong and confident by age five. By age eleven he'd begun to sprout whiskers. By age twelve he'd been seduced by a chowkidar's young wife. By fifteen, Balbir was a man—a man who knew what he was looking for. And it wasn't for a life in the army.

His showdown with the now promoted Major-General took place just after he'd finished school. Driving back from Gwalior to Delhi his father had informed him of his plans for the future.

'These holidays are going to be important ones. We have to start you off with the right grounding. The entrance exam for Khadakvasala is a few months from now. I want you to pass with distinction.'

Balbir, fresh from the impressive farewell ceremony at school, had made the mistake of laughing out loud. His father had looked at him sharply and asked, 'Did you hear something funny? I didn't crack a joke.'

Balbir, still shaking, turned to his father with eyes brimming over. 'I don't want to go to Khadakvasala, Dad,' he'd said placing his hand familiarly on his father's uniformed knee.

Jasjit Singh had slapped the boy's fingers away smartly before saying in a low, firm voice: 'That decision does not rest with you. It was taken the day you were born.'

Balbir had looked at his father defiantly and in a steady voice he told him he had no intention of ever joining the army. Jasjit Singh had stared out at the flat, traffic-free road ahead without the slightest expression. He was only too conscious of the driver in the front seat. Father and son had already created enough of a scene to make it to the Mess grapevine. He had no desire to contribute further to his own embarrassment. Balbir was disappointed that his father had terminated the conversation so abruptly. He'd looked forward to a long man-to-man talk for a change. They rarely got the chance and here they were stuck in a long car ride together. Such an opportunity was unlikely to present itself in a hurry. Besides, Balbir had done surprisingly well in his school leaving exam. He'd scored in other areas as well: house captain, cricket and squash captain and the boy adjudged most likely to succeed in later life by his classmates. He'd led his school to several convincing victories on the sports field besides having credited himself as a director and actor at the annual theatre festival. He'd done it for himself, not for his parents. Balbir was a natural achiever. It mattered to him to win. And in most situations, he did. He'd expected to demolish his father on this touchy point as well. A point that had become a recurrent source of conflict within their small family. Staring moodily at the relentlessly bleak landscape outside the car window, Balbir had brooded over the small fracas he'd just had. There would be time to make up and renegotiate, he'd finally concluded. Balbir's charm when he so decided to harness it, was boundless. Even his father would find it hard to resist.

*

That had been the first of Balbir's many miscalculations. It wasn't that he was unrealistic or that he over-estimated himself. Balbir was just so full of confidence and bravura, it never occurred to him that the word 'no' existed in anyone's vocabulary and that a few of the people who used it actually meant it. This got him into innumerable tricky situations especially with women, but he would often escape by grinning sheepishly and saying, 'We were taught in school that when a woman says "no" she always means "yes".'

Jasjit Singh never forgave his son for letting him down. Amrita stayed neutral as she always had, letting the two men in her life sort out their differences without involving her. Balbir's charm, which she did have a weakness for, had not worked this time. She stared at her son soulfully as he appealed to her to intervene and suddenly saw a stranger she didn't know or particularly like. All she could say to him was a shocked, 'You have changed. I cannot recognize you any more.' With those words Amrita had withdrawn into her air-conditioned bedroom (which denied entry to the Major-General except during emergencies) to nervously pluck dried petals from her prized roses and drown herself in Begum Akhtar. Balbir had stormed out of the house taking his golf clubs, tennis racket and Lacoste T-shirts with him.

Jasjit Singh had forbidden his wife from trying to locate their missing son. 'The bounder will be back,' he'd thundered, his face dark with fury. Amrita had fluttered around near the phone, wondering whether or not to call the mothers of his schoolfriends. She'd eventually decided against it, nervous at the thought of prolonged explanations and lengthy conversations. Besides, in some strange way she felt she'd already said her goodbye. The boy who had nearly torn her apart as he emerged from her loins, had grown into a man she couldn't recognize or even get herself to care about. As she pressed pretty lace hankies daubed with cologne to her ivorine, unlined forehead, Amrita had sadly acknowledged her failings as a mother. And then, as a wife. But they didn't seem to matter. Nothing really did. The heat had been oppressive in their large Prithviraj Road bungalow as she wandered out into the garden to check how the dahlias were doing.

*

Balbir headed for Bombay and his best friend's house. When Nitin saw him at the door of his Altamont Road apartment, he wasn't really surprised. Neither was his mother. Balbir had spent nearly all his vacations with them. The Shahs had taken to introducing him as their 'second son', a remark that invariably led to sniggers given Balbir's hirsute, turbaned appearance. Nitin was Balbir's exact opposite: a studious, shy, gangly boy entirely in love with his computers—their only shared interest. Nitin played no games other than chess and listened only to classical music. And yet, their friendship had survived through six turbulent years. Balbir had mocked everything Nitin stood for, including vegetarianism. Balbir had smoked, drunk and whored as a schoolboy, while Nitin stayed back in the dorm desperately covering up for his wild and wilful friend. Balbir was a carnivore who often shot crows with his air gun to eat them. Nitin shuddered at pictures of bloody steaks and all but puked when Balbir insisted on ordering them at restaurants. But it was really Nitin's family that cemented their relationship after the first holiday Balbir spent in their secure, quietly-ordered home.

*

Mrs Shah had welcomed him warmly and taken care not to ask any questions. It had been obvious to her that Balbir's unannounced visit wasn't a spontaneous holiday decision. Whatever crisis it was, she wasn't going to pry. Balbir had been visibly distraught and had walked straight past her, unable to meet her eyes. She'd waited for him to emerge from Nitin's room making sure the servant took him a tall glass of fresh lime juice to cool him down.

Nitin had left almost immediately to seek admission into Sydenham College. Nitin knew what he wanted in life. He would get his commerce degree, follow it up with a degree in law and join his father's very successful firm as a junior partner. The Shahs had never had to worry about their son, but they'd spent many hours wondering about his hot-headed friend. And there he was locked up in a room with the music at a deafening volume, probably crying his eyes out.

When Nitin had returned hours later, he was exhausted. His admission was still a question mark. He could tell that something major had upset his friend, but was sensitive enough not to probe. Balbir had told him soon enough. Recounted the incident in broken sentences and halting words. Nitin had heard him out without interrupting. When Balbir was through Nitin had walked across to his over-stuffed cupboard, thrown out half the things and said casually, 'Here, keep your stuff on these shelves.' And that was that.

*

If Mrs Shah worried about Balbir's influence on her timid son, she didn't express her concern to either of the boys except on one occasion when they'd staggered home at four a.m. dishevelled and drunk.

'Where have you been?' she'd asked anxiously.

'Whoring,' Balbir had roared.

Mrs Shah had covered her ears and commanded, 'Stop. Don't say another word. I find your conduct despicable and disgraceful.'

Nitin had tried clumsily to apologize but his mother had turned around and walked out of the room saying,

'I didn't raise you to hear these ugly words. I'm so ashamed. And so sad. For you.'

The boys had looked at each other sheepishly and retreated to their room.

*

It had been Nitin's first time. Balbir had mocked, 'What are you saving all that semen for? Don't believe those sex-books. It doesn't turn into blood, you know. Come on, let me show you some action.'

They had cruised the seedy bars along Colaba Causeway, starting at Leopold's, where Balbir had got into a fight with a couple of Nigerian students, and had eventually ended up in the darkened and smelly Sassoon Dock area which Balbir seemed totally familiar with. He had led Nitin up a flight of wooden stairs and into a curtained room where he was greeted by name by a blowsy woman in her forties.

She had looked at Nitin indulgently and teased, 'So, Balbir, you've brought us a *chikna* friend, have you? Let's show him our prettiest girls.' She had called out raucously, 'Laila, Twinkie, Bubbly, Madhoo—come out and see what we've got for you.'

Four young girls clad in impossibly tight mini-skirts had sashayed out from the innards of the place and surrounded Nitin. Two of them knew Balbir and had promptly bummed cigarettes off him. Nitin hadn't dared to look into their interested, teasing eyes; finally, one of the girls had seated herself on his lap and begun to rub the back of her hand across his crotch making appreciative noises and saying, 'Look at what a big gun he's hiding inside. It's a cannon, man.'

Nitin had recoiled at the stench of her cheap scent combined with sweat and hair spray. He had noticed the dark patches of perspiration under her armpits and saw the strap of her frayed black bra as it strayed outside the neckline of her red sweater. The girl had plastic clips in her tangled hair and far too much make-up. Her jaw hadn't stopped working. Neither had her hands with chipped pink polish on her dirty fingernails.

Nitin had tried appealing to Balbir with his eyes. But Balbir had been far too preoccupied flirting with the older woman and patting the generous rumps of the younger ones. Hoarsely, Nitin had whispered, 'Let's get out of here, I really don't want to. Some other time. I've got a terrible stomach-ache.' But Balbir had winked at the girl in Nitin's lap and shouted, 'Take him in and give him the works. The full treatment—a fuck he'll remember on his deathbed.' Giggling stupidly, the girl, Madhoo, had dragged Nitin into a tiny cubicle, shut the door, pointed to a water basin in a corner and said, 'Wash, wash. First get clean. Then wear a condom. After that we fuck, OK?'

Nitin had wanted to open the tiny ventilator in the cubicle and crawl out. Instead, he had obediently taken off his pants, folded them up and waited. When he saw her outstretched palm he hadn't known what to do—was he supposed to shake it, was she extending her hand in some sort of a weird gesture of friendship? He had blushed and stared till the girl said sharply, 'Money. You give me the money first. And then we fuck. Those are the rules.'

Nitin had lunged for his wallet, eager to impress her with the fact that he wasn't a cheapskate and wanted to play by the rules. He had pulled out the few notes he had and asked uncertainly, 'How much?'

Greedily, the girl had grabbed the lot and said, 'So much,' and briskly peeled off her clothes, wiped herself with a washcloth and reclined on the narrow bed, legs wide open. 'Come on, *yaar,*' she urged in a bored tired voice.

Nitin had looked at the stubble on her thighs, noticed an angry looking rash near her groin, noticed the shrivelled up little breasts with their scrunched up brown nipples and had muttered, 'It's all right. Really. I mean we don't have to do anything. But. . . but. . . you can keep the money. I won't tell anybody. Promise.'

She had laughed and then asked nervously, 'You're sure it's OK, *na?* Later on you won't tell her that I didn't do a thing? See, I'm still offering. You want to do, go ahead. Makes no diff, *yaar.* Try it, you might like it. But don't say I cheated you or I'll be in shit trouble.'

Nitin had assured her his lips were permanently sealed. She had asked him to sit on her bed for a few more minutes while she faked a loud and blood-curdling orgasm, complete with moans, groans, shrieks and screams: 'Otherwise they'll get suspicious. It usually takes twelve to fifteen minutes. That is, for first-timewallahs like you. Otherwise it's all over in less than five. We girls know our job,' she'd explained. Then she'd taken a few quick drags at a cigarette, doused it, changed back into her ghastly work-clothes and signalled to Nitin that it was all right to walk out and join the others.

Balbir had looked up expectantly and boomed, 'Kaisa hua? Did she give you a good time?'

Nitin had shrugged nonchalantly and said, 'The best.' Madhoo had lit a cigarette and winked at Balbir. Nitin had prayed fervently that his friend wouldn't grill him on the way home. Mercifully, Balbir didn't.

*

There was no question of Balbir returning home and the Shahs didn't even consider the possibility. The moment he'd flung his gear down and stormed into Nitin's room, Mrs Shah had known instinctively that Balbir was there to stay. And that's exactly what he did. Stayed. Curious friends of the family were told Balbir was studying with Nitin (which was a lie—Balbir was bumming around restlessly looking for something to do).

'I must earn my own bread,' he announced after a week.

Mr Shah agreed that it was a good idea but also tried to impress upon the young boy that an incomplete education wouldn't get him too far.

'Look at Bill Gates, an entrepreneur at sixteen, a billionaire at thirty-two. And he is a drop-out,' Balbir had answered stubbornly. Within a couple of months Balbir had managed to attach himself to an ad film maker who'd earned a formidable reputation as the best knock-off whiz kid in the business. Pradeep Khosla forcefed himself on MTV and then recreated the biggest hits for local consumption. Balbir had succeeded in impressing him with his knowledge of computer graphics—something he'd picked up through his long-term association with Nitin and a natural flair for hi-tech gizmos.

Within three short years Balbir had gone independent picking up ten major accounts and four prestigious awards along the way. People who hired him knew they'd get quality combined with a technical wizardry that was hard to better. Balbir had what he wanted—nearly. A great apartment reconverted from a dilapidated, rundown loft in a crumbling mansion, plus all the girls he could handle. But his parents still didn't speak to him. On frequent trips to Delhi, Balbir would try in vain to wangle an invitation to dinner, but each attempt would be met with a snub and a dismissive, 'We have nothing to do with you. Please don't bother us.' Nitin's parents were the only 'family' he had, but even they were getting on. Besides, with Nitin working for a law firm in Seattle where he'd decided to immigrate after marrying a Canadian college mate from Harvard Law School, the Shahs spent longer and longer periods abroad. Balbir longed for 'continuity' as he called it, but it eluded him. His relationships with girls who floated through his busy life remained at a need-based, superficial level. And while other men envied him his 'score card', Balbir remained dissatisfied and alone.

*

It was at this point that Rashmi had entered his life briefly—a little too briefly perhaps. She'd teased him at their first encounter. 'What's it going to be: a one-night stand or something meaningful?' They had met at a party on the terrace of the house of a high-profile liquor baron. Pips had produced a snazzy audio-visual in collaboration with Balbir. Rashmi had seen the two working late into the night oblivious to anything but the slides clicking in and out of a dozen trays. While they mixed and matched music with a keyboard genius, Rashmi, clad in a bikini top with an Indonesian sarong tied loosely around her waist, drifted in and out of the room bringing the men coffee and toast on large lacquer trays. The party at Mr and Mrs Moolbhoy's house was the first time she'd spoken to Balbir. At that point, Pips and she had been going through one of their regular showdowns, often descending to gutter level sniping that left them both feeling wretched later. Balbir had witnessed quite a few scenes with such remarkable equanimity that he had immediately interested Rashmi. 'That friend of yours,' she'd commented to Pips, 'is made of rock. Does nothing real register with him?' Pips had replied nastily, 'Sluttish is not real.'

And suddenly that pre-monsoon, May evening, fragrant with flowering creepers trailing over bamboo trellises, they'd met at the Moolbhoy bar where Rashmi was getting herself her third rum of the evening and Balbir was getting bombed at his own speed. He'd reacted to her teasing remark with an indifferent shrug, but the hungry look in his eyes as they shifted swiftly from her exposed cleavage hadn't escaped Rashmi. The barman was taking his time fixing a tray with Scotch. Rashmi swayed her hips to the taped music and rearranged her off-white Kerala mundu. It had become her look that season and everybody complimented her when she donned the deceptively simple garment, edged with gold.

'I hear you're quite a guy,' she continued, humming along with the song.

'What if?' Balbir replied, this time staring pointedly down her emerald green blouse.

'I like guys like that,' she said, reaching for a cigarette.

'Look, cut it out,' Balbir snapped, 'you are Pips' woman and that's how I see it. Go find yourself some other sucker.'

Rashmi had laughed full-throatedly saying: 'It's funny how honourably bastards behave when they're shit scared. I didn't know you suffered from scruples. If Pips doesn't mind, why should you? Besides, he screws around on the side.' Balbir picked up an unopened bottle of beer and tried to walk away without responding. 'Hey, big boy, don't you turn your back on me. I fancy you, I thought I'd made that clear. The question is, do you want to fuck me or not? Straight and simple.' Seeing his way blocked, Balbir looked over her head and at Pips, who was busy talking to Mrs Moolbhoy animatedly, one hand placed intimately on her bare shoulder. Rashmi followed Balbir's glance. 'See, what did I tell you? We can slip away right now and he won't notice. What's even worse—he won't care. We are a very *liberated* couple you know. We don't believe in being possessive. Hasn't Pips told you his space theory?'

Balbir put the bottle of beer down roughly on the granite bar. 'Let's get out of here,' he said, removing the cigarette from between Rashmi's lips and placing her drink on a low wrought-iron table. She shivered slightly when she felt his fingers touch her bare midriff as he manoueuvred her past guests coming up to the terrace through a narrow passage. She giggled as Balbir stopped to kiss four or five trophy wives arriving on the arms of their proud husbands. 'Bet you've slept with all of them,' she whispered as they ran down the stairs not waiting for the lift that opened directly into the host's plush penthouse.

'Health Club friends,' he answered guardedly, before they found themselves on the street outside.

'I want to go for a horsey ride,' Rashmi announced unexpectedly. 'Let's leave your car here and go home by victoria. Haven't done that in years.'

Balbir and she started running down a steep slope towards the main road. It was a still night, but perfectly illuminated with a low-slung, buttery moon rising lazily over the silhouettes of newly constructed skyscrapers. 'Forget about fucking,' Balbir announced firmly, 'this is so much more fun.' Rashmi looked up into his eyes naughtily. 'Hang around. Hang around. I'm a woman with lots of sexy ideas.'

The old mare clip-clopped her way past sleeping forms huddled on the pavements. Nobody looked at Rashmi and Balbir as they kissed deeply and long. The buggy-man pulled on his beedi indifferently. He'd seen it all before.

Thirteen

Rashmi and Balbir's affair ended brutally and abruptly, surprising no one, not even the two of them.

Rashmi recalled the scene with a small laugh as the others listened. Swati said she had to make a phone call and disappeared into a tiny study crammed with untouched leather-bound volumes and plush coffee-table books. She took off her point-toed, ankle-high boots with a sense of relief and wiggled her toes, raising her legs up to look at them. The pedicure was still perfect—no chipped polish, no dead skin. She peeled off her stockings and felt her legs, running her fingers lightly along her shins. The lighting in the room was perfect, bright enough to take in details yet sufficiently low to hide harsh shadows and unflattering contours. Swati lit a cigarette and took a long, deep drag. She asked herself whether the lunch had come off the way she'd wanted it to. Outside, she could hear raised voices as Rashmi re-enacted the big brawl, with Balbir interjecting from time to time. Swati didn't really have a call to make—all she'd wanted at that point was to get away from an atmosphere that had become unbearably stifling. It was an unexpectedly charming room, she mused, looking around at the happy chintz upholstery on stuffed settees, the warm tones of the beige deep pile carpet, the comforting buzz of the air-conditioner, the soft glow of a well-picked lamp. Next to her chair was a low granite-topped table with a hi-tech telephone complete with an answering machine. Idly, she switched it on, shut her eyes and leaned back. The first few callers were obviously Reema's kitty friends—familiar voices that didn't bother to identify themselves. It amused Swati and reminded her of some London friends—the ones who plunged into instant conversations without salutations or greetings. Reema's callers followed the same pattern of easy recognition that was so convenient and comforting. Dreadful accents, Swati thought, as one woman went on and on about a maid who'd upped and left after pinching a huge bottle of Creation. Another woman complained about a hair-dresser getting uppity and refusing a tip. A third wanted a quick recipe for 'something different' (she didn't specify what).

Gradually, Swati became aware of somebody standing close to her. She didn't have to open her eyes to recognize Aparna's perfume combined with the smell of leather, cigarettes, coffee and starch that she always exuded.

She kept her eyes shut and breathed in deliberately taking a lungful of air and exclaiming, 'It's you, isn't it?' Aparna didn't answer but sat down on the settee across Swati. 'Why have you been avoiding me all afternoon?' Swati asked, her eyes half-open, her body stretched out languorously.

Aparna lit a cigarette and stared back at her steadily. 'Some things just never change. Why are you listening to Reema's answering machine? That's an awfully intrusive, sneaky thing to do, besides being ill-mannered, offensive and obnoxious.'

Swati switched off the machine and said lazily, 'You know, you should've been either a teacher or a preacher. You're so good at lecturing and moralizing.' Aparna continued to smoke. Swati shifted her bottom in the chair and laughed, 'So much in control—huh? Or pretending to be. God what a tight-arsed bore you've become. A corporate woman, an *Indian* corporate woman. A businesswoman. My, my!'

Aparna put her feet up on the settee and stubbed out her cigarette. 'I still haven't figured out why you set up this ridiculous lunch. Do you mind telling me? Or is it too much to expect from you—an explanation, I mean?'

Swati laughed her practised laugh, throwing her head back and pushing her breasts out—it was a little trick she'd picked up from an actress friend and it always worked. 'Why can't you just accept that I wanted to meet everybody. No tricks. No motives. It's been years.

Besides, if I'd phoned just you, you wouldn't have come. Admit it. The truth is I organized this *tamasha* only to be able to meet you again. Specifically you. I knew you'd have refused a direct one-on-one invitation—you with your ego hang-ups. So much remains unsaid—don't you agree?'

Aparna looked out of the large wood-framed glass windows. 'Maybe it's best that way. I certainly don't want to rake up stuff I'd rather forget.'

Swati interrupted her swiftly, 'But the whole point is that you haven't forgotten. And neither have I. Why don't we get it out of our systems once and for all? I'd like to be free of it—whatever it is. But first—show me what you got for this afternoon—the souvenir, memento—it's important OK?'

Aparna shook her head. 'I don't want to. Maybe I didn't get anything at all. What the hell! You still imagine you have some kind of power over us, don't you? You think all you have to do is snap your fingers and the rest of us will jump. Forget it. I was a fool once. But I've changed, yes, changed.'

Swati tilted her head to one side and asked, 'Have you really, Aps? We're all schoolgirls playing adult games. Besides, we know each other so well. Don't we, Aps? I don't think you've changed. Nobody changes. Not that much. I haven't either.'

Aparna smiled, her face softening for the first time. 'Don't I know it? I realized it the minute I saw you.

250

You were just the same. You'd merely changed the packaging. But you still haven't answered my question. Why this afternoon? Why all of us? Why this particular bunch? Why Reema? Why Noor?'

A soft knock on the door interrupted the two women. It was one of the servants sent by Reema to ask whether they required anything. He went into the adjoining bathroom to check whether there were sufficient hand towels and fresh soap. The two women waited silently for him to leave.

'You still don't trust me, do you?' Swati asked, putting on her best little-girl pout and voice.

'And I never will,' Aparna answered. 'You were a bitch as a young girl and you are a bigger bitch now. Merely a matter of scale.'

Swati pouted some more. 'You do hate me still, don't you? I thought that was sorted out and behind us. I did write and apologize? Didn't you get my letter?'

Aparna nodded. 'Oh yes, I did. But, my dear sweet Swati, it really didn't matter. You'd destroyed my life so completely by then—and you thought all it needed by way of compensation was a juvenile, insincere letter?'

Swati went over unhurriedly to where Aparna was sitting and tried to put her arms around her. 'Forgive me, Aps,' she said, with a silky edge to her voice. 'I'm begging for your forgiveness. It was horrid of me. I realize that now. And that's why I'm here. Say you'll forgive me.'

Aparna stiffened as she felt Swati's soft, pampered hands on the back of her neck. Swati was deftly massaging the tense knots at her nape and crooning softly. It felt wonderful. For one brief moment Aparna suspended her rage, shut her eyes and abandoned herself to the magic of Swati's fingers as she pressed the pressure spots and worked her way to the base of Aparna's head, gently pushing the hair away and moving the heel of her hand behind her ears. 'It's a Chinese method I picked up from a Hollywood therapist,' Swati said, 'just relax. It feels so good. Remember we used to massage each other after our hockey matches? Remember the time Uma had cracked your shin? What an awful blue-black patch that caused! And the swelling—remember? We went to my house and applied cold compresses. You were in such pain but you didn't cry. No tears—I remember so well. I was the one crying for you.'

Aparna shook herself free. 'Stop it, Swati. Stop being so bloody theatrical. You are doing it again. Your tricks haven't changed either. I don't get so easily distracted or disarmed any more. Why are you trying to manipulate me? It won't work.'

Swati raised her hands in a gesture of mock surrender. 'OK. OK, look—no touch. Stop being so bloody suspicious, Aps. Why don't you ask yourself one simple question: what on earth could I be after? What is it that I'd get out of you or out of any of these girls for that matter?'

Aparna took her time before replying: 'There isn't one thing in the world you'd do for nothing. You didn't in the past and you certainly won't now. I have asked myself that question but no reply so far. And that's why I'm so furious—more at myself than at you. No, Swati, you may have fooled the others, but not me. You were and are the most dangerous person I know.'

Swati shrugged. 'He wasn't worth it, you know. He didn't deserve you. I probably did you a favour—ever looked at it that way?'

Aparna sprang to her feet, her face contorted with anger. 'How dare you, Swati? How dare you bring that up? It's a closed topic. It's taboo.'

Swati got up to face her. 'Maybe it is. For you. But not for me.' Slowly, she reached for her bag and brought out a couple of envelopes. 'Here, take a look at these. I've been carrying them around for years, waiting for a chance to give them to you. Go ahead, open them. Read. You'll find the letters pretty interesting. They're from him. And they're about you.' Aparna stared fascinatedly at them, but she didn't make any move towards Swati's outstretched hand. 'Don't dare?' Swati taunted. 'Shall I read them out in that case? I've waited a long time for this moment.'

Swati picked one out at random. She struck a pose and spoke in a man's deep voice: 'Swati dearest, I did something stupid and entirely out-of-character last night. I sneaked out of the bedroom and tried to call you in

London just to hear your voice. I didn't plan on a long conversation—what with my ever-alert Aparna tossing and turning just a few feet away. But I knew that just your "hello" will do the trick, turn me on, make me hard and keep me that way long enough to perform my conjugal duties and be done.'

Swati raised her eyebrows, changed her stance and voice. 'More?' she demanded and without really waiting for Aparna's answer, she started reading from another letter, 'Listen you horny little bitch, I can't bear it any more. I smell you everywhere and it's driving me crazy. What is it that you exude? Whatever it might be, consider bottling and selling it worldwide—you'd make a fucking fortune. Call it "Sex"—straight and simple. Enjoyed last night—you've picked up a few new tricks, I notice. Why don't you give Aparna a few quick lessons? She could do with a crash course or shall we try a threesome soon? Miss you, miss you, miss you. Hate you too. Pantingly yours, Rohit—the—rod.'

Swati tapped her foot and started whistling 'Singin' in the rain'. 'Funny, isn't it? So many men have mentioned my special smell. Balbir too.' Aparna stared expressionlessly at nothing in particular. Swati began sifting through the small pile in her hands, 'I'm looking for the one that describes a brilliant bed encounter with you. It's hilarious. Really, really funny. Cruel, of course. But that was Rohit's speciality, wasn't it? And definitely a part of his attraction.'

Aparna thought her legs would collapse under her. She reached out weakly to support herself against a marble pedestal. Swati was pacing the room in her bare feet, playing with the envelopes in her hand, not taking her eyes off Aparna.

'He was such a swine, baby. I don't know what you ever saw in him. A selfish swine. You should thank me for saving you.'

Aparna tried to recover. She found her voice but couldn't really recognize it. 'Why have you kept them all this while? Why didn't you post them to me earlier when they would have mattered.'

Swati asked archly, 'You mean they don't any more? Stop kidding yourself, Aps. Rohit continues to be the most important person in your life. Face it. He mattered then and he matters like hell even now. My advice to you is don't read these letters. You'll feel hurt all over again. Old wounds should be left alone—don't you agree?' And Swati started to replace the envelopes in her bag, looking quizzically at Aparna while doing it.

Aparna shook her head in confusion. She felt hot tears coursing down her flushed cheeks. 'You should never have shown them to me, Swati. Never. It was a cruel, mean thing to do.'

Swati sat down next to her again. 'I had to, don't you see? I had to. I wanted you to know for yourself exactly what kind of a man he was. A two-timing bastard. I wanted to expose him. I wanted you to open your eyes and see him warts and all, get him out of your system once and for all. But more than anything else I wanted you to know that it wasn't me who betrayed you—he did. Here—it's all here. The proof that you once asked for and which I refused to give then. In Rohit's handwriting. He didn't love you—ever. He felt sorry for you. And he used you. The woman you discovered he left you for, he didn't love her either. But I suppose you've figured that out by now.'

Aparna was weeping openly, unable to stop her sobs and yet embarrassed by the flood of tears. 'You are lying,' she said, blowing her nose. 'I don't believe you. I knew Rohit better than he knew himself. Yes, he *did* love me. Only me. Nothing you say will alter that. But Rohit was scared and he was ambitious. Had it not been for you and that woman you introduced him to, we'd still have been together. We would have worked it out somehow. You destroyed our marriage. You killed me. What did I ever do to you that you turned on me like a viper?'

Swati patted the letters in her handbag taking her time over it. 'I'll tell since you've asked. . .'

*

Strange how deep adolescent slights go. Swati thought she'd forgotten the hurt, forgotten the humiliation and perhaps even forgiven Aparna after so many years. But

the memory of that wet and grey afternoon when Swati
saw the one thing that mattered to her go to Aparna,
continued to torment her even though in the balance
of things, the trophy itself had been marginalized a
long time ago. Today, Swati could only look back and
wonder why she had valued it as much as she did. Why
it had devastated her so completely then that she'd thought
of dropping out, running away from school, from home,
never to return? She still didn't have the answers and
the nightmare returned periodically to ruin her sleep
and remind her that there was a period in her life when
her most cherished dream had been shattered.

All the girls in senior school had heard of the dreaded
'black ball', the veto power invested in the balloting
committee that often decided the course their life would
take in future. Only Swati had not expected it to descend
on her, affect her as directly as it did. She knew she
wasn't well liked by the teachers. She knew the principal
(who resembled a weathered twisted oak) detested her
but Swati had been banking on her popularity with
her peers, the ones who decided on their leaders in
the final year at school.

For four years Swati had concentrated single-mindedly
on her target. She would be head-girl—she was the
only one who deserved the honour. She would walk
away with the Best Girl of the Year shield. And she'd
worked at it, systematically, thoroughly with a oneness
of purpose that had surprised her friends and family.

Swati was a natural achiever with few self-doubts and while others around her sweated blood, she'd always found the going comparatively easy. It hadn't even occurred to her that the elusive shield could go, *would* go to anyone else. But it did. It went to Aparna.

*

'I don't believe it,' Aparna said quietly. 'You've held that against me all these years. Why? Was it my fault? Did I snatch it from you? I was as surprised as you were—remember?'

Swati stared blankly ahead of her. 'It was all I wanted, Aps. It was all that mattered. For four years I could think of nothing else, dream of nothing else. I had gone over it in my mind countless times—the announcement and then the presentation. I'd imagined the look on my parents' face. And I'd thought about the rest of you staring at me enviously. I wanted that sash. I wanted it desperately. It was so wasted on you. Did you even value the honour? I don't think so. You took it casually, as if it meant nothing at all.'

Aparna shook her head sadly. For the first time a few things about Swati's animosity began to make sense to her. They'd been such good friends that Aparna had wanted Swati to get the shield, had expected her to get it. Not because she herself lacked ambition, but because Swati had brainwashed everybody around her into taking her winning it for granted. She had *booked* it for herself well in advance and not considered anyone competition. When Aparna's name was called out, her first reaction had been to look at Swati next to her, fearing that she'd get up and shout, 'That's not fair,' with tears stinging her eyes. Instead Swati had forced a smile, leaned over and kissed Aparna on the cheek.

'It was the most difficult thing I've ever done,' Swati told her, her voice cracking at the memory. 'I'd felt numb initially. And then angry. It was irrational, I know. But just the sight of you walking towards the stage, climbing the wooden stairs, going to the dias, bowing for the sash and then turning to face the entire school's applause was enough to make me want to kill myself. This is the first time I've found the strength to talk to you directly about it, by the way. And wait. . . hear this. . . I did try and kill myself. Not that night but in the summer vacation before all of us applied to different colleges. I couldn't even pull that off successfully. Stupid me. I tried swallowing rat poison—just a pinch of it made me throw up. I spent the whole night retching while my parents were at a bridge party.'

Aparna looked at her sympathetically for the first time that day. Funny, but her memories of the occasion were completely different. She remembered the applause and her own elated state very well. She remembered Swati's crumpled face too. But the aftermath remained hazy. Maybe because the honour hadn't been all that important to her. She turned to Swati, 'You could have tried to fix me then itself. Stopped talking or something. But if I remember correctly yours was the first card I received. You'd made it yourself with fluorescent paints. It said "Congratulations" in several colours. It was very pretty.'

Swati laughed, 'Of course I remember it. I also remember how I felt inside while drawing those doodles. With each stroke of the brush, I wanted to hurt you. But couldn't. In my heart of hearts, I knew it had nothing to do with you. You hadn't cheated me out of anything. But I still couldn't forgive you. My London shrink found it incredible! I talked about you endlessly. I did that with a former husband too—the one who understood me best.'

'Why did you leave him in that case?' Aparna asked.

'Long story,' Swati snapped. 'Besides, it was the other way—he left me. No. Not for another woman. He felt I was far too self-absorbed (his word) and that I'd stopped respecting him. Or so he said in his divorce petition. Besides, that was the time my career was really taking off. You remember? I was in the papers every single day.'

'You were also having several well-publicized affairs. I suppose it's fair for a husband to interpret that as lack of respect.'

Swati giggled. 'Come on, sweetie. Stop being so prissy and judgmental. That was our deal when we married. We were buddies, the best of buddies. He had no business turning possessive and all that.'

Aparna lit a cigarette and took a couple of disinterested puffs. 'Doesn't sound like such a great marriage to me. So where's the catch?'

Swati looked at her through the corner of her eyes almost teasingly. 'The catch, darling? Does there always have to be one? We were a civilized British couple in the early seventies. Living in London. Every marriage that we knew about ran along similar lines. Separate but friendly lives. There was nothing unique about ours. We loved each other dearly but we led strictly individual lives. And I missed him like mad when we finally split. It was awfully hard on the dogs. You know how sensitive animals can get. And we absolutely doted on our Dalmatians. He got custody, of course.'

Aparna couldn't stop herself from laughing. 'Custody? Of dogs?'

Swati looked at her in mock horror and scolded, 'Don't snigger. Gatsby and Daisy were our big bond. We used to schedule our lives around them. One of us was always home to make sure they weren't neglected. And then he goes and bad-mouths me in court. Calls me a negligent bitch. The press lapped it up.'

Aparna sighed. 'That's what happens when you marry a title. Wasn't he a Lord or something?'

Swati smiled. 'Big deal, Aps. Nearly every second bloke one meets there is titled—major or minor. It

doesn't mean much. At least, it didn't mean anything
to me. I had an old bat for a mother-in-law. She detested
me, naturally. But she quite liked the lolly I made.'

Aparna asked incredulously, 'Was His Lordship broke?'

'They all are, darling. Well, most of them, anyway.
Besides, I'd created such a huge sensation at that point
with my first album and that number which shocked
the pants off everybody. I was really big, big, big then.
That was the time of that major concert—I forget what
or who it was in aid of—Ethiopia? Lepers? Famine?
Water? I was on stage with the supernovas of the music
world. I'd been offered a Broadway role. So much, too
much was happening all at the same time. My agent
was pushing me to push myself. . . .'

Aparna nodded knowingly. 'Yeah, I know. While
you were pushing coke. Didn't you get busted
or something?'

Swati shot to her feet indignantly. 'Hey, wait a
minute. I was framed. That was a set-up, OK? Sure I
did drugs—nothing hard. But that incident, look, forget
it, I'm not prepared to go through with all that shit
right now. Just take it from me the press blew it up.'

Aparna continued, 'You blew your career with that
too, didn't you?'

Swati hesitated before replying: 'In a way, yes. It
was an expensive hit. I had to pay my lawyers a fortune.
And my European tour got cancelled.'

Aparna asked, 'Who set you up?'

Swati said softly, 'I never did find out. It was horrible. I was so depressed. My brain conked out too. I was in therapy, of course. Goodness—I can hardly think of a time when I haven't been with a shrink. The money was running out rapidly. I hung out in Paris with a girlfriend. We did nightclub gigs. Modelled a bit. Whored a bit, yes, that too. Don't look so shocked.'

Aparna laughed. 'Nothing you say or do can ever shock me, friend. Absolutely nothing. But tell me how you pulled out of this mess. I'm deeply interested. You've always employed ingenious ways to crawl out of tough situations, as I recall.'

Swati smiled, a wide open smile and looked like a schoolgirl in that one instant. Aparna stared at her, stunned temporarily by Swati's unique appeal, disoriented by the effect it still had on her. Swati pulled out a scarf from her bag—a large silk square with colourful butterflies fluttering all over it. She draped it over her head and lowered her eyes demurely, 'Darling, darling—that was when I landed *Maharani* and my life changed.'

Aparna nodded. 'Oh yes. I remember *Maharani* turned out to be bigger than *Far Pavilions*, right? You were it, weren't you? The exotic, bejewelled Maharani with an insatiable sexual appetite. I hate to say it, but you were fantastic in that serial. Terrific. Gorgeous-plus. Blue-blooded and a nympho, too. Sounds like your ultimate fantasy.'

Swati giggled. 'A case of perfect casting. Everybody said so. It was a major break for me. Great things were supposed to happen after that. They did, actually. But by then I'd become ambitious. I wanted more and more. I wanted everything.'

*

When Swati was cast as the Maharani the British Press had initially sounded sceptical. It was to be a super-spectacular shot on location in India. The story revolved around a young, beautiful princess caught in a family feud. After Princess Mayadevi's father is killed in battle leaving her at the head of the Nagarpur army, Mayadevi takes an oath to vanquish her father's enemy and restore her family's honour. Trouble starts when she falls in love with the enemy while on a royal hunt. Rana Mahadev Singh and Mayadevi meet over the carcass of a tiger they both claim to have shot from opposite sides of the forest. The romance appears to be doomed from the start. Princess Mayadevi's marriage is fixed by her scheming aunt to another neighbouring ruler—a widower twenty years her senior. Rana Mahadev decides to abduct his lady love on a moonless night but his attempt is thwarted by a palace spy—the princess' lady-in-waiting who reveals the plot to the dowager aunt. The Rana is captured and imprisoned in the dungeon as the aunt steps up the preparations for Mayadevi's impending wedding. The princess is devastated but not defeated. She escapes from the palace in the middle of the night on horseback. Being an accomplished horsewoman, nobody, not even riders from the crack cavalry unit, can catch up with her.

She manages to slip into her husband-to-be's kingdom on a stormy night. Disguised as a lowly maid she secures employment on his personal staff. Meanwhile, the Rana is busy in his cell, organizing a palace coup. The old widower notices the beautiful new maid and suspects her identity. She is much too refined to be a servant. He confronts her during a pre-nuptial feast in his palace. She breaks down and confesses everything. Touched by her youth and beauty, he vows to help her. Together they plan to attack her state and free the imprisoned Rana. A stray arrow gets her. She falls off her horse with the Rana's name on her lips. One of her old guards recognizes her. She is hastily removed to his humble home while the battle rages on.

Meanwhile, the Rana, with the help of men loyal to Mayadevi, manages to get out of the dungeon and join the battle. He is told the princess is dead. He is about to give up all hope when he spots her beautiful veil fluttering in the distance. Mortally wounded, he rides out towards the veil only to discover his love is alive but only just. The two lovers hold each other and await death. They can hear the battlecries outside. They know it's only a matter of time before they're discovered and killed. Suddenly the door bursts open and the old maharaja rushes in. 'We have won the war,' he tells them. 'Your aunt is in our custody,' he informs Mayadevi. There is no time to waste. The court physician is summoned. Mayadevi whispers her love to the Rana whose life is steadily slipping out of him. The widower king summons a priest and issues instructions for a quick wedding ceremony that will unite the lovers in death. The heat of the flames as the priest prepares the holy fire, revives the Rana and he clasps Mayadevi to his heart. 'Don't leave me now,' he implores as the princess struggles to survive. An itinerant mendicant comes in and saves both their lives with a herbal potion. The serial ends with the coronation of the Rana as the head of the two kingdoms with his consort, Mayadevi, by his side smiling proudly.

*

Though the storyline of *Maharani* was simple enough, it was the manner in which it was filmed that gave it a special gloss, a certain magic. Week after week, viewers sat transfixed in front of the telly as the serial unfolded lavishly and at a leisurely pace. Swati was practically in every episode and her costumes all but stole the show from her. It was thanks to the popularity of *Maharani* that the opulent, pampered Oriental look swept Britain over two summers as swanky stores competed to outdo one another in merchandising the Mayadevi look. Shop windows festooned with silks and embroideries attracted drab, overworked suburban housewives who thronged for makeovers à la Swati, heavily kohl-lined eyes and all. As for Swati herself, she revelled in the attention and was often spotted clad in gorgeous ghagras going from one gala to the next on the arm of a titled gent or a high profile entertainment executive. She was between marriages and looked absolutely ravishing. Swati made it to the covers of most major fashion magazines and *Vanity Fair*, the number one society monthly, featured her in an eight-page profile which had her lolling languorously against a painted elephant, wrapped in cobras, semi-naked on a bed of nails and making eyes at a tiger. After the feature appeared, Swati got dubbed 'The Oriental Express'. A perfume called Maya was launched by her in Europe, while women vied to display their midriffs, jewelled belly-button and all, in the best Swati mode.

Then, at the height of the *Maharani* mania, Swati mysteriously disappeared. Nobody knew where she was or what had happened to her—not even her harassed press agent. There were stories galore about her disappearing into the sea off the coast of Malta where she'd been holidaying. Others insisted she was in Borneo, filming another exotic, secret film to launch a range of 'Wild and Wonderful' cosmetic products. Still others claimed she was suffering from a terminal disease and was back in India waiting to die anonymously. Through all the furore her mysterious absence had created, Swati was, in fact, enjoying herself hugely on an unscheduled honeymoon at a remote resort in South America. She'd met and married an eccentric millionaire who'd made his money buying and selling mega corporations. It had been as dramatic as anything Swati had acted in—perhaps even more so.

Juan Mendonca was from the Honduras. His interests ranged from sugar, rubber, coffee, teak, to the recording industry. A powerful man in his country, who was known to play politics as fiercely as he traded on international exchanges, Mr Mendonca was a recent divorcee when he met Swati on a Trans-Atlantic flight. He recognized her instantly. He'd been mesmerized by her image on the TV screen in his hotel suite as he'd watched reruns of *Maharani* on cable.

'It is you, Mayadevi, yes?' he asked leaning over her seat politely. Swati was immediately impressed by his expensive tan, great clothes and well-groomed appearance, besides reacting very positively to his soft and sexy accent. By the time the flight landed at Kennedy airport, she'd changed her travel plans and decided to visit his country.

'It's my luck. I wasn't on a chartered flight,' Juan commented as he helped her with her smart, custom-made luggage. But this time, his private jet was waiting to transport him to Buenos Aires where he had business to attend to.

A crazy, delirious week followed on his sprawling ranch in Argentina during which Juan played out every sexual fantasy that the two of them could conjure—making love on horseback, in a stream of gurgling water, on a bed of hay under an eggshell blue sky, while watching a stud bull in action, standing up against the rough wall of a barn, hanging from a low rafter, in Juan's office with the door unlocked, wearing fancy dress and drag—after a point they lost count. And slept straight through for eighteen exhausted hours. At the end of seven days, Swati reluctantly told him she had to leave. Her agent would never forgive her if she failed to show up for her L.A. meeting. Swati was in America to sign the biggest contract of her career—a move that would place her amongst the top entertainers of the world. The deal was for three years and would cover everything from videos, films, concerts to product endorsements.

Juan looked at her longingly as he reached for the phone. 'Tell you what, Swati,' he said slowly, 'let's forget about this particular contract. I'm offering you a better one. More permanent. Life-long in fact. Why don't you marry me?'

Swati, taken aback by the suddenness of the question, started giggling nervously. Juan made it easier for her. 'I think I should tell you at this point that I own the company you were going to sign up with. And just to make you feel better I'll double their offer right now if you say yes. My lawyer is only a buzz away. All I have to do is to instruct him to draw up a marriage contract. As simple as that.'

Swati asked for time. Twenty-four hours. And got it. She calculated swiftly. What Juan was offering her would make her a very rich woman. Rich and secure. Besides, he wasn't asking for anything in return. Nothing at all. Just her hand in marriage and her body in bed. She'd be an absolute fool to refuse. Besides, she'd discovered Juan was a tiger in the boudoir. An attentive, giving lover who made her feel wonderfully desirable. She loved his home. His style. What did she have to lose? Nothing at all. If it didn't work out, she'd still get to keep the money. Most of it, anyway. Swati was nobody's fool. She'd negotiated tough contracts before. All by herself with only technical assistance from lawyers. She was known to be the sharpest customer going. And she was proud of her reputation. Before her deadline was up, Swati, snuggled into Juan's arms, and whispered seductively, 'Where's the dotted line for me to sign on?' He leapt out of bed and ran into the adjoining salon to telephone his lawyer forgetting the fact that he was stark naked and very aroused.

Swati decided to thank her mentor in the only way she knew. While he spoke in Spanish to his lawyers in Los Angeles and New York, Swati took him into her warm mouth. Later, she slipped into a warm bath and soaked herself in oil of jasmine—a heady, clingy ittar that drove Juan wild. He found her wet and glistening when he came back into the room. The night was still and moonless as he slipped into the bath with her. Swati rolled herself over him gracefully and began massaging his neck, pinching and puckering the taut muscles. 'Aah . . . heaven,' Juan murmured as he closed his eyes. She was like an agile dolphin moving over him constantly, her oiled skin helping her to glide effortlessly, expertly, in and out of his demanding embrace. She entwined her long, smooth limbs with Juan's and rocked her warm body gently, creating tiny ripples in the perfumed water.

Juan whispered, 'Now . . . now . . .' his eyes still closed. Swati kissed his mouth, his eyes, his throat, his navel and stopped. She could hear Juan groaning, begging.

'Take me in your mouth again please . . . don't do this to me.'

Abruptly Swati slipped out of the sunken marble tub and walked to a mirrored cabinet slowly. Juan opened his eyes to ask, 'Where are you going, princess? Come back or I shall die.'

Swati placed a finger on her lips and said, 'Sssh, I have a surprise for you.'

Juan turned around to check whether the champagne flutes were where they always stood—within easy reach. They were in place. His eyes followed Swati as she bent to pick up something from a low shelf. 'Did you know you possess the greatest ass in the universe?'

he asked, adding, 'The thought of your divine bottom distracts me at work. Why don't you just hang around all the time, so I can conclude at least some business sanely?'

Swati had obviously found what she'd been looking for. She walked back to Juan and said, 'Here's a treat for you, for us.' And she showed him an enamelled box. Juan tried to wave her away saying, 'No, baby, we don't need that stuff. Let's not ruin it.'

But Swati had slipped into the water once more and started stroking him till he hurt. 'I've been a good girl for far too long now, darling. I want to be bad tonight. Wicked, really, really wicked. Trust me. Let's celebrate. Let's take a hit each only this one time.'

Juan was most reluctant. He moved his hand sharply and threw the little box away. It feel into the sudsy water and sank to the bottom of the tub. Enraged by the suddenness of his gesture, Swati started to beat Juan's chest with her fists. At first he dodged her blows and tried to hold her wrists down. But Swati was like a wild, out-of-control cat as she flailed at him with her nails, grabbing his hair and scratching his face, her voice, a shrill, high-pitched shriek. Suddenly, she felt his strong, broad, flat palm striking her cheek with a sting that left her reeling. She rushed at him, ready to pounce and pound the man who by slapping her hard had succeeded in arousing her in an extraordinarily exciting way. Juan held her moist body against his own sopping wet one. 'My beautiful beast,' he murmured against her mouth, 'you do like getting hurt, don't you, well, let's see how much pain you enjoy.' He twisted her arms roughly behind her back and opened her firm thighs with his knee. Swati let out a sharp cry and squirmed in his brutal grip. Juan let go of one of his own hands and covered Swati's breasts with it—his touch hard, and unyielding. Swati felt him pushing against her with an urgency that scared her. Juan brought his mouth down on her rounded shoulder and bit into the soft flesh, his teeth leaving deep marks. He continued to nip her with small, sharp bites all over her body, concentrating on the insides of her thighs, her buttocks and the elegant slope of her breasts. After a point, Swati found herself ignoring the pain and yielding to the pleasure that followed. Her breathing became shallower and heavier and she allowed her head to hang over the edge of the tub, while her pelvis thrust itself up to meet Juan's. Swati could feel the bath gel stinging the welts that were rapidly coming up all over her body. The salt from her tears was making the scratches on her face smart and yet, Swati had never felt more aroused or more desirable. She swung her legs over the side of the tub and begged of Juan to enter her, release her from the sweetness of the agony. But Juan wasn't through with his game yet. It was his turn to walk away in search of a new . . . weapon? Toy?—Swati would soon find out. She lay back in the tub, her body aching and sore, her heart thumping, every fibre in her body receptive to the cruel attentions of her crazy lover.

Soon Juan was back carrying a tiny black leather whip in his hand. 'Ready?' he asked Swati.

'For anything,' she responded, her voice thick and husky. Juan walked over and pulled her out, sopping wet. He carried her over to their large bed covered with black satin and threw her face down on it. In one swift move he bound her hands and feet with his silk ties. 'No, Juan, no,' Swati pleaded, 'don't, don't hurt me, please.'

Juan hissed: 'We are only beginning, my love, close your eyes, you're going to adore this. It's the sweetest, greatest pain in the world. You will never forget the pleasure it brings.'

Swati thought she was going to lose consciousness. There was no strength left in her slim body, no resistance, no fight. Each time the whip came down across her burning flesh, her body twitched involuntarily. She let the tears streak the sensuous satin of the sheets. Just when she thought she wouldn't be able to stand another second of Juan's peculiar ministrations he'd entered her smoothly from the back, his hands caressing her breasts, his fingers seeking the inside of her mouth. And Swati, amazed that her body's nerve-endings were still capable of responding, found herself opening up to Juan, taking him deeper and deeper into her, wondering what it was about this strange, magnetic man that captivated her to the extent that she suspended reason itself.

Later, satiated and serene, she lay in Juan's arms while he soothed and stroked the deep welts and cuts over her punished body.

'How was it?' he enquired tenderly. Swati nodded her head weakly and lay back against the cushions—her posture indicating complete surrender. Just as she was falling into an exhausted sleep, she felt Juan's tongue sliding down her body and between her legs. 'Like petals of an orchid,' he sighed, burying his face between her thighs. Surprising even herself Swati started moving even though minutes ago she'd felt more drained of energy, of feeling than ever before in her life. 'Are you in heaven yet, my love, as I am?' Juan asked, looking up into her heavy eyes. Swati reached down and tousled his hair. 'My beautiful bird of paradise,' Juan sighed contentedly, 'I have you trapped at last.'

Fourteen

Sounding wistful Aparna said to a visibly fatigued Swati, 'You've led quite a life, girl. I'll say that.'

Swati, struggling with obvious tiredness, managed a small smile while saying, 'It hasn't been such a ball, Aps. Not really. I've had to pay the price too.'

Aparna asked gently, 'So, what went wrong with the Juan thing?'

'Everything. We were completely mismatched except in the bedroom. And guess what? Both of us knew that with our special talents in that department, we'd always get compatible partners. Soon after the hush-hush wedding, Juan went back to his polo ponies in Argentina, businesses all over the world, besides panting women at each turn, a few men, and God knows who or what else. Maybe a couple of frisky emus and lamas too. I was expected to look a Maharani and behave like one whenever he was in town and in the mood to show me off. My career fell to pieces and I was virtually isolated from my friends, my life in England.'

Aparna didn't look very sympathetic as she asked in a voice sharper than she'd intended it to be, 'But you got to keep the money right?'

'Yes and no,' Swati said. 'I got sufficient pocket money. But strictly no credit cards, no joint accounts and no access to Juan's real wealth. With my terrible habits, it didn't take me too long to blow it all up. And guess where most of it went? Straight up my nose!'

It was Aparna's turn to regard her friend with shock and disbelief. 'Are you telling me you snorted a fortune away?'

Swati shook her head miserably. 'There was nothing for me to do. I was like a captive animal—part of his zoo. By the way, his major passion in life was to collect endangered species. He used to pay the earth for creatures on the World Wildlife Fund's protected list. I began to feel like a snow leopard or something. One of his trusted aides, who was my bodyguard, offered me some coke one evening while amusing me with backgammon tricks. Juan was out of town and I was in a reckless mood. That was it. You can't imagine how quickly that stuff can get one hooked. And how swiftly it disappears. Later, much later, it took me years of expensive therapy to pull out. Besides months spent in a drying out clinic in California.'

Aparna looked at her watch pointedly. 'Whew! This has been quite a day. It's too late now to reopen closed chapters, but I wanted to ask you whether you remember this?'

Swati gasped as Aparna pulled out a printed muslin dupatta with pretty beads stitched into its corners. The expression on Swati's face was difficult to fathom even for Aparna, who knew her so well. But that little gasp had given her away and she realized it quickly. Swati regained her composure before asking casually, 'How come you're still hanging on to that old thing? I thought you must've thrown it into an incinerator.'

Aparna shook her head and laughed bitterly. 'No way. Each time I look at this dupatta I'm reminded of. . . of you know what.'

Swati shot to her feet and started pacing the small study. 'I told you earlier, it didn't happen the way you're probably imagining it.'

Aparna sat back quietly and said, 'No? Well then, how about telling me what did happen? I think in all fairness you owe me that much.'

Swati took a deep breath and continued to walk around the room. This was one episode she wasn't hazy about. No, Swati had no trouble recalling the details—the smallest ones. At the end of it all, Rohit hadn't been worth the time or the effort. But in any case, Swati's target hadn't been Aparna's man—it had always been and still was Aparna herself. The smart,

cool, efficient, together Aparna. The woman Swati
secretly longed to be, but never could become.

*

Aparna worked late and hard. Often, Rohit would get
home before her and start pottering around the neat
kitchen, checking the fridge to find out what was going
for dinner. Sometimes he'd chill a bottle of beer or
two. And occasionally help with preliminaries by
chopping and cutting vegetables or getting a large,
cheerful salad ready. Rohit also specialized in aloo parathas
and dry bhindi—two dishes that had kept starvation
at bay in his hostel days. Aparna was always appreciative
of these gestures even if she knew in her heart of hearts
that Rohit did it all for himself—he enjoyed cooking.
And he liked his beer. He also preferred dinner on
time. And a menu he could control. Besides, as he
often reminded Aparna, she may have been the world's
greatest ad lady but she was no cook. And, of course,
her mother never failed to remind her, 'Thank your
stars Rohit helps you with housework. Look at your
father. Or any of the other husbands. All they do is
come home, put their feet up and order their women
around. "Get me this! Do that. Do this."' 'Not modern
ones, Mama,' Aparna would say gently making her
mother snort, 'Believe me—all men are just the same.
And Indian husbands, the worst. Look at that German

couple in the next block—see how much work the man does. Why, the other day while strolling downstairs, I saw him feeding the baby. Changing his nappy. Even playing with the kid! Have you seen any of our men doing that?'

It made Aparna happy that her mother seemed as ga-ga over Rohit as she herself was. Yes, no question about it—Rohit was very, very special in her besotted eyes. And Aparna felt blessed. This was a side to her personality—her *soppy* side—as she identified it, that she was unable to fathom. Rohit brought out her suppressed sentimentality on a scale that often scared her. Aparna carried his pictures in her bag and didn't require too much encouragement to pull them out. Friends told her she gazed at him with an 'I adore you' expression that was almost embarrassing in its intensity. And yet Aparna was realistic enough to realize that Rohit as viewed by the rest of the world was by no means an exceptional person. He was just a regular sort of chap. Good-looking but hardly irresistible. Average. Yes, that was the word. Average height. Average looks. Average achievements. But to her Rohit embodied all that she'd ever longed for in a man. When asked by curious colleagues to define those qualities Aparna would blush deeply before saying evasively, 'It works for me, whatever it is. And that's all that matters. Besides, every other male bores the hell out of me. Either he's busy being supermacho, super-stud, super-prick, or he turns out to be a slobbering slave. No thanks. I think I belong to the fortunate few who have actually found the mate of their dreams.' Rohit gave the appearance of being easygoing—even likeable. He was smart-talking, amusing, slightly lazy, good-humoured and inoffensive. A sly flirt with an innocuous rogue's easy charm, Rohit was known to chat up Aparna's more attractive friends after a beer too many. But nobody minded since it was assumed he didn't intend his attentions to be taken seriously. He'd declare boozily at the end of the evening, 'I'm just a party-flirt, girls, ignore me. But do take my compliments seriously.' Everybody would smile indulgently, including Aparna. But what Rohit didn't know or refused to acknowledge was that even these light, breezy, social flirtations bored little holes into Aparna. And each time he looked into another woman's eyes and fed her some silly line or the other, Aparna would recoil with hurt and pain and end up blaming herself for not being a sport. For not being sufficiently tolerant. Or worse—for not being interesting enough in Rohit's eyes.

*

She'd sensed a certain something between Swati and Rohit the first time they'd met during one of Swati's early trips back home. But she'd reminded herself sternly that Swati was her oldest and closest friend and an incorrigible tease who didn't mean a thing when she parked herself on a man's lap and announced, 'Darling, when was the last time you got this lucky?' This was supposed to be her style. An act that nobody was meant to take seriously. Rohit obviously enjoyed the attention, and which man wouldn't, Aparna reasoned. Besides, Swati was just an occasional visitor to India and one of the few mutual friends they both enjoyed. An evening with Swati was always so fizzy and fun, Aparna didn't mind putting up with her playing games with Rohit. Anything that was so blatant was obviously innocent and certainly not to be taken to heart. Swati couldn't help being Swati. Rohit agreed when later, lying in bed reviewing the evening, Aparna would bring up some of Swati's more outrageous comments and check Rohit's reaction to them. 'She's a kid, darling. That woman has never really grown up,' he'd say with a small laugh.

There were times Swati would pop by unannounced, straight from the airport, carrying a bottle of wine, some imported cheese and french bread. Occasionally she'd drag in the boyfriend *du jour* as well. While Aparna didn't exactly welcome these impromptu affairs, Rohit seemed to perk up at the intrusions.

'Let's party, guys,' Swati would announce making herself comfortable on the carpet while her escort filled up the ice bucket and Aparna fixed a meal that was more substantial than usual. There were also a couple of times Aparna would get home late from work and find Swati giggling away happily with Rohit. They'd greet her cheerfully and carry on with their interrupted conversation, making her feel like an interloper.

'Hi, sweetheart,' Rohit would raise his hand in greeting, while Swati would continue to loll around, displaying her legs, stretching her limbs and holding out her glass to Rohit with a pout, 'Darling, be an absolute doll and throw some cubes in there, please.' There'd be a perfunctory explanation thrown in Aparna's general direction, 'Was on my way to the hotel and I saw the light on. Couldn't resist checking out the scene. Don't mind do you, darling?'

'I bloody well do,' Aparna had been tempted to scream once or twice. But never did. And she felt far too ashamed to voice her annoyance to Rohit. What would he think of her? How petty she'd appear. And it wasn't as if Swati was just any old woman off the streets. Besides, as the sound of their laughter floated into the bedroom while Aparna wearily got out of her office clothes and went in for a bracing shower, she'd feel relieved that Rohit was being entertained by someone as exuberant as Swati. Aparna often felt she was a bit too serious, a bit too earnest for her own good. A bloody bore in other words. Maybe Rohit needed someone bubblier, someone who laughed at his corny jokes, told a few dirty ones herself, someone frothy and fun, someone less uptight, less inhibited, someone like Swati. Anxiously, she'd ask Rohit about it, trying to make her worries less weighty by sounding as off-hand as she could. Rohit was always exceptionally prompt with his reassurances. He'd clasp her in a bear hug, ruffle her hair and say, 'Forget it, love of my life. If I need to be entertained I can always reach for my *Playboy* joke books. Don't be silly. I adore you just the way you are—grim and starchy and tense and intense and terrible.'

*

'I'd come to collect my dupatta, the one I'd forgotten the previous time—remember? You'd liked it—pink bandhni. That was it. I hadn't gone to your place to seduce your man. Damn it. I was surprised to find him at home at that hour.'

'Really?' Aparna said bitingly. 'My version is slightly different. I heard you called him from London while he was at work and fixed it all up thinking I was *en route* to Delhi for the new cola launch. Only, the two of you miscalculated. My flight was late and it finally got cancelled. Too bad I came home, huh? And the look on your face—do you think I'll ever be able to forget it? What was it, come on, tell me. Triumph or guilt?'

Swati, pretending to study a small chip on her carefully lacquered nails, asked softly, 'And what about the look on Rohit's face? What did you make of that?

Blandly, Aparna said, 'Shit-faced. That's exactly how he looked. Shit-faced. I could've killed the two of you.

Strangled you both with your pretty dupatta.' Aparna
fingered it lightly. 'You forgot to take it with you in
your hurry to get out of the place. I kept it as a memento.'
Aparna spread it out slowly taking her time. Swati watched
fascinated, like it was an object she'd never seen before
or a deadly snake raising its hood out of a basket. 'Miss
it?' Aparna asked. 'I've preserved it the way I found
it. It even smells of you, at least of the way you did in
those days. What was it you always wore? Some cheap
stuff. Charlie?' Aparna held the dupatta to her nose
and sniffed it. 'It's there—everything, the whole story.
Here, hold it. Feel it. Smell it.' She handed it over to
Swati whose instinctive reaction was to draw back
from it like it was something live, something that could
bite her.

Recovering rapidly, Swati picked it up and draped
it around her shoulders. 'Isn't that how I used to wear
it? Loosely tied like a large scarf? I loved bandhni things
in those days. Still do. But now they make me feel tacky.
Very Janpath, if you know what I mean. But back then
all of us lived in Rajasthani stuff—remember? And all
that chunky silver jewellery. You were famous for your
powder bindis and I had more kajal in my eyes than a
Kathakali dancer.' Aparna smiled at the memory despite
herself. Swati came over to sit by her. 'Hey, all this
was a long, long time ago. We've all moved on, changed,
grown up. Or don't you agree? You shouldn't have
kept it, you know. What was the point in hanging on

to this wretched thing? Bad memories. Nasty ones. Horrible, just horrible.'

Aparna nodded. 'True. But Rohit was my husband, not yours. Perhaps your little affair was nothing more than a casual screw to you. But it destroyed my marriage, my life. Had I been more like you I might have moved on, found someone else. I tried to. But it didn't happen. I wanted Rohit. Longed for him. In a way, I still do. I've got so many of his shirts, a tennis racquet, shoes, shaving things, a discarded wrist watch, coffee mug, books, music, speakers, he still lives there, you know. It sounds crazy, but after so many years I haven't got over him.'

Swati patted her hand. 'There were others. I wasn't the only one he betrayed you with. He told me so himself. And these letters, they're unbelievable. He's boasting like a bloody schoolboy . . . trying to impress me with his conquests—"body counts" as he calls them. Pathetic. I really don't know what it was—is—that obsesses you about that scumbag.'

Aparna's eyes flashed as she hissed, 'Don't call him that. You brought out the ugly side in him. The Rohit I knew was different. A caring, attentive, sensitive person—the only man I respected. In many ways he was the only man who made me feel wonderful and I'm not talking only about sex, you know. He brought out my femininity, made me feel, you know, a woman in the best sense of the word.'

'Aa-ha, now comes the truth. You've always had a problem about that, haven't you?' Swati asked, her eyes glinting.

'About what?' Aparna countered, a defiant edge to her voice.

'About being a woman—that's what,' Swati replied.

A long silence followed. A silence that was filled with the filtered noise of desultory conversation from the next room. Aparna's face was mask-like as she fought unsuccessfully to keep her emotions at bay. Swati watched her keenly, revelling in the discomfort she had successfully created. Finally, when Aparna spoke, it was with sorrow: 'I don't care if you know or who knows any longer. Yes, I have problems, but then, who doesn't? Maybe you are very secure about your sexuality. I've always been confused—always. Way back in school too.'

Swati said, 'Don't I know it? You fall into the classic butch category.'

Aparna shook her head. 'It isn't that simple. Had it been so uncomplicated, I might have been able to come to terms with it. It isn't just about liking women and hating men. It's far more complex. Besides, I don't really hate men. Maybe I hate myself, at least certain aspects of myself. But the fact still remains—I'm uncomfortable about being born a woman. It seems . . . so . . . so . . . I don't know . . . unfair. Rohit was the only person who understood this and accepted it. It was so comforting, so wonderful. Maybe it was this very quality that made him irresistible to other women—to you or to the one he finally left me for or to the countless others I'm sure he bedded.'

Swati was reflective as she replied, 'Yes, Rohit was sensitive to women. Simpatico as the Spanish put it. But more than anything else, he was great in bed. And coming from me, baby—that's a mega compliment.'

*

And then back we were to looking at each other and wondering—was it always this way? When did it change? In school on that one day when we became competitors and ceased being friends? Or was it later? It was so tough to decide, so bloody tough. I wanted to get up and leave right then but something stopped me. Something in Swati's eyes. I tried to figure out what it was about her that still continued to haunt me all these many years later. Why hadn't I succeeded in exorcising her ghost? And those eyes—those awful, terrible, beautiful, hypnotic Swati-eyes that could make you, force you, to do whatever she wanted you to, without your even knowing it. And it was happening again. I was staring at her and she was regarding me coolly, as coolly as she always had. It unnerved me—again—as it had in the past. This was ridiculous. I wanted to escape. But I also knew she'd blocked all the exits. There were only dead-ends now.

Aparna stared dully at the entry in her old diary, the one she'd stuffed into her bag despite herself. Strange that the paragraph could've been written by her so many years earlier. She debated with herself whether or not to share it with Swati moments after their marathon conversation. A conversation both of them had postponed. A conversation they ought to have had years ago. She flipped through a few more entries and was amazed to see how many of them featured Swati. Her diary that significant year was neatly divided into two distinct periods—Rohit and post-Rohit. Swati figured equally prominently in both sections. Today, the pain had not dulled, nor blunted. Aparna watched the woman in front of her with the same mixture of revulsion and fascination as she had over the years. She reluctantly acknowledged the power Swati still exerted over her and to a lesser degree over the rest of them.

Unexpectedly Swati announced, 'How would I look with a zigzag perm? I'm thinking of getting one as soon as I am back in London. New publicity stills and all that.' Her voice, with the laughter lurking just under the surface, broke through Aparna's reverie.

'What the hell are you talking about? What the fuck is a zigzag perm?' she asked disinterestedly.

'Don't you keep up, babes? Everybody is sporting it right now.'

'Who's everybody?'

'Everybody in the entertainment business, you know, Whitney, Cher, Annie. . . I'm working on a hot, new look for myself. Chances are I'll be signing a biggie soon. Mucho moolah. Hongkong-based company. Keep your fingers crossed, girl. This is going to be the big one—a make or break deal. And I'm determined to bag it.'

Aparna sniffed, 'I'm sorry, but I'm not clued in at all. Besides, I don't really give a damn about your hair.'

Swati threw back her head and laughed. 'No, of course you don't. What do you give a damn about, Aps? Have you thought about that? Or is it too tough a question to handle?'

'Matter of fact, it is. I haven't had the time, the leisure, to draw up a detailed list. But broadly speaking, I'd say I care sufficiently about stuff you consider entirely unimportant, irrelevant perhaps. Like ethics.'

'Oh, oh, oh, oh,' Swati swirled around, 'we are getting all uppity again, are we? All right here it comes. I don't give two fucks for your kind of tight-assed ethics, your morality shit. Screw you and screw the others. Do you think I don't know how much all of you despise me? But you know what? I think you're jealous. You with your bleak little mediocre lives. Playing safe and yet cheating, sneaking on the side. Tell me, which one of you here is all that pure—as pure as the driven snow you'd love to compare yourselves with? But guess what? I think I'm far more ethical, yes, ethical, than the lot of you.' Aparna raised one eyebrow and stared coldly at Swati. 'Don't you dare look at me like that. I hate that bloody expression of yours. I remember it from school. But think about this: Look where I am and look where you are. Nowhere.'

Aparna glanced out of the large window and asked quietly: 'Was that the purpose of your grand visit then? To tell us all—us, miserable little vermin—how big and important you've become? But we already knew that, and you know what, we still aren't impressed. At least, I am not. You should've spared yourself the elaborate effort.'

Swati flew at her, eyes afire and arms flailing. 'You superior bitch, look at you, look at your clothes, your hair, your nails, your skin, your lousy, neglected, unfucked body. I bet your boobs hang down and merge with your belly. I bet you're grey down there. I bet you haven't waxed your legs in months. I bet you pluck your upper lip. Who the hell would want to sleep with you?' Aparna held her wrists as Swati continued to scream hysterically, 'As for the rest—I wouldn't spit on them. They with their hypocrisies and petty lies. Bitches all. Betraying everyone, fooling everybody, pretending they are virtuous virgins. Give them half a chance and they'd screw themselves from here to Timbucktoo. And you dare criticize me!'

Aparna said calmly, 'I think you need a glass of water. You always did get hyper when you were tense. Remember how nervy you were before our school finals?

Your stomach cramps nearly always prevented you from sitting for the first paper. I'd given you cold water from my bottle that morning. And you'd thrown up. Remember? It's OK. Sit down. Calm down. Let me get you a drink.'

Swati's chest was heaving as she stood rooted to the spot staring at her image in an ostentatiously framed gold leaf mirror on the wall. 'There is something I have to tell you . . .' she started to say.

Aparna laughed. 'You mean after all this you still have more left?' Swati nodded. Aparna noticed her clenched fists and saw the veins standing out prominently on them. 'Forget it, Swati,' she said quickly. 'I'm sure it can wait. Perhaps you could unload the rest of the baggage on your next trip—whenever that is. Let's leave it for now.'

'No!' Swati's voice was sharp and harsh—but before she could continue, Reema walked into the room to announce cheerfully, 'Girls, this is so exciting. Imagine, it's nearly dinner time. I called my husband at the office and told him to eat at the club. Why spoil our fun? He was so sweet, he agreed immediately. So, now no problem. No tension. Let's really relax. Let our hair down. Swati, I know you're a busy girl. Big celebrity and all that. Maybe you have to attend *hajar* cocktails in Bombay. But come on, *yaar*. We're all old friends. This evening will never come again. Please stay. You too, Aparna. Don't say no.'

They exchanged glances. Aparna was undecided. Something told her this was an awfully bad idea and that she should leave right away while the going was good. But Swati held her arm in a vice-like grip and hissed, 'Don't you dare leave now. No way. I have a feeling this is going to be an awesome night. A night to remember.' Then she turned sweetly to Reema and purred, 'Thank you sweetheart you've been so kind. Of course, I'd love to stay. I can always cancel my other plans. Who cares two fucks about those overdressed society bitches dying to show me off at their parties? I'll just keep them chewing their nails and wondering when I'm going to show up. That will fix them.'

'Good,' cried Reema enthusiastically. 'Let's go join the others. Balbir's left. So has Surekha. Her mother-in-law phoned. So did her husband. But Rashmi's still around. And Noor just woke up.'

Swati put on her boots and they trooped back into the living-room. Aparna was exhausted. She'd never experienced such bone-tiredness before. Rashmi looked bombed, devastated. Aparna guessed Balbir had raked up too many old, buried memories.

'Where is your daughter?' Swati asked casually.

Reema pointed to a closed door and giggled. 'Locked in her room. Talking to her boyfriend, I'm sure. Her father will kill her when he finds out. And then kill me.'

'Why?' Swati demanded.

'Well, it's like this. I had an arranged marriage. My husband would like our daughter also to have an arranged marriage. That's how it works in our community. No love marriage nonsense. Our girls are brought up very strictly.'

'What if she elopes?' Swati asked curiously.

'Nobody elopes. These girls aren't such fools. They know what's good for them. But, I feel, let the poor girl have a little fun before she gets into prison—as long as her dad doesn't find out. She tells me everything. It's innocent, yaar. Better this way. Look at me. Did I elope?'

Aparna cut in, 'Oh Reema. . . that was then. Nearly twenty years ago.'

'Maybe. But some things don't change. At least among us.'

'Good for you,' Rashmi muttered. 'Fortunately I won't have that problem. My son Pips can fuck anyone. Marry anyone. Leave anyone. He's a guy after all.'

Aparna snorted. 'That's the most hideous thing I've ever heard. How can you say that? Don't you care about the girls he'll use and discard?'

Rashmi shot back. 'Did anybody care about me? I was also someone's daughter once.'

Swati let out a long sigh. 'Why does our dialogue always end up sounding like a Hindi film or a lousy, third-rate soap?'

Reema laughed. 'Funny. I don't know whether we pick it up from the movies. Or those fellows pick it up from us. But even my card group sounds like this. Especially when we're gossiping and not concentrating on the game.'

Swati perked up. 'What do you girls discuss? Is there anything new left to say?'

Reema smiled a slow, smug smile. 'We never run out of conversation. Or let me put it more frankly, gossip. There is so much, so much we like to share.'

Swati asked slyly, 'Do you talk a lot about sex?'

Reema pretended she was shocked before shrugging. 'Also. Not only. But also. Who else can we discuss these problems with? Most of the women are like me—married early to men they didn't know. Didn't like. They're bored with their husbands. Nothing new happens in the bedroom. At least by talking about it we know that this restless feeling goes on everywhere. Every woman longs for . . . I don't know what. Then there are times when one of the women is attracted to something else, someone else. Only she comes and tells us. We advise her sensibly. Our motto is: Say no to divorce. Never break up the home. Have your fun quietly somewhere. But don't leave the family. That is the sensible way of handling the situation.'

'Balls,' Rashmi yelled, 'back we are to your sanctimonious lectures. Reema, I thought you'd changed. You were the same in school—goody-goody on the surface and a smooth operator behind the scenes. Don't you feel ashamed to even admit all this?'

Reema looked genuinely hurt. 'Just because I'm frank with you people you are attacking me. You think every woman should behave like a bloody whore. Sleep around. Show her boobs to the world—get fucked by any passing fellow. Balbir could've slipped it into you right here in front of all of us. You have such a terrible reputation, even my husband has heard of you through his health club friends. Just the other day one of the men told him, "I'm trying for Rashmi. Vikram had her last week. She gave him a good time. Now it's my turn." That's how men speak about you.'

Rashmi ground her cigarette into a crystal ashtray and reached for her bag. Her eyes were ablaze, her body aquiver, she could barely stop her hands from trembling as she groped for her sling-back sandals which she'd kicked into a corner earlier. 'Bitch! Bloody fucking, stinking, rotten bitch!' she spat through clenched teeth.

Swati put an arm around her. 'Don't darling. This is most cathartic. All of us need it. I'm feeling purged. Let Reema have her say. Then you have yours—believe me you'll feel a whole lot better. It's been such a therapeutic evening.'

Rashmi was shaking with rage as she fussed with her sari. 'These bloody women with their false sense of propriety, their so-called security—what do they know about the real world? I have to fend for myself, for my kid. I don't have some sucker's protective umbrella

296

over my head. Yes, I sleep around. But I do it openly. And not for money or a fucking bauble. I get nothing out of it, except maybe a sexy evening. Whereas the Reemas of this city extract a price from their own husbands—"You can fuck me darling but don't forget the diamonds." Don't talk to me about your phoney friends. Sneaky bitches betraying their husbands. Living under a man's roof, blowing up his money and screwing him behind his back. And they have the nerve to be judgmental about me.'

Swati soothed her, 'Nobody is being judgmental, darling. We all have our lives to lead, Reema has found her way of dealing with her frustrations. You've got yours. And I've got mine. Big deal.'

Aparna interjected, 'I still don't know why we are all frothing and foaming like this. It's been an overlong session. Nothing gets resolved by merely talking about it. I've been a participant in dozens of these so-called pop psychology encounter groups. Nobody expects to achieve anything at the end of the day. It's an empty, futile, stupid, boring exercise which makes money for the person conducting it. That's about all.'

Swati turned to where Noor was sitting huddled up under Reema's shawl. 'Hey! Wakey-wakey. You've been so quiet, all of us had forgotten you were there.'

Noor answered ruefully, 'Hasn't it always been like that? All of you have always behaved like I didn't exist. Or if I did, I was just a harmless retard sitting in a corner with nothing registering. But guess what girls? I've been awake and alert through all this rubbish. And guess again. I've found out a couple of things on my own. Some secrets. Not about the past—that's over. But about now. Something happened today that only two people in this room know about. I found out accidentally. But if I were to open my mouth, it would probably lead to bloodshed.'

The room was very quiet suddenly. The sound of the quartz clock from the living-room could be distinctly heard. If they strained their ears they could also hear Reema's daughter whispering into the phone. Noises from the kitchen told them the cook was in a bad mood. The sound of car horns floated up clearly. A few raucous teenagers on the ground floor were shouting out to friends in the adjoining building. Someone's television set needed the volume adjusted. One of Reema's servants was listening to a popular film music request programme on a transistor. The groan of elevators rushing residents up and down created constant vibrations. The memsaab upstairs was obviously getting ready to go out—the sharp click-clack of metallic stiletto heels on marble flooring filtered down as she went from one room to the next. The long pause seemed to go on and on. But only one woman looked tense. Only one woman stood stiff and watchful. Only one woman's eyes never left Noor's. Swati's.

Spitefully, Swati swung around and shook Noor, grabbing her by the shoulders. 'Why don't you shut the fuck up, you little bitch? I don't like the sound of that whiny voice of yours. Thin and reedy like a badly scratched record. You don't know a thing. Not a thing. So, save us all the bother of having to listen to your shit. Sneak. You little sneak. Still the same snoop you were in school. There's no hope for you, Noor. No matter what you do—including snitch on friends— you'll never have one of your own. You'll never be one of us.'

Noor began to shrink visibly and whimper. Swati continued, her voice low and urgent, 'Look at yourself in the mirror, you miserable wretch. You are so pathetic. Just so pathetic. Your entire life is fucked up—and it shows. Are you even a woman? A complete woman? You certainly don't look like one, you brother fucker. Has any man other than Nawaz ever touched you? Nobody would. Nobody normal. You're a freak. Hear me? Freak. You are finished. Washed up. Nobody gives a shit about you—and nobody ever has. Not even that grand-bitch mother of yours.'

Noor crumbled on to an adjoining pouf, her whimpering amplified to a loud whine that emerged from her gut. She drew her legs up to her narrow chest and covered her head with her arms. 'Don't, Swati, don't,' she pleaded like a child who's being beaten by the neighbourhood bully.

Swati stood over her, straddling Noor's frail body and prodding her ribs with the hard toe of her boots. 'Get up you piece of shit. The damage is done. I really don't know what you live for. Or even why. There's no justification for your sad little existence—nobody needs you. Not even that horny brother of yours.' And with that Swati delivered a final kick in Noor's side and tried to walk out grabbing her bag from where it lay.

Noor reached out feebly and caught hold of Swati's ankle. 'Sorry . . . sorry. . . please . . .' she started blubbering. Swati jerked her leg out of Noor's weak grasp and spat—the gob landed on Noor's left eye. Noor blinked stupidly and wiped the spit away carefully with a lace edged handkerchief. Swati hissed, 'Pathetic. Yes—that's exactly what you are: A pathetic nothing. A zero. A non-person. I wish I could feel something, even pity for you. But I don't. In the past you used to revolt me, disgust me, put me off. I used to puke at the memory of you grovelling at my feet— not anymore. You aren't even worth my vomit.' Swati turned her cold, hard face away leaving Noor to hide her eyes behind her hands while emitting short, sharp cries of pain.

'Bye girls,' Swati sang out, 'I'm out of here. Great evening. Great food. Great booze. A pity our little Noor fucked up. As usual. Ideally, we should all have stayed on till dawn, had some more champagne over breakfast and sailed home flying high. Well, I don't know about you guys but I have things to do.'

Fifteen

Swati was about to leave the room, when Reema suddenly exclaimed, her voice shrill with excitement: 'What's that, Noor?' Aparna came over for a closer look. Only Swati stood aside, a sneer on her face.

Noor looked up unexpectedly and in an unnaturally strong voice she said, 'Why don't you tell everybody what this is?' She dangled what looked like a tiny ear-plug from her extended hand.

Swati snapped: 'How the hell should I know?'

Noor rose to her feet and swiftly walked the room, searching under surfaces, looking beneath tables, in flower arrangements, along lamp shades. 'I've managed to find five so far,' she said to the others. 'With Swati's help, I might locate some more.' Swati began moving towards the door.

'Wait, you have a lot of answering to do,' Aparna stopped her. 'From what I can see these look like bugs to me—electronic bugs. Why have you been snooping?'

Swati whirled around, her chest heaving. 'Fuck you! I don't have to answer any of you. What is this—an investigation? Are you the Gestapo or something?'

Rashmi shot to her feet, her voice rising, 'We won't let you leave so easily, Miss Fancy Airs. What's going on with this shit? You've bugged the place like it's the fucking Kremlin or something. Where are the tapes? Give them to us immediately.'

'What tapes? That female Noor is batty. She has always been loony. You people are equally crazy to believe her. How can you take Noor's rantings seriously all of a sudden? We all know she's completely mad and ought to have been certified ages ago. I mean—just look at her . . . . Nuts. If I were you, I'd call the asylum and ask for a strait-jacket. She really should be put away. Such a menance to society, this one. What have I to gain by bugging this joint, huh? It isn't exactly Princess Diana's bedroom or anything. Just stop this nonsense and let me get the hell out of here. By the way, I intend reporting this ugly incident to the press and police. Noor, darling, don't tell me I didn't warn you. Let the world read about your insanity . . . your sordid little secret. That brother of yours fucked you up good and proper but that doesn't mean I'll allow you to fuck with me. I've got your sick little love-notes too, what fun. Imagine how they'll appear in print. You'll be exposed for what you are and always have been—a suicidal psychotic bitch. You're nothing, Noor. Nothing

at all . . . As to those damn things—bugs or whatever—
you're going on about, I don't know what they are. I
haven't seen them before. I haven't a clue what
everybody's getting so bloody hysterical about. This is
crazy . . . mad . . . lunatic. Like that snivelling little
bitch. I'm getting out of here.'

'Not so fast,' Reema warned. 'You are in my house.
I want to know what you were up to.'

Swati looked at her witheringly. 'Why don't you
tell us what you've been doing? Maybe you're the one
who has planted the bugs. Maybe Noor did. Or Aparna
or Rashmi. Why on earth would I bother?'

Reema moved towards her menacingly. 'I'll call the
police if you don't confess. I know you've been up to
some slimy trick of yours. Tell us . . .'

Swati extended a graceful arm and stopped her.
'I have a feeling your husband has organized this,
I'm sure he'd love to know what his vulgar, cunning
wife has been up to. Maybe that's how the poor man
gets his kicks—listening to all your cheap antics.'

'How dare you,' Reema snarled.

Swati continued smoothly, 'Tch! Tch! Don't get so
worked up. You'll need half-a-dozen facials to fix your
face after this. Don't worry. Today's secrets are safe
with me.' Swati smiled.

Aparna spoke to her in a voice full of quiet authority:
'Swati, you know you are being perfectly absurd. You
can't get away with this. I know you have the tapes in

your bag. Or maybe you've hidden them somehere. Wherever they are, hand them over. And get the hell out. What were you planning this time—blackmail? We'll all treat this like our worst nightmare and never mention it again.'

Swati widened her eyes and said mockingly, 'Oh there you go again hoity-toity and propah as ever. How I loathe that superior attitude of yours. How I detest that expression in your eyes. Do you think you are still the head-girl and this is a prefects' meeting, huh? Forget it. I have what I want. This is what I came here for. You women performed so in character, so predictably, it's pathetic.' Rashmi walked up and tried to snatch the voluminous bag from Swati's shoulder. 'Hold it, you two-bit tart,' Swati said, stepping out of her way agilely, 'I've spent a great deal of money and time on this little expedition. Don't spoil everything now. And in any case, what are you afraid of? You have no reputation to safeguard. And your bastard son must know he has a whore for a mother.'

Rashmi went for her blindly, hitting out, grabbing fistfuls of Swati's lustrous hair. The two women went crashing into Reema's glass and chrome coffee table breaking an onyx lamp and sending all the antique silver clattering onto the marble floor. 'Bitch! Bitch! Bitch!' Rashmi screamed as Swati started to slide out from under her, all pounding fists and dagger-like nails. 'I'm going to kill you,' Rashmi yelled while Aparna and Reema fell over both of them, in an effort to pull Rashmi away. Rashmi was bleeding from cuts in her arms and legs. A thin stream of blood began trickling slowly from a gash in her thigh.

Noor rushed out of the room, her face covered with her hands. Nobody noticed her leaving. Reema shouted for her servants. The small, soft click of the latch as Noor shut the bedroom door behind her went completely unnoticed. Reema's bearer stuck his head out of the swing door that connected the kitchen with the dining-room and nearly dropped the drinks tray he was carrying. Unexpectedly Reema shouted out, 'My decanters. Help!' Startled, the man took an involuntary step back and a beautiful Czech specimen with countless shining facets fell noisily to the floor.

Reema started wailing, 'My husband's going to kill me. That was his favourite. From Heathrow duty free. Oh God! What am I going to do!' Another servant padded out, took in the scene and went in search of the ayah who was watching a Hindi film on cable TV in Reema's daughter's room. The woman came rushing out, saw the bleeding Rashmi and the others and started screaming *'Bachao! Bachao!'* her hands over her ears, her eyes shut. Aparna rushed to the phone. They needed to summon help and immediately. 'Oh shit!' Aparna cursed as she dialled the wrong number. She tried again. This time the circuits were busy. She wasn't even sure why she was dialing the police, when in fact, she ought to have been trying the Emergency Ambulance number. And even then, what for? One of them could have driven the injured Rashmi to hospital. As she waited for the phone to connect, pieces of the Swati puzzle began falling into place. The tapes. It was so obvious. Swati was looking for fresh material. That was it. Earlier, she'd talked of a 'fabulous offer' she'd received from Hong Kong. An offer to produce a serial on a contemporary subject dealing with women—Indian women. Her British script writer had begged off insisting it was a subject beyond his scope and understanding. Swati didn't really have too many contacts left in the entertainment industry in India. Besides, she was a great one for challenges. And here it was—her big opportunity to prove she was more than just a glamorous, wanton actress. With the right kind of inputs, she could put a proposal together—she could write, direct and produce a bold, meaty series on the exciting world of the Nineties Indian urban woman. She was shrewd enough to realize that this break would take her a long, long way—if she played it right. But to make it happen, she needed voices—authentic voices, familiar voices, confused voices. Voices that would ring true. She also knew it was difficult to conduct cold-blooded research into a subject like this. She certainly couldn't imagine any of the young, uppity research assistants from London being successful at getting under the skins of Indian urban women—women such as her friends. As she looked at her friends—Reema supporting the bleeding Rashmi—it slowly dawned on her just how callously they'd all been used. Aparna let out a huge, resigned sigh. Wearily she asked herself why they'd put up with Swati. Tolerated her. Why they'd allowed themselves to become guinea pigs in her laboratory? But most of all Aparna cursed her own lack of perception. She too had fallen for Swati's seductive spiel. She too had been taken in by her stated purpose. ('Just a get-together to catch up on old times.') Of all the women conned that day, Aparna should have seen through Swati. Guessed her motives. Armed herself against her machinations. Resisted her sneaky manipulations.

Aparna had guessed right. As if waking out of a dream she heard Swati's sibilant voice confirming her hypothesis. *Sisters of the Subcontinent*, for that was what Swati intended to call her serial, would elevate her to the sort of fame and money that she needed. As she tapped her foot impatiently and dialled over and over again, Shonali slipped into the room quietly, her face drained of colour, her voice barely a whisper. Aparna replaced the receiver and turned to face the young girl. This whole scene must've been most unsettling for Shonali, she thought to herself as she held out her hand. Shonali surprised her by rushing into her arms and holding her round the waist tightly. Her words were broken, practically incoherent as Aparna strained to catch them. 'The . . . the . . . other aunty. The . . . the

. . . one who looked sick . . . I can't get her name just now . . . that one . . . Noor or something . . . she has locked herself in the bathroom . . . I'm scared . . . I think I heard some funny sounds . . . I can't find Mummy . . . I don't know what's happening.'

Aparna glanced about the room. While the young girl had been talking to her, Reema and Rashmi had disappeared. Deprived of her audience Swati, the only one left, had fallen silent. Without another word Aparna ran towards the bathroom. Damn! How come nobody had noticed Noor's disappearance? The door was locked from the inside. Aparna pounded on it calling out to Noor over and over again. She turned to Shonali and asked her to summon a male servant. Shonali came back to say they'd all gone down carrying a bleeding Rashmi in their arms.

'Aunty couldn't walk. There was so much blood— Mummy had to drive the car herself. They've gone to the hospital.'

Aparna looked around desperately. 'Do you have a hammer or something in the kitchen? Quick. Bring me a rod if you can find one.' Shonali nodded obediently and went off to look for the implements. Aparna continued to struggle with the door, urging Noor to open it. 'Don't be stupid, girl. This doesn't have anything to do with you. Open up. I promise everything will be all right. Please just let me in, please open the door.'

Swati who had followed her said in a low and sardonic voice: 'She can't, Aps. You are asking for the impossible as usual. Noor is dead. Take it from me. She's dead. She was already dead when she decided to come here this afternoon. I saw it in her eyes—didn't you? I'm surprised you didn't—you the all-seeing, all-knowing one. She had death written all over in block letters.'

Aparna snarled, 'Shut up, you bitch. Stay out of this. And stay out of our lives. You've done enough damage to last forever. If Noor is dead it's because of you. Why don't you get the hell out now. You've got what you came for, haven't you?'

Swati leaned tiredly against the door. 'I'm leaving. I'm leaving. Hell! This wasn't worth the trouble. I don't know what I was looking for but if it makes you feel any better let me tell you I didn't find it. It was a colossal waste of time. Energy. Money. Everything. Besides the lot of you turned out to be such bloody bores. You especially. Aps, my girl, I really don't know how I could ever have agonized over not being you. And in case you want them you can have the bloody tapes.' But Aparna's attention was distracted just then by Shonali who had reappeared carrying a menacing-looking crowbar. 'I found it with the car things,' she explained.

'Good girl,' Aparna said quickly as she went to work on the heavy door. The sound of water flowing was now very distinct. 'Noor, Noor. Are you OK?' Aparna cried out as she hammered against the obstinate latch.

She heard it give way after what seemed like an eternity. She turned to the young girl and instructed her briskly, 'Darling, you'd better go and try the ambulance number. It's in the phone book.'

Shonali smartened up enough to say, 'Oh, I know the number. We are made to memorize important numbers in school. Is Aunty really dead inside?'

Aparna didn't reply. But Swati did. 'You bet,' she said through twisted lips that suddenly made her look cruel and ugly. 'She has taken her time though. That kid should have died years ago. Before her accident. Before anything. She was born with a death-wish. Something to do with bad karma.'

Holding her breath, Aparna pushed the bathroom door open. The sight that greeted her didn't surprise her at all. Noor's body was sprawled on the floor at an awkward angle, her limbs contorted, face down. She resembled a marionette whose strings had been cut mid-performance—she was as awkward and ungainly in death as she had been in life. Reema's husband's razor had fallen out of her limp hands and rolled towards the round drain near the bath tub. Noor's dupatta was carelessly draped over the toilet. And the magnificent ring which had fallen out of her bag lay close to her body, defiantly flashing fire from its centre as it caught the light from the adjoining room. The pool of blood was growing around her fragile frame. It looked unreal. . . as if a careless painter had overturned a can of scarlet by mistake.